GONE

REAGAN KEETER

Irresistible Publishing
Marietta, Georgia

This book is a work of fiction. Names, characters, places, and incidents are either the product of the author's imagination or are use fictitiously. Any resemblance to actual persons living or dead, events, or locales is entirely coincidental.

FIRST EDITION

Printed in the United States of America

ISBN 978-1-7343945-2-8
ISBN 978-1-7343945-3-5 (ebook)

GET AN EXCLUSIVE COPY OF THE LAYOVER

Connor Callahan has been through a lot. More than anyone should. It has left him with an overdeveloped sense of justice. Perhaps that is why when he sees a man discreetly tag a stranger's suitcase with a black magic marker, he sets out to discover what is going on. It's a decision that will thrust Connor into a conflict far more dangerous than he could have imagined, and when it's over he will know one thing for sure: You're not always safer on the ground.

Details can be found at the end of this book.

CHAPTER 1

ET. OUT.

That was the first message Ion had sent when Connor tried to hack his machine. It appeared suddenly in a black window in the center of his screen as all of his applications shut down.

Whoa, was the only thought Connor could manage at the time. He was studying computer science at Stanford University, but had been hacking into other people's computer systems for much longer than that. His fingers had been practically attached to the keyboard since he was four years old. Until that day, nobody had caught him in the act. Or, at least, nobody had kicked him out. He wouldn't have even thought it was possible to do what Ion had done.

That wasn't the end of it, though. Two days later, he got an email from ion@truthseekers.com. He recognized the domain as the one he'd tried to hack and deduced Ion must be the handle for the guy who had kicked him out. It contained only one line: *Stay out of my system or I'll make sure Matt finds out what you've been up to.*

The message bothered Connor for a lot of reasons. First, it meant Ion had hunted Connor down, found out who he was and how to contact him. Second, despite all that work, all the research Ion must have done, his email referenced someone named Matt, and Connor knew no one by that name. So who was Matt?

Connor wasn't a malicious hacker. His targets were not financial institutions or government entities. He didn't send out phishing emails or try to steal anyone's identity. He was a hacker of, as he saw it, the most righteous type. He sought out sites that dealt in misinformation and did what he could to disrupt them. There were "the sunners," for example, who actually claimed that a secret society had harnessed the sun's rays and was using them to monitor people's outdoor activity. It was an absurd notion. Connor hated the idea that these fools were out there spreading lies and, as hard as it was for him to believe, gaining followers.

For three days, the sunners' website had shown a popup to every new visitor that said, "This is a lie. Do not buy into their half-truths."

Connor knew, though, that he would never be able to stop a group of people like that permanently. Everyone he attacked eventually fixed their sites, patched the holes Connor had been able to exploit. But the way he saw it, if he kept even one person from slipping down a rabbit hole that would twist their view of the world into something untrue, possibly destroying their lives in the process (as he understood it, many sunners had found themselves alienated from family and friends), then he had done something good.

TruthSeekers was one such site. It didn't peddle in sunners theories, though. It had no such single focus. It had posts on Bigfoot and aliens, modern-day vampires and possession. A smorgasbord of crazy, in other words.

Connor had stumbled upon the blog by accident. A Facebook post on blood diseases had caught his attention. It had had enough truth to sound legitimate, but something had smelled wrong. He'd followed a link in it to another site and a link there to TruthSeekers.

But he didn't go after the site right away. He had other things to do. He was home from college for the summer, working for a house flipper named Austin during the day, and was just too tired to bother with a mere blogger who posted stories so obviously false.

At least, that was how he'd felt when he found the site. But he couldn't stop thinking about the lies TruthSeekers was spreading. People believed them. Some did, anyway. If they didn't, there wouldn't have been an article on Facebook that eventually linked back to the site. One visit, and the algorithms that served up content might then use that information to deliver more insidious lies.

And, for that reason, TruthSeekers was just as bad as all of the other sites he had attacked.

Stay out of my system or I'll make sure Matt finds out what you've been up to.

Connor had read the message over and over the night he had received it and, tonight, a week later, had pulled it up again. The gnawing, relentless question wouldn't leave him alone. *Who's Matt?*

He was sitting at his computer in his attic bedroom, still wearing the clothes he'd put on for a day of painting with Austin: a pair of old khakis and a Cure tee shirt he had found at a thrift shop in Greenwich Village. He had taken to showering at night since he had started working with Austin, and his blond hair stuck out every which way.

From downstairs, he could smell dinner cooking. His mom, Kim, liked to use a lot of spices. Nutmeg and oregano were her favorites. But unless his nose deceived him, tonight's meal would feature basil.

He could also hear his parents going at it again, something that, this summer, had become almost a nightly occurrence. His mom would tell his dad, Frank, to stop being so mean, to stop sulking around the damn house all the time and at least *act* like he was happy to see her. Kim would say something was wrong, she could feel it, and why won't he just talk to her? Frank would tell her she was being paranoid. He'd say nothing was wrong, and maybe he would be in a better mood if she would just stop bothering him every night with these stupid questions. And on and on it went. Sometimes one of them would mention Connor—"He's right upstairs. He can hear us."—and they would call it quits for a while. Other times, they'd get so heated they'd forget he was there.

Connor slipped on his AirPods with the intention of drowning out the argument, but no music played.

The old oak desk he sat at stood in stark contrast to the sleek monitors and souped-up laptop on top of them. It reminded Connor of an era long since passed. A time when people still wrote letters regularly and did so with a quill instead of a pen.

Connor scoured the desktop, shifting fast food wrappers, crumpled paper towels, loose sheets of paper, books, dishes, and a whole manner of other junk in search of his phone. Then he remembered he had shoved it in the top desk drawer to his left specifically because there was nowhere on the desk to put it.

He opened the drawer, removed the phone. It was dead. At least that explained why there was no music playing.

From outside, he heard the squeal of tires and a thump, like a car bouncing over a curb. Not the sort of thing you would expect to hear in a quiet suburban neighborhood. Certainly not when you were in the cul-de-sac of said neighborhood.

Connor crossed the attic bedroom to a small window that faced the front of the house, careful not to hit his head on the slanted ceiling, and looked out. At first, he saw nothing but the dark and quiet tree-lined street that arced away from their house and disappeared around a curve. Then he heard a bang from downstairs. It sounded to him like somebody had opened a door fast, let it slam into a wall. He instinctively looked from the street to the yard and saw a nondescript panel van parked on the grass. Blue or black—it was hard to tell in the darkness. The rear doors were open.

"What the . . ." he heard Kim say.

"Who are you?" Frank said.

Then there was another thud, and Kim screamed.

CHAPTER 2

CONNOR BEGAN TO panic. His hands shook. His mouth went dry. *What the hell was going on?* He had to call the police. He looked at his phone, then remembered it was dead. *Shit.* Well, he had to do something.

There was more banging, like furniture getting toppled over and the sounds of footsteps—one person chasing another.

"Please, please, please! Leave us alone!" Kim shouted. "Take what you want and go!"

There were two doors between Connor and the rest of the house: one that led out of the bedroom, and the other at the bottom of the attic stairs. He bolted out of the bedroom door, ready to attack the intruder. As he ran, Connor imagined jumping on top of him, pinning him to the floor, beating him unconscious. Then, just at the top of the stairs, he stopped, realized the intruder might have a gun.

New plan.

He crept down the stairs. More banging.

"What do you want with me?" Kim screamed.

Connor turned the doorknob quietly, pushed the door open an inch, two. From here, he could see the living room and most of the dining room. Frank was sprawled out on the floor. A marble bust of Hippocrates, perhaps ten inches tall, lay beside him. Connor recognized the statue from their foyer where, until now, it had sat on a side table, atop a small stack of medical books.

The couch was askew. The coffee table and dining room chairs were overturned.

More screams from his mother. Demands for the intruder to get out. It sounded like she might be in the kitchen. Then he heard dishes breaking, and his suspicions were confirmed. She was, no doubt, grabbing dishes out of the cupboard and the sink, tossing them at the intruder, doing whatever she could to defend herself.

Why didn't she go for the block of knives by the fridge? Was she afraid to turn her back on him?

Probably. Connor would be.

Think. What are you going to do?

If the intruder had a gun, if he planned on shooting anyone, he would have done it already. He wouldn't have needed to use the Hippocrates bust to knock out Connor's father. His mother wouldn't be so bold as to run or throw dishes at the man.

But what was *he* going to do? Even if the intruder didn't have a gun, going after him empty-handed would be stupid. He needed a weapon of some sort. He quickly assessed everything within sight without actually focusing on any one item. Although the Hippocrates bust was certainly heavy enough—if it could knock out his father, it could knock out the intruder—he would also have to get right up on the intruder to use it. That didn't seem wise.

Then he saw what he was looking for. The fireplace poker. That would work. He would just have to get to the other side of the living room. That was doable, right? In his heightened state of alarm, he wasn't entirely sure. The other side of the living room seemed to be twice as far away as it normally did. Three times, maybe. And it wasn't a straight line, either. Even if his father wasn't in the way, even without the toppled furniture and broken knickknacks that could slice into his bare feet, it wouldn't have been a straight line.

Still, those things weren't going to stop him. He would just have to be careful. Careful and fast. He could do this. At least, that was what he told himself.

It was what he was still telling himself when the thump-thump-thump of footsteps started coming rapidly in his direction. They were approaching from the jointed side of the door, so there was no telling who it was. But odds were good that even if it was his mom, the intruder would be right behind her.

He pulled the door shut. Since it had only been open an inch to begin with, he was hoping the intruder hadn't noticed.

Chickenshit.

Then, right outside the door, he heard a loud crackle and the buzz of electricity, his mother screaming, and another thump. This one was not that of a foot. This was a whole body going down.

Connor wasn't sure what had just happened. He suspected the intruder might have a Taser. Either way, there was no point in showing himself now. Let the intruder take what he wanted and go.

Connor's hand had been on the doorknob when he heard his mother hit the floor. It fell slowly to his side. He stayed there for a minute, maybe two. Still and quiet. Ready to launch himself onto the intruder if he opened the attic door. He heard the intruder leave, come back, and leave again.

After he left the second time, Connor hurried back up the stairs, to the window, to see . . . well, whatever he could. The intruder sounded like he was taking furniture out of the house, which didn't make any sense. How much furniture could you put in the back of a panel van? Maybe it was the TVs. Connor peered cautiously out the window.

It was neither.

The intruder had left the house the second time with Kim in his arms. He dumped her in the back of the van, leaned in to do something. Connor thought he saw the end of a rope.

No, no, no, no, no.

The energy in the words put his feet into motion. He ran back down the stairs, bounding straight through the door at the bottom of them. He had to find a phone. He had to call the police. Fortunately, his father always had a phone on him, and it was always charged—

But his father was gone, too.

Connor's panic grew. He could feel it in his blood now, coursing its way through his body. He looked left, then right. For something. Anything. A solution. Help.

The fireplace poker.

Connor grabbed it and ran for the front door. He would stab the intruder straight through if he had to. This man wasn't leaving with his parents.

He hadn't quite made it to the door when the intruder stepped back inside for the third time. The man was slim, six feet tall, wearing black jeans, a black turtleneck, a ski mask, and leather driving gloves.

Connor froze. This man hadn't come for just his parents. He had come for all three of them. Why?

The intruder pulled a Taser out of his pocket, aimed it in Connor's direction. He fired it up for just a second, and Connor jumped back a step, dropped the fireplace poker. Then, perhaps sensing Connor would stay where he was, the intruder leaned over and picked something up. A cellphone. Was it the one that belonged to Connor's dad? Had it fallen out of his pocket when the intruder was carrying him out to the car? It had to be. But why? Why did the intruder want his father's cellphone? Why had he abducted Connor's parents? What the hell was going on?

The intruder put a finger to his lips and made a shushing sound. Then he backed out of the door slowly and closed it behind him. The message was clear: *Don't scream. Don't follow me.*

Connor did neither. He stayed where he was until the van's engine turned over and the sound of it faded away.

He ran to the door, just to make sure the intruder was gone, then back upstairs to get his own cellphone. He plugged it in, waited for it to charge. He hated himself for not having the guts to run the fireplace poker straight through that son of a bitch.

The little white apple appeared on the center of the iPhone. "Come on," Connor mumbled, willing the phone to launch faster.

Seconds later, he was on the line with 911.

CHAPTER 3

THE HOUSE WAS overrun with police. CSI and the like. They seemed to be everywhere, examining everything. Connor had seated himself on the bottom stair that led to the attic, mostly so he could be out of their way. Hovering over him was a detective who had introduced herself as Olivia Forbes. She was a squat woman in a black suit. Her hair was parted down the middle and tucked behind her ears. Every so often, several strands would work their way free, and she would push them back into place without stopping her flow of questions or, it seemed to Connor, even realizing she was doing it.

"So the intruder," she said, reading from her notes, "was dressed all in black. Ski mask, gloves. The whole deal."

"His gloves were brown."

She looked over the top of her glasses, thick spectacles that made Connor wonder how much she could really see. "Excuse me?"

"He was dressed all in black except the gloves. They were brown. They kind of looked like driving gloves, you know? With the holes on the knuckles?"

She wrote something down in her notepad. "How did he get in?"

"I don't know."

"Did he crawl through a window?"

"No. He came through the front door. Parked his car right out on the yard. And . . ." Connor trailed off. He had already told several officers what had happened. Each time had been harder than the last. As things stood, he was barely holding himself together. And, really, why put himself through it again if he didn't have to? Certainly one of the officers he had told would have repeated the story to Olivia. Why was she asking him the same questions all over again? He shifted gears, decided instead to address the ambiguity of his last answer. "I mean, I don't know how he got through the door so fast. I was the last one home. I locked the door, I know it. I always lock the door. But it seemed like as soon as he got to the house, he was inside."

"You have a key hidden somewhere? Underneath a fake rock? Something like that?"

Connor shrugged. "Sure. But how would he know where it is?"

"Can you show me?"

Connor pushed himself up—it seemed to take everything he had to get to his feet—and led the detective out the front door. He searched the bushes along the right side of the house and closest to the stoop. Then he pulled up an artificial stone, turned it over, and slid a panel open. He dropped a key into his other hand. "Like I said."

Olivia had put her notepad back in her coat pocket and was standing with her hands on her hips. She shook her head, just a little, as if at some private thought. "What about the van? You said it was a blue panel van."

"I think so."

"You *think* so?"

"It was a panel van, for sure. And it was old. Kind of rusty. But I'm not sure if it was blue or black."

"Did you catch the license plate?"

Connor tried to remember. "No."

"Did you happen to notice what state it was from?"

"No." Connor put the key back in the fake rock and put the rock back in the bushes.

A uniformed officer stepped out of the door. "Detective?"

Olivia turned her attention to him. "Yes?"

He held up a cellphone, and the movement lit up the screen. There was a picture of a cat playing poker on it. "Found this under the sofa."

She looked at Connor. "You recognize that?"

"It's my dad's," Connor said. So the intruder hadn't come back for his father's cellphone. That meant it had to have been his. Dammit. If he had bothered to look toward the front door when he exited the stairwell, he would have seen it. Even if he had thought it was his dad's at the time, went for it only to call 911, he would have realized what he had as soon as he picked it up. It would have been all the evidence the police needed to find the intruder. He could have slipped out the back door, run to a neighbor's. If he had just paid attention to his surroundings, everything would have been different.

"Okay," the officer said, and walked back into the house.

"Wait. What's he doing?" Connor asked.

"The tech guys are going to install some monitoring software on it that will let us listen in, in case the kidnapper calls. You'll just have to activate it. Privacy concerns, and all that. Speaking of which . . ." Olivia held out her hand.

Connor gave her his phone, and Olivia gave it to another officer who was on his way into the house.

"Set this one up, too," she told him.

The officer nodded but didn't stop.

"Do you know anybody who would have had a bone to pick with your parents? Either one of them?"

He considered that. "Not that I can think of."

"Both parents work?"

"Yeah."

"Where?"

"My dad works for Leewood Construction, and my mom's a surgeon in the William Marks ER."

Olivia nodded, made a note. Then she paused, as if deciding where she wanted to go next with her questions, before simply asking, "Can you think of anything else that might be important?"

Well, there's the money, Connor thought. But he wasn't going to mention that.

CHAPTER 4

THE MONEY CONNOR was thinking about was a stack of loose bills in a plain white envelope. He had found it on the dining room table after the intruder had left and before the cops had arrived. He hadn't mentioned it because he didn't know for sure whether the intruder had left it. That money might have belonged to his parents. (Although it wasn't like them to carry around stacks of cash. Especially not stacks of hundred-dollar bills.) And if the intruder had left it, then that would only lead to questions he couldn't answer. It might look to the police like he was involved.

No, thank you. That was not a complication he needed to introduce into the investigation. Best to keep that information to himself. At least for now.

Olivia stayed until the crime scene investigators had finished their work and, on her way out the door, told Connor to keep both his and his father's phone on him. (They hadn't found his mother's.) "Sooner or later, somebody's going to call," she said confidently.

Connor, though, had his doubts. Why would you leave an envelope of cash and then call with demands? "What if they don't?" he asked.

"They will, and when they do, we'll be listening." Olivia held out a hand to shake Connor's and he obliged. "I'll be in touch."

He watched her trek across the front yard, straight over the tread marks left behind by the intruder's vehicle. When she was halfway to her car, she turned around and said, "You got anybody you can stay with?"

Perhaps because he hadn't been alone for more than a few minutes since the abduction, Connor hadn't given any thought to what it would be like once the police left. Now facing a night by himself in a house that, as familiar as it was, seemed foreign to him, he wished he had. Then again, what difference would it have made? He had a few friends at Stanford he could stay with if this had happened on the West Coast. But here he had no one he was close to. He had grown apart from his friends here, and good riddance, as far as he'd been concerned at the time. "I'll be fine."

Olivia shrugged and continued on her way.

Connor went inside, closed the door. Locked it twice, just to be sure, and latched the chain. He walked from room to room surveying the mess. In the living room, whole shelves of stuff—books, knickknacks, photos—had been knocked off the built-in bookshelves that lined the wall on each side of the fireplace. Some of those items, like an antique plate handed down from parent to child for God-knows-how-many generations, were broken. Others, like the angel made from Swarovski crystal, had shattered. The sofas were askew, the coffee table turned over.

The dining room and formal living room were almost as bad, but the kitchen had gotten the worst of it. No surprise, since Kim had used stacks of dishes to defend herself.

Each room connected to the next, and Connor was able to survey the entire floor without backtracking. When he was done, he dug the envelope of cash out of his waistband and sat down on the sofa to count it.

He made his way through the stack of hundreds. At nearly six thousand dollars, he lost interest. He felt numb and broken and scared, and at that moment the money just didn't have any meaning to him. With just a glance at the stack of bills remaining to be counted, he estimated the total came in somewhere around twenty thousand.

He shoved the money back into the envelope and placed it on the mantel over the fireplace. It was the only flat surface that didn't need to be cleaned. And he had to clean. As strange as it seemed, even to him, he had to bring order to this mess. It was almost as if by doing so, by returning the house to some semblance of normalcy, he might be able to bring his parents back.

Connor started with the big things, pushing the furniture into place and righting the chairs. Then he got the broom, swept up the broken dishes. Operating on a sort of autopilot, he carried one bag of trash after another to the bin outside. By the time he had filled his third bag, he had cleaned up most of the mess and, he realized, overfilled the bin as well.

He stood there in the dark looking at that last bag—half-in, half-out, the bin's lid resting on top of it—and felt defeated. The zombie-like state that had carried him through the last several hours finally crumbled, and the torrent of emotions it had been keeping in check flooded out.

Connor screamed and slammed his fist on the bin's lid. Over and over, he hit it. He used all of his weight to try to force it closed. When nothing worked, he pushed it over, let the damn bag of trash roll out, and stormed back inside.

THREE WEEKS LATER

CHAPTER 5

MARK WILSON DIDN'T care much for the city. He only came into town to catch a Broadway show with his wife once in a while. Tonight, they had come to see *Wicked*. His wife called it a "spectacle" on the way out. She meant it in a good way. He would have called it a spectacle, too, if she had asked. He wouldn't have meant it in a good way. They didn't agree on a lot. But that was what made their relationship work.

Hillary had gotten pregnant not long after they'd started dating, and originally they had stayed together for the child. Twenty-one years later, with their son at Princeton, they now stayed together because they loved each other. He couldn't say for sure when their love had taken on the depth it had now, but he was sure those differences had been a part of making that happen.

On the way home, Hillary found a playlist of the musical's songs on Spotify and put it on. By the time they reached their house in Westchester, they were both singing at the top of their lungs and laughing at how bad they were.

A rusty blue panel van was parked along the curb across the street. Mark looked at it and grunted. "Looks like the Sizemore kid got herself a new ride."

"She should park that thing in the driveway," Hillary said. "It's such an eyesore."

"Her parents probably don't want to look at it any more than we do."

"Yeah, well, she's their kid."

Mark pulled into his garage. "I'll talk to them in the morning."

"Good luck with that."

"Luck?" he asked, then leaned in and put on an accent. "I don't need no stinkin' luck."

Hillary laughed as he kissed her neck. She opened the car door. "Take that to the bedroom."

They entered the house through an adjoining door. Mark turned off the alarm and Hillary headed straight for the stairs. She would expect him to follow, and he did.

Or he started to, anyway.

He was halfway up the stairs when a knock on the door caused him to stop. The small hairs on his arms jumped to attention. It was too late for visitors. He should probably just ignore it.

The visitor knocked again, louder this time, and rang the doorbell.

"What's going on down there, honey?" Hillary shouted. "Who's at the door?"

"I don't know," Mark called back. "Maybe the Sizemore kid heard us talking about her."

"Well, it's too late for visitors. Just ignore it. Whoever it is, they'll go away."

Exactly what I was thinking.

Mark started up the stairs again, this time reaching the bedroom. He came up behind Hillary, kissed her neck. She leaned into it.

Then that damn knocking was back. And the doorbell. *Ring. Ring. Ring.*

"Son of a . . . !" Mark charged down the stairs. His wife again

22

encouraged him to ignore the visitor, but he couldn't. This was going to stop now.

Mark turned the deadbolt, yanked open the door. "Listen. I don't know who you think . . ." Although his words trailed off when he saw the man on the patio, the thought finished playing itself out in his head: . . . *you are, banging on my door like that. What's the matter with you?*

It was as if his mind needed time to finish processing the reality before him. This man—this stranger—was dressed all in black. Scuffed black work boots, black jeans, black turtleneck (despite the fact that it was the kind of sticky hot tonight that made Mark want to strip naked and stand in front of a fan). Even a black ski mask. Were it not for the brown leather gloves with holes on the knuckles, he'd look like a living shadow.

Mark tried to slam the door shut, but the man in the ski mask stepped forward, pushed his weight against the door, and shoved.

Mark stumbled back several steps. "Call the police!"

"What?" Hillary shouted as she came out of the bedroom. "Honey, who is it? You can't shout at me from downstairs. I can't hear you." Then she, too, saw the intruder and was likewise stunned into silence.

The intruder lunged at Mark, his right hand held out in front of him. It wasn't until then Mark realized the man was armed with a Taser. He heard the crackle of electricity as the intruder activated it. He tried to move out of the way, but he wasn't fast enough. The current shot through his body, scrambling his thoughts and sending his muscles into spasms. He fell to the floor. If he could have thought at all, he would have thought he smelled his flesh burning. Then he felt a white-hot wave of pain wash over him as the intruder whacked him on the side of the head.

Hillary was frozen with fear. She saw the intruder hit her husband square in the chest with the Taser. She could tell Mark had tried to get out of the way but was unable. She watched in horror as her husband collapsed to the floor. The intruder looked up at her, then walked deeper into the house and, as such, out of sight.

She thought about running down to Mark to see if he was all right. She thought about returning to the bedroom to get her phone so she could call the police. Both choices felt wrong. How could she leave her husband alone down there while she went to call the police? But wasn't calling the police exactly what she should do?

Hillary tried to think through her own chaotic emotions.

Call the police, she told herself. *Do it now.*

She was just about to follow her own instructions when the intruder returned with a wrought-iron candlestick. Hillary recognized it as one of two from their dining room table.

Call the police!

The intruder swung the candlestick at Mark's temple. There was a sickening thud when it connected, and Hillary screamed again. Finally, she ran. Back to the bedroom. She looked around frantically. Where was her phone? Not on the side table. She grabbed her purse off the bed, shook everything out of it. Makeup, her wallet, a bunch of receipts, a Snickers bar she'd forgotten about . . . and her phone.

Hillary could hear the intruder charging up the stairs as she dialed 911. She ran into the master bathroom, pushed the button on the doorknob to lock it. That wasn't going to hold long, but, God willing, it would hold long enough.

She leaned against the door just to make it that much harder for him to get inside and held the phone up to her ear.

An operator was already on the line. "Hello? Can you hear me? This is nine-one-one. Hello?"

"There's someone in my house." She sounded out of breath, terrified, and hearing herself that way only made her more scared. "You've got to get someone out here."

"Ma'am, are you all right?"

The intruder slammed into the door on the other side. Hillary felt the wood shake and screamed. "Please, hurry. My husband . . . Right now . . . I don't know."

The intruder slammed into the door again.

"What's the address, ma'am?"

"Don't you have that?" she shouted.

"Ma'am—"

Hillary cut in, rattled off her address. Then the intruder hit the door hard enough for the lock to give way. The door swung inward, knocking Hillary off balance. She dropped the phone, felt all fifty thousand volts the Taser delivered pump through her system.

CHAPTER 6

CONNOR HAD MADE only one call the night his parents were abducted, and that was to his uncle, Henry Snider. He had decided Olivia was right—he shouldn't be alone. Henry was his mother's brother and was, of course, horrified. He had caught a plane that night to LaGuardia and arrived at Connor's house just after three a.m.

Connor, who couldn't sleep anyway, didn't mind the late hour. In fact, he appreciated Henry coming as quickly as he did.

Henry was a big man, taller than average and, as Connor's mom politely put it, well fed. He had lost most of his hair a few years back and, upon his wife's advice, shaved the rest of it off. It did not make him look as cool as he thought it did.

His pressed gray shirt was tucked neatly into a pair of black slacks. When he entered the house, he loosened his tie and undid the top button of his shirt. Connor wasn't sure why Henry always made a point of dressing up. It seemed unnecessary, especially on a night like this.

Then again, he had rushed straight to the airport. Perhaps these were simply the clothes he had worn to the office.

That first night, they had stayed up until dawn, drinking coffee and watching the cellphones that sat on the kitchen table between them. There were a lot of questions from both of them. Why would someone do this? What did they want? Were Kim and Frank all right? And there was the one question Connor suspected they were both thinking but neither said: Were Kim and Frank still alive?

There were no answers.

Connor didn't tell Henry about the money because he hadn't told Olivia. Eventually, he figured, he would have to tell somebody. But he needed some time to think it all through first. Two very long days later, though, during which Connor and Henry did nothing but putter around the house hoping for a call, he still hadn't figured out what it meant and realized it would be even harder to bring up then. Because now Connor wouldn't just be faced with the question of what the money meant but also why he hadn't told anybody about it sooner.

Olivia checked in a couple of times. When Connor asked if she had any leads, she said they had one, but not to get his hopes up. A patient had recently died on Kim's table, the hospital staff had told her. Olivia hadn't been able to reach the family yet. According to the neighbors, they were out of town. Once she could, she was going to talk to them to rule it out. That sort of thing happened from time to time, she explained, and as far as motives went, it was weak.

Three weeks after the abduction, Henry told Connor he had to go home. "You should come with me," he said. "I hate the thought of you being here by yourself." He was, by chance, wearing the same gray shirt and black slacks he had arrived in, although they did not look as fresh as they had.

Henry delivered the news over breakfast. Bacon and eggs. It was the only time their morning meal had consisted of anything more than black coffee and Wheaties. Often it hadn't even been that much.

Connor shook his head. "I can't do that. I need to be here. Just in case."

"Just in case what? I'm as worried about them as you are. But it's been three weeks. If anyone was going to call, we would have heard something by now. I hate to say it . . ." Henry's gaze fell from Connor to his coffee cup. "We need to start thinking about what you're going to do . . . next."

"*Next?*"

"Jesus, Connor, don't make me say it."

Connor slid the plate of food away. He had appreciated the hot meal when he had come downstairs. Now he saw it for what it was. A way to soften the one-two punch. Henry was leaving. His parents were dead. Enjoy your eggs.

"Kim made Sarah and me your godparents."

"Yeah, well, it's not like there was anyone else."

"I just want what's best for you."

"I'm not leaving."

Henry dropped his head, sighed, pushed his chair away from the table. "Are you done with this?" he said, pointing at Connor's plate as he got up.

Connor didn't respond.

Henry must have taken that as a "yes" because he picked up both plates and carried them to the sink, which was already full with an assortment of cookware. "I'll clean it up before I go." Then, lumbering like he always did, he made his way from the kitchen to the dining room. Before he was out of sight, he turned around. "I can't make you come with me if you don't want to." He waited for Connor to say something, but Connor wasn't sure what he should say. "Sooner or later, we're going to have to deal with all of this." He pointed a finger and waved it around as if to indicate not just the house but Connor's entire life. "You can't afford this place on your own, and it wouldn't be a good idea for you to stay, even if you could."

I can afford it for now, Connor thought.

Connor knew the statistics as well as anyone. It seemed like every talking head would repeat them anytime the news covered an abduction. The most important of those statistics, and the one Henry had been driving at, was this: If a victim wasn't found within the first day or two, he was probably dead.

Connor wasn't ready to accept that possibility when it came to his own family, and going with Henry to Florida would be tantamount to not only accepting the possibility, but accepting it as fact.

Still, he shouldn't have acted like a jerk. Henry was only trying to help.

Henry huffed and puffed his way down the hall, his suitcase held out in front of him. Connor met him in the foyer.

"I'm sorry," Connor said.

Henry let his suitcase fall by his side. "It's all right. I wish I could stay longer."

"I'll be okay."

Henry's phone chirped. He fished it out of his pocket, looked at the screen, then at the door. "My Uber's here. Call me, all right?"

Connor nodded. He wanted to give Henry a hug. He thought Henry might want one, too. But they had never had that kind of relationship, so with a handshake and an awkward pat on the back, Henry was out the door.

Connor locked the deadbolt behind him, slid the chain into place. Then he made sure the garage and rear doors were also locked. He checked the windows, set the alarm.

This is my life now, isn't it?

Always wondering, always worrying.

Connor called Austin to say he was ready to come back to work. Hanging around the house with Henry had been bad enough. Now there wasn't even the minimal conversation Henry had provided to comfort or distract him.

He pulled the envelope of cash out from the back of his sock drawer, counted it again. It was all still there. Twenty thousand dollars to the penny. He hadn't spent any of it and wasn't sure he would. He counted it not because he thought Henry had found it and secretly pocketed a couple of hundred dollars for himself—Henry would have come right out and asked him about the money—but more as a form of meditation. Slowly going through those bills, one by one, he let his mind drift. Wondered again what the money meant. Hoped that an answer, anything that made sense, would occur to him.

Once again, though, he came up empty.

Connor returned the money to its hiding place. He went into his parents' bathroom, opened his mom's medicine cabinet, and took an Ambien from a bottle of pills. She had trouble sleeping and had been taking the drug for as long as he could remember.

Connor stretched out on his bed. He looked over at his computer. He could find out more about the man who had died on his mom's table if he wanted to. It wouldn't be hard to hack into the hospital's system, find the man's records. But he decided against it. He hadn't tried to hack his way into anything since the night his parents had been abducted. Part of that was because he had been too wrapped up with worry and heartache to think about it. The other part was that message he had gotten from Ion: *Stay out of my system or I'll make sure Matt finds out what you've been up to.*

It still creeped him out.

Besides, the Ambien was already starting to take hold.

But there was one thing he did want to do before he passed out. He forced himself to sit up, then stand, then cross the room to the only window. It was here that he had stood when he saw the panel van parked on the front yard. It was also here that he had stood for several minutes every night since, looking for . . . well, he wasn't sure what. It was a little like pulling back the shower curtain just to make sure there wasn't a killer on the other side.

He was certain by now that if the intruder was going to come back for him, he would have done so already. He also knew it was unlikely, if the killer did come, that he would be looking out the window at the exact right time to see him before he entered the house.

Still, it made Connor feel better, so he looked.

He could still make out the tire marks on the grass. But there was something else out there this time, too, that didn't belong. A man.

CHAPTER 7

THE MAN WAS standing at the end of the driveway, facing the house. He was little more than a shadow in the darkness.

Connor began to panic, his terror overpowering the Ambien. It was the killer. (*Your parents aren't dead. Don't think that way.*) He had come back, after all. Maybe he had been watching the whole time, waiting for Connor to be alone.

Connor ran to the stairs before he knew what he was doing. But he did know this much: If the intruder thought he was going to take Connor by surprise like he had his parents, he had better think again. As he reached the bottom of the stairs, he thought about the sound of his mom tossing dishes at the intruder. He remembered thinking she should grab a knife from the block on the counter.

He detoured to the kitchen—the fireplace poker was a fine weapon, but a knife would be better. Especially that large carving knife they used only on Thanksgiving and Christmas. He circled around to the foyer, barely stopping long enough to pull the carving knife out of the wooden block.

He charged out the front door. "Who are you?" he shouted. "Tell me where my parents are or I swear—"

"Whoa! Whoa! Whoa!" The man's hands were out in front of him. Connor could see him better now. He was in his early thirties, Connor suspected, and wearing pleated tan slacks, loafers, and a striped dress shirt. His hair was carefully styled into that "I pretend I don't care but I do" look Connor hated. "Put that thing down, would you?"

Connor slowed to a stop as he realized this man wasn't the intruder. But still he demanded to know, "Who the hell are you?"

The man pulled a business card out of his pocket with an efficiency that suggested he was prepared for a confrontation like this. Then he rambled off his name so fast Connor couldn't understand it.

Connor sized him up. He let the knife fall to his side, but still watched the man warily. He crept forward, snatched the business card out of the stranger's hand. The name on it was Isaiah Cook. His title: Producer. And the show he produced? That was on there, too. *Uncovered.*

Connor knew it well. It was among his favorites. Or it had been, until his parents were abducted. Since then, he'd had trouble concentrating on any TV shows long enough to follow a plot, and the last thing he wanted to watch was true crime.

"What are you doing out here?" he asked.

"I wanted to talk to you—"

"Why were you just standing there like that, looking at the house?"

"Oh, that." He smiled. It seemed a little forced, like he was trying to put Connor at ease. "I just wanted to get a feel for the place. Trying to picture how it might look on camera, you know? Good, I think. These traditionals almost always play well. They're the kind of home just about anyone can imagine themselves living in. Makes the whole story more relatable."

"What are you talking about?" Connor suspected he knew where this was going, but he still wanted to hear Isaiah say it, just to be sure.

"We heard about what happened to your parents. That's a strange thing. You don't have a lot of cases like that—someone just coming in and snatching two adults out of their home. And you saw him, right?

The guy who took your parents? And he saw you. But he just let you go. That's strange, don't you think?"

The question sounded rhetorical. But since it seemed like Isaiah was looking for a response, Connor nodded. "Yeah. I mean—yeah, I thought so."

Isaiah glanced over each shoulder. "Do you mind if we go inside?"

Looking for his competition, Connor thought. A series of reporters had made their way up to the house over the two weeks that had followed the abduction. First in a big wave the day after it happened, then in ever-dwindling numbers until they had stopped coming altogether. Connor hadn't spoken to any of them, and Henry had been good about shooing them away. Some had baited him into answering a few basic questions, like how long Kim and Frank had been married and if he knew why they had been targeted. Since Henry hadn't been present during the abduction (and since he had no idea why his sister and her husband had been targeted), they never got much out of him. Certainly not enough to make it worth a return trip.

Connor thought it over. "Sure." Then he turned around and led Isaiah into the house.

Connor stopped in the foyer, but Isaiah did not. He made his way to the living room as if he had been invited and took a seat in a large, pillowy chair that, as it happened, was intended for guests.

Connor followed him. He took a seat on the sofa, put the knife down on the coffee table between them.

"How's the investigation coming?" Isaiah said.

Good question, Connor thought. "You'd have to ask the police."

"They haven't told you anything? No leads they're working? Nothing like that?"

Connor shrugged, and repeated what Olivia had told him about the man who had died during surgery.

"That's it?"

"That's all I know about."

"That's not a good sign, you know."

"What do you mean?"

Isaiah leaned back in the chair. "She told you about the incident at the ER because it's all she's got. She wants you to know she's working the case, but she also wants you to know it's not going anywhere."

"What makes you say that?"

"She basically told you that. Has she even followed up with the family yet?"

Connor shrugged again.

"You would know if she had." Isaiah crossed one leg over the other. "So I guess it's a good thing I stopped by."

Here it comes. The big pitch. Connor had been expecting it ever since Isaiah had commented on how the house would play with his audience. He wasn't sure how he felt about it. There was a reason he hadn't done any TV interviews or even given a quote. God knew he'd had the chance if he'd wanted to. Being in the spotlight just wasn't his thing, and would it really do anything to help his parents? He doubted it.

"Have you seen our show?"

"I have."

"Then you know what we could do for you."

"Actually, Mr. Cook, I'm not so sure I'm interested in doing any TV at all."

Isaiah rocked forward. "What? Are you serious? Do you know how many calls a show like ours can generate?"

It probably did generate a lot of calls. But there was a more important question. "Has it ever closed any cases?"

"Are you kidding? I can think of a dozen cases right off the top of my head that were put to rest because of the tips that came into our show. You know the story of that kid—Nick Parsons—taken straight out of his backyard in broad daylight? Barely a toddler. You remember that?"

Connor wasn't certain. It sounded familiar. But this time Isaiah didn't give him a chance to answer.

"The guy who kidnapped him was in jail a week later thanks to our show. Sick fuck was part of some baby-snatching ring."

Connor's eyelids started to close. With the adrenaline wearing off, the Ambien was starting to take effect again. "I appreciate you stopping by," Connor said as he stood up. "I haven't slept well. Could I think about this?"

"Oh, sure. Of course," Isaiah said, likewise standing. "I understand. Really do think about it, though, and call me. I'm back and forth between here and California a lot. But trust me, unless I'm in the air, I'll answer. Anytime, day or night."

Connor led Isaiah to the door and closed it behind him. He was starting to understand why Henry had made a point of keeping the reporters out of the house. Were they all as bad as this guy? Connor considered that and decided they were probably worse. If a reporter had managed to get inside, he would likely have kept firing questions until he was physically thrown out.

Connor went upstairs, barely made it to bed. The last thing he thought about before falling asleep was the man who had died during surgery. He was sure Olivia would talk to the man's family eventually. But it was Connor's parents who were missing, so why shouldn't he track them down and talk to them, too?

CHAPTER 8

CONNOR WOKE UP feeling disoriented and tired. The morning sun sliced through the blinds of his one window, hitting him smack in the face. He squinted, checked the clock. He had been asleep for twelve hours. Good. He had needed it. Once the Ambien finished wearing off, he would probably start to feel a little better.

He sat up, vaguely remembered the conversation with Isaiah from the night before, and checked his pocket for the man's business card. Okay, so that hadn't been a dream. Connor tossed the business card onto his nightstand and made his way to the bathroom. He washed his face, ran his wet hands through his hair, trying to tame the worst of it, and applied deodorant. Then he traded one tee shirt for another and called himself done.

Austin would already be at 213 Powder Lane, likely in the midst of tearing out the wall that separated the living room from the kitchen, and Connor had promised him he would be back at work today to help. Anything was better than wandering around this empty house like a ghost. He particularly liked the idea of spending the day smashing drywall with a sledgehammer.

He put his father's cellphone in the right front pocket of his jeans and his own cellphone in the left. Then he grabbed the keys to the old Ford Fiesta and headed out of the house. The car had been a hand-me-down from his mother, who, when he had complained it wasn't new, said no first-time driver needed a new car. She had been right, too. He'd had more accidents than seemed fair, and they had left the vehicle a beaten-up shell of the car she had given him. These days, it barely managed to limp along from one location to the next.

He made the ten-minute trip to Powder Lane in silence. He had no interest in music right now and feared if he turned on talk radio he might accidentally stumble upon a report of his parents' abduction.

Connor had been lucky to get this job. It paid quite a bit better than any other summer gig he had considered, and Austin, who had only started flipping houses, could afford just one assistant. If Connor had been required to compete with other applicants, no doubt somebody with experience would have won out. But Austin had never gotten so far as to take applications. Connor had run into him when Austin was putting up flyers in the neighborhood, advertising the open position.

Actually, he hadn't quite "run into him." That would imply they had met by chance. In truth, Connor had seen Austin tacking a flyer to a telephone pole from his bedroom window and had gone outside to investigate. He came up on Austin from behind while the man was in the middle of hanging his second flyer on a pole even closer to Connor's house.

It said "HELP WANTED. HOME RENOVATION. $30/HR. NEARBY" and included a phone number.

"What's this about?" Connor said.

Austin turned around, startled. He was rail thin, hadn't shaved in a week or more. His blue eyes were sunk deep into his skull. His stringy blond hair hung to his shoulders. Connor had thought he must be in his sixties (later he learned Austin was only a year older than his mother). But he also smiled easily and was wearing a white Polo shirt tucked into a pair of blue jeans. "Sneak up on people much, do you?"

Connor smiled back. "Depends on the day." He pointed to the flyer. "You're looking for help?"

"It seems that way."

"Why don't you put an ad online?"

Austin turned back to the flyer, placed the staple gun on the last remaining corner, and fired, securing the flyer in place. "I wanted somebody local. Thought they might be more reliable. Are you interested?"

Connor frowned, thoughtfully. He wasn't big on manual labor. Then again, any job he could get would put him on his feet all day, and at least this wouldn't force him to interact with an endless stream of customers. "What would I be doing?"

"The flyer kind of spells it out, doesn't it?"

"I mean specifically."

Austin tucked the stack of flyers under one arm. "Look, I'll level with you. I needed a change. My old job—I was on a computer all day long and I just needed to *do* something. So I bought this house on the cheap, figured I could get in on the whole flipping game. I'm not much of a handyman. But, I thought, 'I'm smart. I can figure it out.' So here I am—figuring it out. But it's just too much for one person to do alone, and I need some help."

"What did you do?"

"I was a software developer."

Interesting, Connor thought, noting the similarity between Austin's former career and his future one. "I don't have any experience with all that renovation stuff."

Austin shrugged. "Didn't you just hear my story? Neither do I. But you're young. You look strong enough. Could I count on you to show up?"

"Sure."

"Then the job's yours if you want it. I don't feel like interviewing a whole bunch of candidates. Plus, even if I find someone with experience, I don't have the time to find someone else if they flake out on me. You just do what I tell you to and we'll be fine."

Connor liked the way that sounded. Soon, he was going to have to spend every day on the computer. Probably working long hours to prove himself. Why not use these three months to do something completely different?

He pulled up to the house on Powder Lane and parked along the street. It was an old Victorian. Two stories. A wraparound porch. Probably a hundred years old, Connor thought, and it had all of the wear and tear that would come with a house of that age.

It was an ambitious project for any house flipper, and especially for one who had never flipped a house before.

Austin had already hired a plumber and an electrician to get the major systems working. And for the house itself, he had paid cash. So, aside from Connor, all it was costing him now was time, which he had plenty of, and materials, which he could afford.

The property didn't have a garage, but it did have a shed at the end of the driveway that was big enough to be one. Austin planned to convert it.

Connor entered the front door. The house was quiet, which was not what he expected. "Austin?"

"Yeah. In here."

Connor followed the sound of his voice to the living room. The bulk of the wall that separated that room from the kitchen had been punched through. Most of the drywall Austin had knocked down was spread across the kitchen tile—once white, now gray, and another thing they would eventually have to tear out. Dust was everywhere.

Austin was standing with his hands on his hips and looking at a part of the wall he had left standing. From where he was, Connor could see two-by-fours inside it that stretched from floor to ceiling. "I think this is a support beam. Probably better to leave it."

He wiped his forearm across his brow, crossed the wooden floor in the living room to a cooler he had set in one corner. He pulled out a bottle of Dos Equis, used his Swiss Army knife to open it, then used the cooler as a chair.

After he took a long drink, emptying half the bottle, he looked at Connor. "You're late."

"I was just . . ."

Then he smiled, waved his hand dismissively. "I'm kidding. I'm just glad you decided to come. It's been hard going without you. How are you holding up?"

Connor shrugged.

"They'll figure it out. Don't worry. Who are you staying with?"

"No one now. My Uncle Henry came up for a few weeks, but he had to go home. He asked me to go with him, but I think I need to be here. You know, just in case."

"Where's home?"

"Florida."

"That's a long ways away."

"That's why I couldn't go," Connor said, but Austin was still talking.

"It's not a good idea to be by yourself right now. Don't you have a friend you can stay with?"

Connor shook his head. "No, not here."

"Well, look, you can stay with me if you want to. I've got an apartment in the city. Two bedrooms, even, so you'll have your own space. I don't like the idea of you being all alone."

"I'll think about it."

Austin stood up. "Don't ever get old. Everything hurts," he said as he stretched his elbows in toward his spine. "While you're thinking, how about you help me clean this mess up?"

Connor put on a pair of work gloves. He started with the largest pieces of drywall, carrying them out to the dumpster Austin had rented. It was one of those big ones used on construction sites and it took up most of the driveway.

"Any word from the police so far?" Austin asked as he helped Connor toss the drywall over the lip of the dumpster.

"Not yet." The question reminded Connor of his conversation with Isaiah, who had asked pretty much the same thing. He wondered, now that he had had a little sleep, if he was making a mistake. He needed a second opinion. "Have you ever heard of that show *Uncovered?*"

"That's like *48 Hours*, right?"

"Something like that."

"What about it?"

"I had a guy visit me yesterday. A producer for the show. He said he wants to use my story."

"So, like, interview you? Film a recreation in your house? That sort of thing?"

Connor tossed the last of the drywall into the dumpster, then patted his gloves together to shake loose the dust. "I would assume so."

"I don't know if that's a good idea."

"Why not?"

"Do you really want to watch them recreate the abduction of your parents? I can't imagine that would be good for you right now."

That was exactly what Connor had thought when the idea had first been presented. And as far as he was concerned, hearing his first instinct repeated back to him confirmed he had been right.

CHAPTER 9

LETTING GO OF *Uncovered* did not mean Connor was letting go of everything, though. He'd had an idea when he'd been lying in bed last night, and it, unlike the TV show, seemed better and better the more he thought about it. He wasn't going to let the abduction of his parents end up getting labeled an unsolved case.

When Austin called it a day, he again encouraged Connor to stay with him, said they could even go up to Austin's cabin over the weekend and do a little fishing. Something peaceful. It would be good for him, Austin insisted.

Connor again said he would think about it, but instead went home, powered up his laptop, and hacked his way into William Marks Hospital. It didn't take him long to find the records tied to his mother's name. The patient she had recently lost was one Carlos Hernandez. His records included an address, mentioned a wife named Adriana and a daughter named Rosa. Armed with that information, Connor figured he knew everything he needed to.

He found a small, ramshackle house at the address in Carlos's records. It had been squeezed onto a particularly small plot of land, in a part of town Connor had never visited. The white wood siding had grayed and cracked in places, succumbed to rot in others. Most of the window screens were missing or torn. The curtains appeared to be bedsheets. The grass—weeds, mostly—was overgrown.

But it also didn't seem much worse than the houses around it.

He made his way up to the front porch and knocked. Waited. Knocked again. Rang the bell. Then, after he looked around to make sure there was nobody staring at him, he squeezed through the bushes in front of the closest pair of windows. He cupped his hands around his eyes, leaned forward so that he was touching the glass. He didn't have much hope of seeing anything with the bedsheet in his way. But maybe there was a tear, and maybe it would be enough to give him a glimpse into Carlos's world.

And what will that tell you?

Nothing, he knew. Still, he looked, and perhaps a second after he connected with the glass, a Rottweiler pushed aside the curtain, landed with his paws on the glass, and started barking.

Connor leaped back, got tangled in the bushes, and fell. Once he was on his feet again, the dog was still there, still barking. He didn't want to draw more attention to himself than he already had, so he returned to his car and tried to decide what to do next.

The neighbors had told Olivia the family was out of town. Connor doubted they knew any more than that. But there had to be somebody taking care of that dog. And that person—they probably would know something.

Connor decided to wait. Give it a couple of hours, at least. See if anyone came.

But, parked directly across the street from the house, he couldn't stay where he was.

He drove around the block, parked at the corner. From here, he could still see the cement path that led to the Hernandezes' front door, but not the house itself. It was enough.

The sun started to set. Connor wasn't sure it would be a good idea to hang around this neighborhood after dark. He was about to call it quits, maybe come back in the morning, when he saw a child appear on the path in front of the Hernandezes' house. She hauled a bag of trash that was almost as big as she was to the bin at the end of the driveway and struggled to get it inside. Then she returned the way she had come.

Connor hopped out of the car, ran toward the house. He was sure he hadn't seen anyone enter, so where had this girl come from?

The front door came into view just as the child stepped through it.

Once she was out of sight, the house looked as still and quiet as it had before.

Had somebody been there the whole time? If so, why hadn't they answered the door?

He returned to the house, knocked again and, like last time, no one came. He knocked louder, rang the doorbell repeatedly. The dog started to bark. Good. He intended to make a nuisance of himself.

Finally, it worked.

He heard the lock turn. The door opened as far as the security chain would allow. "What do you want?" a woman said in a thick Mexican accent. She looked worried, tired, anxious. Connor could relate.

"I need to ask you about Carlos."

"I have nothing to say."

She began to close the door, and Connor instinctively pushed on it from the other side to stop her. "Wait. It's not about him exactly. It's about his doctor. Dr. Callahan?"

She stopped trying to close the door, and Connor stopped trying to hold it open. She looked at him in a way Connor couldn't quite describe. "The surgeon?"

"Yes."

"You don't look like police."

"I'm not."

"What do you want?"

"I need to talk to you. Could you let me in?"

The woman looked at him a couple of seconds longer, then closed the door, unlatched the chain, and reopened it. "Come."

Connor stepped inside.

As soon as he had, the door was closed and bolted shut again.

The living room he found himself in felt dark, even with the overhead light on. That was more likely a trick of the mind than fact—a result of having sheets (mismatching sheets, Connor now noticed) nailed over the windows. An overturned crate served as a coffee table. A small TV sat on the floor. The sofa was old, supported by a brick where one of its feet should have been. But the house was also tidy. Connor could tell the floor had been recently swept and all other surfaces had been dusted.

The Rottweiler barked ferociously from another room. Connor tensed up.

"He's locked up," the woman said, perhaps noticing the subtle change in Connor's stance.

"Is your name Adriana?"

The woman nodded.

The little girl who had taken the trash to the street peeked out through the kitchen doorway.

"And that's Rosa?"

At the sound of her name, the little girl disappeared. Adriana nodded again.

"What do you want?"

"The police have been by here to talk to you?"

"Every day. They come every day. I don't talk to them."

Connor thought about what Adriana had said before she opened the door. *You're don't look like police.* "Why not?"

Adriana glanced at the kitchen, and Connor suddenly realized he already knew the answer. "She's not legal, is she?" It was possible neither of them was.

"You said this is about doctor. Tell me what you want," Adriana said.

"She's my mother."

"So?"

"I know you probably don't like her. I understand. Believe me, I'd probably blame her too, for what happened to Carlos, if I were you."

"I don't blame her for what happened to Carlos."

"What?" Connor said, surprised. "But—" He wasn't sure what he was going to say next, and before he could figure it out a timer went off in the kitchen.

Adriana went to take care of it. Connor followed.

She turned off the timer on the stove and pulled a plate of cookies out of the oven. Oatmeal, Connor guessed, from the look of them.

Rosa appeared from the only other doorway that led into the kitchen. She spoke to her mother in Spanish and in that sort of pleading tone children got when they wanted something.

"English, only," Adriana said as she used a spatula to transfer the cookies from baking sheet to plate.

Rosa's eyes cut to Connor and then back. "Can I have a cookie? Pleeeeeeeeease?"

"You are still hungry, *mi cielito*?"

Rosa nodded.

"Okay, you can have one cookie."

Rosa snatched it off the plate and ran back the way she had come.

"They're hot!" Adriana called after her. "Don't eat it too quickly." She sighed, returned her attention to Connor. "Speak. This doctor. Your mother. What about her? Why are you here?"

"She's missing."

"The police. This is why they come by? They think I have something to do with her missing?"

"They just want to talk to you," Connor said. Of course the truth was they thought she *might* have something to do with it, but saying that to a woman who was already hostile toward him seemed like a bad idea. "They're trying to find out where she is."

Adriana threw the spatula into the sink. "They want to talk to me because they think I am responsible."

"Please, Mrs. Hernandez, do you know anything that could help them find her?"

There was a breakfast table in the corner with three chairs, just enough for the family before Carlos had died. The window adjacent to it was also covered with a sheet. Adriana sat down in one of the chairs. She sighed. "You know why Carlos was in hospital?"

"No." It was probably in the records, but Connor had only read enough to get the name and address.

A pained expression crossed over Adriana's face, then disappeared. "We needed money. Carlos, he said he could get it. Said he had a friend, needed him to do some work. He wouldn't tell me what, but I knew. He had talked about it before. I told him, no, don't go. We don't need money that badly. We find another way. But he goes. He does it anyway. And now . . . no Carlos. No money."

Connor felt his cellphone vibrate. He knew it was his and not his father's because of which pocket it was in. He slid the phone out just enough to see who the caller was. Olivia. He could phone her back when he was done doing her job.

"What was it? This work he was doing?"

Adriana sniffled, did her best to hold back her tears. "It doesn't matter. But see, your mom, this not her fault. This is . . . ." Her voice wavered and she stopped talking. She straightened up, tightened her fists, then continued, once again in control of her voice. "This is Carlos's fault. Your mom, she came to see me after Carlos died. You know that? She came and stood right over there in my living room and apologized. She said she knows what it's like to lose someone and I told her no, this not her fault. So see? I couldn't have had anything to do with it. This is *Carlos's fault*." She poked the table with each of the last two words, as if merely repeating the statement wasn't enough.

Connor believed her. Adriana had no idea what had happened to his parents. But there was something she had said, something he'd almost missed, that didn't seem right. "You said she came here? That she told you she knows what it's like to lose someone?"

"Yes."

"Are you sure that's what she said?"

"Yes, I'm sure."

"Do you know what she meant?"

Adriana shook her head, then wiped away a tear with her thumb.

Connor wasn't sure what to make of that. Both of his mother's parents were dead, but that didn't seem like the kind of thing you would say when you were talking about a parent, especially since both had died of natural causes. "All right. I'm sorry for bothering you." He headed to the door.

"Hey," Adriana called after him. "You tell the police not to come back here anymore, you hear me?"

Connor turned around, looked her in the eye. "I'll tell them." Then he returned to his car. The sun had nearly set, and a pair of men standing on a porch across the street watched him the whole way.

Connor immediately locked the doors and put the car into drive. He didn't bother to listen to Olivia's voicemail until he was on the interstate.

She had said only, "Call me as soon as you get this. It's urgent."

CHAPTER 10

TRAFFIC ON THE interstate was light, so Connor didn't mind taking his eyes off the road long enough to grab the USB cable curled up in the cup holder and connect it to his phone. Then he clicked the icon beside Olivia's message to call her back.

She answered on the first ring. "Where are you?"

"What? Why?" Connor said.

"Are you at home?"

"No, I—"

"How soon can you get there?"

He glanced at the clock on his dashboard and did a quick calculation. "Fifteen minutes."

"Okay, I'll see you then."

"What's going on?"

"Better we talk in person," Olivia said, and hung up.

Shit, Connor thought. Something had happened. He pressed his foot down on the gas, going as fast as he dared and weaving between cars. Fifteen minutes was how long it would have taken him on a normal night, but he could get home faster.

What does Olivia want? Have the police found something? The suspense was killing him.

When he pulled up to the house, he saw a black sedan parked out front. Olivia stepped out.

"Tell me what's happening. Did you find something?"

She waited until Connor was close enough to speak without raising her voice. "Let's go inside."

Oh, God. This is going to be bad. Really bad.

He was right.

"Can we sit down?" Olivia asked. She was carrying a manila envelope.

Connor felt his legs go weak as he moved to the sofa.

Olivia took a seat beside him. She leaned forward, propping her elbows on her knees and holding the envelope with both hands. "We got a call."

"And?"

She opened the envelope, slid out an eight-by-ten photo and handed it to Connor. "Do you recognize this?"

The photo was of a ring, taken close up and against a white background. In any other setting, the photo would have reminded Connor of the kind of picture he would see hanging in the window of a jewelry shop. Here, though, tonight, it could mean only one thing.

"That's my mother's ring."

He knew this not just because the detective was asking about it. He recognized the distinctive, swirling pattern that had been etched into the band.

"You're sure?"

Connor nodded. "Where did you find it?"

Olivia ignored the question. She held out a hand, requesting Connor return the picture. When he did, she swapped it with another. This time, he was looking at a piece of fabric. Unlike the ring, it consumed the entire frame. But from the look of it, Connor suspected its actual size wasn't much larger than a quarter.

"How about that?"

He couldn't be as certain about the fabric as he was about the ring, but Connor suspected he recognized it, as well. "My father was wearing a shirt like that, I think, the night . . ." He couldn't finish the sentence, so instead he asked, "Where did you get these?"

Olivia again held out a hand to request Connor return the second photo. She put it back in the envelope. "Like I said, we got a call."

"What did they say?"

"They told us where to find your parents."

"Did you find them?"

Olivia looked away, directing her attention once again to the envelope. "Yes."

Connor felt a flutter of excitement in his chest. "What are you showing me this stuff for, then? Are they all right? Can I see them?"

"Slow down. Listen to me. The caller told us we would find your parents at a parking garage in Linwood. So we went to check it out. This was late last night, and the lot was nearly deserted. As we neared the top, one of the officers with me said he smelled smoke. And then when we finally reached the top floor, we found out why. Someone had lit a fire right in the middle of the deck. We called the fire department, locked down the garage. At first, we thought we had been played. Then one of the firefighters called me over." She paused long enough to lean in and shake her head. "The bodies were no longer recognizable. All we managed to recover were a few scraps of clothing and your mother's wedding band."

The nervous energy Connor felt morphed into something dark and unidentifiable, but equally as intense. He got up, paced to the wall. "No, no, no." Turned around. "That can't be right. You're mistaken. You have to be."

"Connor, please. I wish we were. But if you're sure about the ring—"

"Dental records. You can check those, right? We've been going to the same dentist as long as I can remember."

"Not this time," she said softly.

"Why not?"

Olivia sighed, tossed the envelope onto the coffee table. "The killer took their teeth."

"What?"

Olivia shrugged.

"Okay, well, how about DNA?" he said. "You can test that, can't you? I mean, we have to be sure this really is my parents, don't we?"

"This isn't *CSI*, Connor," Olivia snapped, also getting to her feet. Then she seemed to catch herself, perhaps remembering Connor had just been told his parents were dead. "This case just isn't that complicated. The killer told us where to find the bodies. You've identified your mother's wedding ring and your father's clothing. There's nothing the lab can tell us that we don't know already. I'm sorry. But we're going to find their killer, I promise."

"Well, you've done a bang-up job of the investigation so far, haven't you?"

"Excuse me?"

"You tell me you're going to talk to Carlos's family—"

"How do you know the patient's name?"

"—and it's the only lead you've got. And I know you said it was probably a dead end, but still . . . who ends up talking to them? I'll give you a hint. It wasn't you. It was me. I talked to them."

Blood rushed to Olivia's face. "You what?"

"I mean—how hard is it to follow up on *one* lead?"

"Connor, we went by the house multiple times. I told you—they were out of town. When did you talk to them?"

"Today. Just now."

"Then I guess they just got back."

Connor took a deep breath. "You happen to notice that big dog when you went to their house?"

"Of course."

"Did it ever occur to you that if they had a dog, they had to have somebody taking care of it? Because it occurred to me, so I parked at the end of the street and waited. It took a while, but eventually I saw—" Connor realized he was about to mention Rosa and revised his statement. He still wasn't sure whether both of them were illegal, but he was sure Adriana did not want to get her daughter involved. "A woman. She was hauling a bag of trash out to the street. I caught up to her before she made her way back inside. She was Carlos's wife, she said. She told me Carlos had gotten involved in some bad stuff, and that's what got him killed."

"You shouldn't have gone over there."

Connor didn't hear her. He was too wrapped up in his own thoughts, overwhelmed by emotion. "She said my mom even came by to see her after it happened, told her she was sorry. So, yeah, you were right. There was nothing to it. But if you'd just been doing your job, maybe you would have gotten another idea after you talked to her, don't you think? And maybe we'd be having a different conversation right now."

CHAPTER 11

OLIVIA DECIDED IT probably wouldn't have been hard for Connor to dig up Carlos's name. Perhaps Kim had written about it in a diary or Connor had found it in notes she had brought home from the hospital. It didn't matter. He was upset, and she didn't see how it would do any good to ask again.

She did, however, chastise herself for not staking out the house like Connor had done. She could blame it on a long list of distractions: her ex-husband, who was suing her for custody of their child; the long hours; her decision to give up caffeine at this time. She could rationalize the choice by reminding herself she had other cases to work, and all of them demanded her attention. She could tell herself that from the beginning she hadn't thought Adriana was involved. But she knew it really came down to her choices. It had been a mistake, and not one she could afford to repeat.

She let Connor rant until he was done. Everyone had their own way of grieving. Then she apologized again, assured him once more they would find the killer, and told him someone would be in touch when they were done with the bodies.

What Olivia didn't tell him was the bad stuff Carlos Hernandez had gotten involved in. She knew about it because there was a file with his name on it.

According to the report inside, Carlos had entered the One Point liquor store in Windroff Park wearing a Halloween mask and carrying a Colt Python. He was barely through the door when the owner, Aden Tindol, had pulled a gun of his own out from underneath the counter and told him to get the hell out of there.

Seconds later, Aden had fired his weapon. A warning shot, he said, which was why the bullet had missed Carlos by a wide margin, instead drilling a hole into the far wall, only inches from the ceiling.

At that point, Carlos ran. Had he run out the store, Aden claimed he would have let the whole thing go. He had been robbed once before and the report he had filed with the police after that incident had led nowhere.

But the would-be robber hadn't run out of the store. Instead, he'd sought cover down one of the aisles. Then there was more yelling—Aden telling Carlos to come out, Carlos telling Aden to drop his gun.

Eventually, Carlos had pushed over a metal rack of shelving, perhaps to create a distraction. It had crashed into another, and that one had crashed into a third. Thousands of dollars of product ruined, Aden said.

Then, finally, Carlos had come out, only he came out running. Gun drawn. It looked like, on the CCTV footage, they were both within sight of each other for a good second and a half. It would feel an eternity in that situation, Olivia knew. But, unlike Carlos, Aden hadn't hesitated to pull his trigger. In fact, he'd pulled it four times. Each round had hit Carlos square in the chest.

During the interview, the report noted, Aden had repeatedly insisted he hadn't had any choice, and that he wouldn't have shot Carlos at all if he had just left the store when he'd told him to. Not that it mattered. There was no dispute about whether Aden had been within his rights to defend himself.

CHAPTER 12

THE MORE CONNOR thought about it, the more certain he was his parents were still alive. It wasn't simple denial. He *knew* that. There was something that Olivia had said, something that didn't sit right with him. It wasn't that the killer had removed the victims' teeth—he'd seen enough crime shows to know killers sometimes kept trophies from their victims. It wasn't that the killer had called to tell the police where they could find the bodies, or even the fire itself. Although all of these things seemed a little strange. It was *something else*.

But what?

Connor reviewed the conversation with Olivia as he went to the kitchen to get a glass of water. The argument with her had left his throat dry, aching. His mind jumped from one part of their exchange to another. She had asked if they could sit down. He had accused her of not doing her job, told her about his conversation with Adriana. He had asked about DNA testing, looked at the photos she had brought, said the scrap of fabric matched his father's shirt, the ring was his mother's.

He filled a glass with water from the tap, and as he was about to take his first sip the answer occurred to him. Could that really be it?

He scurried back to the living room to get his cellphone and called Olivia. "The ring you showed me. How did you know it was my mother's wedding band?"

"We found it on the ring finger of her left hand. It just made sense. Why?"

Connor hung up. He wasn't ready to answer that question yet. He had to be sure he wasn't mistaken.

In his parents' walk-in closet, he found a pair of photo albums and a box. One of the albums was blank and the other was only half full. It was the box that held most of his mother's cherished memories. Although she kept promising she would sort the pictures in it, she never did.

He quickly scoured the photo album, but couldn't find what he was looking for, so he dragged the box out of the closet and dumped the contents onto the dining room table. Connor's old report cards. Elementary school artwork. Photos. Used plane tickets.

The photos had been dated on the back with a black magic marker. Connor picked them out one at a time, noting the dates as he did so. He was only interested in those that included his mother and, in particular, those where he could see her left hand. A photo from three years back confirmed what he remembered his mother telling him about her ring, but he wanted something more recent. Finally, he found it.

The picture was of his father and mother, her left arm draped over his shoulders. Behind them was a Christmas tree. The photo was dated December 24. That was only seven months ago, and probably the most recent picture he was going to find.

He looked closely at his mother's hand. The ring was on her middle finger, just as it had been three years ago.

He remembered her telling him she had lost weight some years back and couldn't find a jeweler to size her ring. Doing so would distort the pattern on the band. His dad had offered to replace it, but she had said no. She liked having the original, and besides—it didn't matter which finger the ring was on.

So, that couldn't have been his mother in the fire. Her ring, yes. Not her body.

The man who had abducted his parents wanted the police to think they were dead. That was why he had set the bodies on fire instead of dumping them in the harbor. *That* was why he had taken their teeth.

His parents were still alive.

Connor grabbed his phone out of his pocket, ready to call Olivia back and give her the news, when he noticed something else—a document, and on it a flash of letters. He hesitated. The document was a marriage certificate. The letters that got his attention spelled out the name Matthew A. Jones. The person he had married? Kimberly D. Snider. Connor's mom.

Stay out of my system or I'll make sure Matt finds out what you've been up to.

He sat back in his chair, feeling a cold prickle on the back of his neck. His mother had been married before, and Ion knew about it.

Then, another memory. Something Adriana had said: *She said she knows what it's like to lose someone.*

Adriana had been talking about Connor's mom. He had already ruled out both of her parents as the mysterious "someone." Now, at least, he had an idea of who his mom must have been referring to. Matt. According to the date on the certificate, they had gotten married three years before Connor was born. He must have died shortly thereafter.

Now that Connor understood who Matt was, he wasn't surprised his mom had kept that to herself. But how would Ion know about him? Had he dug up more about Connor's life than just his email address? The answer to that was an obvious yes, so how crazy was this guy? Was he crazy enough to come after Connor's parents as some sort of payback for hacking into his website?

If the information on TruthSeekers.com was a reflection of the man's mental state, he was out there, for sure.

Connor wouldn't call Olivia yet. The killer wanted the police to think his parents were dead. Maybe he should leave it that way for now. At least until he knew a little more about the man behind that website.

CHAPTER 13

CONNOR HAD COME to the conclusion that Ion must have tunneled his way back into Connor's computer while they were connected. It would explain how he had managed to shut down Connor's system. It would also explain how he had gotten Connor's email and enough information to start digging into his life.

That sort of tracing would have begun with Connor's IP address.

But if Ion thought he was the only one who could locate a stranger by their IP, he was mistaken. Connor started his search for Ion with the email Ion had sent him. Most emails included the IP address from which the email originated, and this one was no exception. The IP address wouldn't take him straight to Ion's front door, but at least it would let him know where he needed to be looking. It would also let him know whether it was even possible that Ion was behind his parents' abduction. If the IP traced back to France, for example, he could rule Ion out without any further investigation.

But it did not trace back to France, or even Boston.

The sender's IP pointed squarely at New York. Watertown Heights, to be exact. Another suburb of the city, and one that was barely an hour's drive from Connor's house.

So maybe he was on to something, after all.

He tempered that hope, though, reminded himself that proximity alone did not make this man the kidnapper. He needed to find out more.

Connor searched the web for the TruthSeekers.com domain registration. Those could be public or private, depending on how much the registrant was willing to pay. When he found the domain, he took a deep breath, worried he might have come to a dead end, and clicked for more information.

Boom.

A name and address: Dylan Naese. 121 Forrest Creek Drive. New York.

He was in business.

Connor went straight to his car, stopping barely long enough to put on his shoes. It took him two tries to get it to start—*piece of crap*—and then he was on the road.

Connor wasn't sure what he'd find at 121 Forrest Creek Drive. He pictured something small, maybe even run down. A manifestation of the man's inner world. He was ready for that. He imagined himself charging straight up to the front door, pounding on it until the man answered. *You're Dylan?* he would ask, just to confirm there was no mistake before demanding Dylan tell him where his parents were.

What Connor found, though, was not small, and not even a little bit run down.

The three-story brick Georgian loomed large in a neighborhood of large houses. It was surrounded by a brick wall and the driveway was blocked by an iron gate, complete with a callbox. Connor drove past it slowly and parked along the curb. He walked up to the gate so he could get a better look. The only lights that were on seemed to be those on the top floor.

The house was at the intersection of Forrest Creek Drive and Park

Lane. Connor put his hands in his pockets and strolled to the corner, turned, then continued to follow the wall until it ended. Ivy clung to the brick, climbing all eight feet and over.

Perhaps there was another way in, he told himself. But there wasn't. At least, there wasn't one that was visible from the street.

When the wall that ran along Park Lane ended, Connor peered around the corner to see if there was an opening along the back of the property, but he couldn't see much from where he was.

He looked over his shoulder—an action, he realized, that couldn't be more suspicious—and slipped off the sidewalk into the darkness behind the property. There were only a few feet between Dylan's wall and his neighbor's fence, not enough space to walk straight ahead. Connor eased between the fence and the wall, palms pressed to the bricks. He considered pulling out his cellphone, using the flashlight on it, but worried that might draw attention.

The wall continued uninterrupted to the far corner of the property, and then turned toward Forrest Creek Drive. Only because Connor had already come this far, he finished scouting the perimeter in its entirety. When he reached the street, he leaned against the wall and dropped his head. He thought about the money this guy must have, the life he must live. He sighed. This was stupid. Connor was wasting his time. This guy wasn't involved.

He went back to the car and called Olivia, told her about the ring, what he thought it meant. He wasn't going to make the same mistake with the ring that he had made with the cash he had found after the abduction. Then he thought about the show *Uncovered*.

"To hell with it," he mumbled. He wanted his parents back, and a segment on that show wouldn't make the situation any worse. It might even help.

CHAPTER 14

OLIVIA WASN'T CONVINCED the ring meant anything at all. The killer might have removed it for one reason or another and simply shoved it back on the wrong finger. She kept that to herself, though. It didn't change anything. Whether the bodies were actually Connor's parents or not, the man who had taken them was still a killer, and, according to the department's forensic psychologist, would likely kill again.

She had traced the phone call back to a burner and the burner back to the 7-Eleven where it was sold. Unfortunately, the buyer had paid cash, so that lead died there. Subpoenaing T-Mobile didn't do her any good either, since the phone was off.

So she was stuck waiting for the lab to see what clues, if any, they might be able to pull from the remains of the fire.

While she waited, she decided to follow up with the owner of the One Point liquor store. On its surface, the report had painted the picture of a man who was no more defensive than most might be after killing someone, even when it was done in self-defense. But Aden Tindol was ex-Army. And although she couldn't put her finger on exactly why that bothered her, it did.

It would probably amount to nothing. Likely she still felt guilty that she hadn't spoken with Adriana before Connor had.

She stopped by the liquor store first, hoping to catch him off guard and ease her way casually into a discussion about the botched robbery.

A woman was sitting on a stool behind the counter reading a book. She was wearing a white wool sweater. (Olivia wasn't surprised. The store was cold, even by her standards.) She looked up when the door chimed, nodded, and went back to her reading. A romance novel of some sort, Olivia assumed, judging by what she could see of the cover.

"Aden around?"

"Not tonight." This time the woman didn't even look up from her book.

"You know where I could find him?"

She shrugged. "I guess he's at home. Is there something I can help you with?"

"You weren't here the night of the robbery, were you?" Olivia didn't remember seeing anything about a woman in the report. Still, she didn't want to assume.

"Oh, you're here about that?" the woman said, closing her book and sitting up a little straighter. "No, I wasn't. Why? Are you a cop?"

Olivia showed the woman her badge.

"I heard it was quite a thing," the woman said. "Aden was particularly upset about it."

"How do you know that?"

"He told me."

"What exactly did he say?"

The woman pursed her lips, looked up at the ceiling for a second, perhaps trying to remember the conversation. "He just said he was upset."

"That's it?"

"I mean—basically. He spent most of the night cleaning up and was back at it the next morning by the time I came in for my shift. He looked tired, complained about the cost of the lost product and the damage to the wall."

The woman's gaze shifted. Olivia instinctively turned, looked in the same general direction. She saw the bullet hole near the ceiling she had read about in the report.

"He said it was a terrible time for something like this to happen," she continued.

"What did he mean by that?"

"I don't know. He just kinda said it and moved on. Why?"

"Never mind. Thanks for your help." Olivia headed to the exit.

"You want me to tell Aden you stopped by?"

"Don't worry about it. It's not that important. I'll catch him later."

Olivia had lied. The more she learned, the more important it seemed she talk to Aden right away. There was something he was hiding.

Aden lived in an apartment building two miles down from the liquor store. She decided to try her luck there next. Unit 217. The building was a looming tower of steel and cement that looked like it had seen better days. It was named Wooden Grove, which struck Olivia as ironic since there wasn't a hint of nature within sight.

The glass doors to the lobby were unlocked. She pressed the button for the elevator and, after waiting for a minute or so, decided to take the stairs. When she exited the stairwell, she looked left, then right, assessing which way she needed to go, and started moving again.

The interior was better cared for than the exterior. That was true of a lot of buildings in this part of town, she thought.

She found the door and was about to knock when she heard shouting coming from inside. Most of it was inaudible, just the blurry noise of angry voices. They belonged to a man and a woman.

Olivia listened, trying to get the gist of the argument. She gathered he had done something that upset her. No, he was *going* to do something. What on earth could he be about to do that would make the woman this mad?

The way they were fighting reminded Olivia of how she and her ex-husband had fought when she found out he had cheated on her. But you don't tell your girlfriend *before* you cheat, do you? So it couldn't be that.

Then she heard the woman scream and decided there was no more time to wait around. Olivia turned the knob, pushed. The door swung open. She pulled her gun immediately.

Aden was barefoot, naked from the waist up. The sweatpants he was wearing were torn at one knee and looked like they needed a wash. He had his hands balled into fists, but they hung by his sides. The woman—a brunette—was holding a hand to her cheek. She was wearing a blue pantsuit and had backed up to the wall. With Aden dead center between her and the door, there would have been no getting around him.

Olivia announced her name, flashed her badge. "Are you all right?" she said to the woman.

The woman nodded.

"You want to tell me what's going on in here?"

"Someone call you?" Aden said defiantly.

The woman looked away, shook her head. Olivia had seen this scenario play out before. Maybe it was bad. Maybe it wasn't. One thing was for sure—she wasn't going to tell Olivia anything. "You want to leave?"

The woman nodded.

Olivia gestured toward the door. "Go."

The woman did, grabbing her purse from the glass console table beside the door as she left.

Olivia pushed her glasses back up her nose, then took them off, annoyed they weren't staying in place. She might not be reading any menus without them on, but she could see Aden well enough.

"You know, I came here to follow up with you about the robbery at your store. But . . ." she trailed off. Olivia thought she saw something on the coffee table—something horrible. "Get on your knees," she said to Aden. And before he even had time to move, she repeated the command. "Get on your knees now!"

Aden did as he was told.

The glasses went back on.

The thing on the coffee table was exactly what Olivia thought it was.

"Are you alone?"

"Yes."

Olivia stepped backward so she could close the door without turning around. She didn't want anybody coming up on her from behind. Then she handcuffed Aden, cleared the apartment, and called in the bomb.

It wasn't fully assembled yet. But it was close enough.

CHAPTER 15

UNDER NORMAL CIRCUMSTANCES, Connor would say his parents were entitled to their secrets. Everyone had a past. However, the circumstances right now were anything but normal. Connor hadn't even been looking for secrets when he came across the marriage certificate. What might he find if he did?

The box Connor had taken out of his parents' closet was still sitting on the floor in the dining room. The things that had been inside it were still spread across the table. He went through them again, this time examining everything. The pictures, dated all the way back to the eighties, revealed little. His mother and father he recognized, but the rest—all strangers to Connor. Friends of his parents, no doubt, who had come in and out of their lives years ago. He didn't spend much time on them. In fact, looking at the pictures at all was mostly a "check the box" activity Connor did so he could tell himself he had been thorough.

He found a faded pair of movie tickets to *The Usual Suspects*, bound together by a rubber band. A drawing of a turkey he had made in preschool by tracing his hand. A plastic bag with baby teeth. High school yearbooks for both of his parents. The plane tickets he had seen before but hadn't bothered to look at. A diploma from Columbia University with his mother's name on it.

It all seemed like sentimental garbage to Connor.

He picked up the plane tickets. They were for Kimberly Jones and

Frank Callahan. Destination: Prague. Connor knew his mother had researched her ancestry years ago and traced her lineage to the Czech Republic. He wasn't surprised she had visited. She liked to travel.

He tossed everything back into the box, slid the box back into the closet.

There was a small bedroom on the first floor that Connor's father had converted into an office. It had been Connor's room before he had moved to the attic. That was his next stop.

He rifled through his father's filing cabinet and found nothing of interest. Nor did he find anything in the desk drawers, the closet, or on the bookshelf.

Connor turned on the computer. At one time, this machine had sat in the living room, been shared by the family. That was when Connor had been little and his parents had wanted to monitor his online activity. He still remembered the password. Rickety Rat. It was a little-known character in a children's book, but one he had loved.

Once he was in, he reset his father's password and logged in again.

He examined the documents on the desktop and scoured the folders marked as "Frequent" by Windows. Nothing and nothing. Then he fired up Outlook and went through that as well.

That likewise appeared to be a big nothing burger until he opened the trash folder. There were only three emails in it. Two were spam. One was from a Roland Cooper.

Subject: Payment
Body: Let me know when and where you want to meet.

Connor read the message twice, and then asked himself the obvious: *What payment?*

He thought about the envelope of cash he had found the night of his parents' abduction, still stashed away in the back of his sock drawer. Could this have something to do with that? It made more sense than anything else so far, so he decided that yes, maybe it did.

He needed to find out more. If this had something to do with the money he had found the night of the abduction, then was it so much of a stretch to think it might even be related to the abduction itself?

He looked up the name "Roland Cooper" online but found too many results for them to be meaningful. Okay. That was fine. The online search was largely reflex. It was not as if there was going to be a webpage called "The Nefarious Activity of Roland Cooper." If Connor wanted to know what the payment was about (and if there really was anything nefarious going on), he would have to find a way to meet the man in person. A phone call wouldn't cut it. Roland could just hang up. And even if he didn't, Connor wanted to be able to look him in the eye so he could judge whether Roland was telling the truth.

He checked the Sent folder to see what his father had said in response but found nothing. Then there was a knock on the door. Connor looked at the time on the computer. It was eight-thirty a.m.

They're early, he thought.

Isaiah Cook entered the house first. "This is going to be great," he said, with more enthusiasm than Connor felt was appropriate.

Behind him came a throng of strangers. They hauled in cameras, audio equipment, and lights. Isaiah rattled off a handful of names as they passed, identifying the ones he felt were important. Connor didn't catch any of them.

Suddenly a man was in his face. And although Connor hadn't

caught his name either, at least he remembered Isaiah had identified him as the director.

"So, let's just get this straight. The guy came in through the front door. And then what happened? Exactly."

Connor took a step back. He was overwhelmed and was starting to wonder if this whole thing was a mistake. All of these people in the house—he didn't like it. Connor wasn't a people person, and these kinds of people—the ones who delighted in (not to mention profited from) other people's tragedy—were the worst. But, he reminded himself, he had agreed to do this for a reason. And even if he hadn't, he also felt like he was stuck now, so he did his best to be helpful.

"He attacked my parents, put them in his van, and took off. I didn't see much. I was upstairs when it happened. My bedroom is in the attic."

The director made a face. "Yes, but you heard something. You saw *something*. According to the police report, you saw a van pull up on the lawn, right?"

Connor nodded.

"Okay. Let's start there."

"I'm sorry, but what do you need to know all this for?"

"The reenactment, of course."

Connor should have known that. *Uncovered* always did reenactments. Hell, Isaiah had *told* him they were going to do a reenactment when he'd called back. Part of him must still be thinking about that email he had found.

"Nothing tasteless. We just want to get a few key shots to sprinkle in during the interview. Now, the van, when it pulled up—how long did it take the guy to get inside the house?"

"Seconds, I think."

"He had a key?"

"I don't think so."

"So the door was unlocked?"

"It must have been." Connor remembered answering similar questions for the police.

"The police report said he was wearing a ski mask. Is that correct?"

"Yes."

Two men entered carrying collapsible lights. "Where do you want them, boss?" asked one.

The director waved the men off. "Just put them down for now."

The men shrugged and all but dropped them on the wood floor. Connor winced.

Then another man walked up. He was dressed in black jeans and a black turtleneck. "How do I look?"

"Fine, fine. Actually, Connor, how does he look?" Then, to the actor: "Put the mask on."

Even though Connor knew the man before him was an actor, and even though he watched the man put the ski mask on, his heart still began to race.

"What do you think?" the director asked again. "How does he look?"

Connor tried to hold himself together. He licked his lips, nodded. Once he found his voice, he said, "Good."

"Nothing's missing?"

Connor looked at the actor's hands. "Gloves. The intruder was wearing gloves."

The actor whipped a pair of black leather gloves out of his back pocket and held them up.

"No. Not like that," Connor said. "They were driving gloves. The kind that are open on the knuckles. And they were brown."

"Shit." The director glanced around. Connor couldn't imagine what he might be looking for. It's not as if a pair of driving gloves would magically appear. "Helen!"

A mousy woman holding a clipboard scurried up to him. "Yes?"

"See if you can find a pair of driving gloves, will you? Brown, if possible. And tell everyone to set up outside. We're going to shoot the intruder coming in through the front door."

Then she was gone.

"If she doesn't find a pair of driving gloves by the time everyone's ready, we'll go with what we have," the director told the actor.

The actor pulled off the ski mask. "Sounds good," he said briskly, and walked away.

At that same moment, a crash from the living room drew Connor's attention. He saw one of the cameras the crew had brought on the floor and a man standing over it, staring down.

"What the hell, Dave?" the director shouted.

Dave immediately moved to pick it up.

"I'll be right back," the director said to Connor. Then he made his way over to Dave, waving his hands in the air dramatically and telling him to be more careful.

Connor went into the half-bath off the hall for a minute of quiet. His heart was still pounding, and he felt like he was on the verge of a panic attack. He took a deep breath, told himself the man was just an actor, and wondered if this was what PTSD felt like. Sooner or later, he might need to talk to a professional if these attacks kept up.

Right now, though, he had a more immediate concern. After taking several more deep breaths to calm down, he pulled his father's iPhone out of his pocket. Since the abduction, Frank had received only one call from someone he knew—his boss at Leewood Construction. He had demanded to know where Frank was, and then apologized profusely when Connor told him what had happened. "You'll let me know if there's anything I can do to help, okay?" he'd said before he hung up.

And that lone call was one more than the number of texts he had received.

But just because his father hadn't received any texts recently didn't mean he had never sent any.

Connor opened the messaging app. Most of the texts Frank had sent were to Kim. There was one, though, that got Connor's attention. It was as covert as the email he had received from Roland, addressed simply to a phone number, and dated the day of the abduction: *Deerfield Park. Noon.*

He knew that park, had been there a bunch of times with his dad when he was a boy.

He did a quick reverse lookup and confirmed his suspicion. The phone number was Roland's.

With that, he realized he had everything he needed to make contact.

His thumbs hovered over the phone's two-dimensional keyboard. What should he say? Would Roland even show up? If Roland had been involved in the abduction, probably not. Especially if Connor pretended to be Frank in the text. But what other choice did he have? He couldn't very well pretend to be a cop. To hell with it. Frank it was. If Roland didn't show up, then Connor would know he was on the right track. If he did, then perhaps Connor could find out more about the nature of their meeting. Either way, it didn't seem like there was anything to lose.

Need to talk. Urgent, he typed. *Same place.*

He was trying to settle on a time when someone banged on the bathroom door. "Don't hog the throne!"

It startled Connor, brought him back to reality. "Almost done," he responded, before adding to the text: *Same time. Tomorrow.*

Connor hesitated again before pressing Send and closed his eyes when he did. "Here's hoping," he mumbled. He watched the screen for thirty seconds or so for a response. When none came, he slid the phone back into his pocket, flushed the toilet, and ran the tap.

As he stepped out of the bathroom, a bearded, heavyset man hurried in with his hands already working his belt free. He slammed the door behind him.

The crew filmed the intruder entering the house, a cheesy-looking chase scene, and approximations of the actual attacks on his parents. Connor had done his best to answer the director's questions, since he wanted the scenes to be as accurate as possible, but hid out in his attic bedroom during the filming (just like he had during the actual break-in). He didn't want to watch another masked man attack anyone in his house, even if the whole thing was staged.

Now he was back downstairs, sitting on the sofa. The actors had cleared out, as had much of the crew. A woman arrived in a sharp yellow suit and took a seat across from him. She introduced herself as Samantha Hawkins, but no introduction was necessary. Connor recognized her from the show.

"Okay, Connor, I just want to prepare you for how this is going to go," the director said. "Sam's going to ask you to tell her what you saw and heard, how you felt. That sort of thing."

As he talked, a makeup artist descended upon Samantha and went to work, fussing over every little thing.

"I didn't see much," Connor said. "Like I told you, I was—"

"I know, I know. But we're going to get it all on film, and we'll decide what we're going to keep in post. She's also going to ask you about your parents' lives and who they were. We want to paint a picture people can relate to, so be open and be vulnerable."

"He'll be fine," Samantha said, barely moving her lips so as not to cause problems for the makeup artist. She cut her eyes to the director. "Should I ask about the other case?"

"What other case?" Connor said.

"You haven't heard about it?"

Connor shook his head.

"Mark and Hillary Wilson," the director said. "They lived over in Westchester. Expensive neighborhood. Big house. The whole deal. Seems a masked man attacked them in the exact same way your parents were attacked."

"What happened to them? Did they get away?"

"No."

Connor thought about the two bodies that had been burned in the fire. They must have been the Wilsons. Olivia would put that together eventually, if she hadn't already. Connor suspected she wasn't telling him everything she knew, which he decided was fair enough since he wasn't telling her everything, either.

CHAPTER 16

OLIVIA LOVED TO watch suspects squirm when she got them into the interrogation room. It was a small space, with cinderblock walls, a steel table and chairs. And, except for the security camera mounted to the ceiling, not much of anything else. It looked exactly like she had imagined interrogation rooms to look before she had joined the academy. She wished she had a reason to get her ex-husband in here.

Aden would have to do.

He was handcuffed to the table, perched upright in the chair farthest from the door, and still naked from the waist up. He hadn't said a word since Olivia arrested him, hadn't even asked for a lawyer. That was unusual. Sure, a lot of suspects kept their mouths shut when the cuffs went on, but they almost always asked for a lawyer.

Olivia could tell Aden was angry. His jaw was clenched so tight she could see the thin veins under his chin clearly. His wiry black hair, which had already been a mess when she had arrived at his apartment, was somehow even worse now.

She fingered the keys in her pocket, thought about releasing the handcuffs, but decided against it.

She sat down in the chair opposite him. "Tell me about the bomb."

Aden smiled. "Is that what you think you saw?"

"Come on, Aden. I'm serious. What the hell were you planning?"

Aden turned his hands over, pulled up on the cuffs as far as he could to make a point. The chain connecting them rattled. "Does it matter?"

"So you're telling me it's over?" Aden didn't strike Olivia as a lone wolf, but she asked the question anyway to see what he would say.

He shrugged.

"The woman in the apartment—does she know what you were up to?"

"Maggie, no. Maggie Magpie is too sweet to do what had to be done. She shouldn't have even been over at my house tonight. Quite an evening for visitors. You'd think I was the toast of the town."

"So if she wasn't supposed to be there, if she was too sweet to do *what had to be done*, what was she doing inside when I showed up?" Olivia made air quotes around the words "what had to be done."

"I let her in."

"Why?"

"I was hoping I might be wrong."

"Why did you slap her?"

Until now, Aden's gaze had been all over the place. Sometimes he had been looking at Olivia, other times past her or down at his hands. He fixed his eyes on hers now in a new and deliberate way. "She said she was going to call . . . well . . . you."

"Me?"

"The police."

"And what has to be done?"

Aden frowned. "I can't tell you that."

"Because it's not over."

Another shrug.

"Who else is involved?"

This time, Aden didn't even shrug.

CHAPTER 17

CONNOR DID HIS best to give Sam what she wanted during the interview, but his mind kept drifting back to what the director had said about Mark and Hillary Wilson: *They lived over in Westchester. Expensive neighborhood. Big house. The whole deal. Seems a masked man attacked them in the exact same way your parents were attacked.*

Maybe if he could find out more about them, he would be able to figure out what the attacker wanted from his parents. Connect the dots, so to speak. At the very least, it would give him something to do while he waited for Roland to text him back.

He sat down at his computer in his bedroom. It didn't take much work to find a news story about the Wilsons on the *Westchester Gazette* website. (He found no such story on the *Times* or *Post* sites.) The headline: COUPLE KIDNAPPED FROM THEIR HOME. It wasn't particularly imaginative. The story was short and poorly written. Not much more than a recap of the police report, as far as Connor could tell. It included a large photo of the Wilsons' house and smaller pictures of Mark and Hillary.

The journalist hadn't drawn the connection between this abduction and his parents'. Likely he didn't even know about what had happened to Connor's parents.

He opened another browser window and scoured the web for

information on the Wilsons. According to LinkedIn, Mark had been a money manager for Fidelity. And according to Facebook (which, Connor determined, was where the *Gazette* had acquired pictures of the victims), he liked tennis and soccer. His most recent post featured a selfie of him and Hillary in the stands at a New York City FC game with the caption "Off to Broadway tonight. Would rather be back at another game."

The photo was close enough to the field that Connor could make out the names on the jerseys of the soccer players behind them.

There weren't a lot of people buying tickets that close to the field.

Connor had known Mark and Hillary were well off as soon as the director had mentioned the neighborhood they lived in. He had known they were rich as soon as he had seen the house. Now he knew they were even more than that. This was a couple who had money to spare. A lot of it.

But that didn't get Connor any closer to an answer. He had already ruled out money as a motive. So what was it that connected this family to his? Could they simply have been selected as stand-ins for his parents at the site of the murder?

Connor didn't think so. The killer seemed to have a plan. He hadn't taken Connor when he'd found him in the house, which suggested targeted abductions. He hadn't killed his parents, while he had killed the Wilsons, which suggested he still needed them alive.

So what was the connection?

He continued to scroll through Mark's Facebook feed until he saw a picture of the couple with a son about Connor's age. They were standing beside a sign that read "Princeton Orientation." All three were beaming. The caption: "He's staying on campus this summer. Aiming for an early graduation. So proud."

Connor wasn't sure whether this was the connection he was looking for, but he did think it was worth finding their son and talking to him.

He did some more online digging and found his name—Olin.

Connor suspected he would have come home after finding out his parents had been abducted. Playing the hunch, he got in his car and drove over to Olin's house.

Olin answered the door almost immediately. He had sharp features, a slim build. He was wearing plaid pajama bottoms and a nondescript blue tee shirt. Both seemed loose on him. The bags under his bloodshot eyes suggested he had not been sleeping (which, from personal experience, Connor figured was probably the case). The short black hair that had been carefully parted to one side in the Facebook photo was now a mess.

"Can I help you?" He kept one hand on the interior doorknob when he spoke, seemingly ready to close the door if he didn't like Connor's answer.

"I wanted to talk to you about what happened to your parents."

"I'm not interested in talking to the press right now," Olin said, then proved Connor's assumption right by stepping back and starting to swing the door shut.

Connor put out a hand to stop him. "Wait. I'm not a reporter. What happened to your parents—it happened to mine, too."

Olin eyed him suspiciously, then eased the door back open. "What?"

Connor sat at a breakfast table that was both big enough and fancy enough to replace the one in Connor's dining room.

Olin grabbed a pair of glasses and poured two fingers of scotch for each of them. He placed the glasses on the table and sat down across from Connor.

"Okay, so what do you mean when you say it happened to your parents, too?"

"I mean exactly that. A man in a ski mask driving a blue panel van pulled up to my house—plowed right through the front yard, as a matter of fact—and took my parents."

"You were at home?"

"I was in the attic."

"So the kidnapper didn't see you."

"Actually, that's the strangest part. He did see me. Once he had taken my parents outside, I came out of the attic and grabbed the fire poker. I was ready to go right outside after him. I thought I could stab him straight through with the thing if I had to. Whatever it took to get my parents back, I told myself. But then he was back. Seems he had dropped his phone. I didn't see it until he picked it up because it was by the front door." Connor shifted in his seat, a little uncomfortable and ashamed of what had happened next.

"And?" Olin asked, filling the silence.

"He had a Taser. He fired it up and I froze. Then he grabbed his phone and left."

Olin slid his glass of whiskey closer to him. He looked at it for a couple of seconds, took a sip. "I would have stopped him if I'd been here."

The sentiment stung. It was easy to think you would be a hero under the right circumstances. Connor had always thought he would be. But that's not always who you were when the time came to prove it.

"How did you hear about my parents?" Olin asked.

"You know that show *Uncovered*?"

Olin nodded.

"They were at my house today, doing a spot on the abduction. I thought maybe it would help. Anyway, the director—he told me about it." Then it occurred to Connor that Isaiah Cook had probably been by to see Olin as well, and so he asked.

"Yeah, he came by here. I told him to take a hike. I said let the police do their job. Didn't see how it would do much good to put the story all over the television."

"Well, that's how I felt at first, too, but my parents have been missing for a month."

Olin's glass was halfway between the table and his lips when Connor made the comment. He returned it to the table. "That long? Who's working your case?"

"Olivia Forbes. You?"

"Don't remember his name. I've got his card upstairs. But he's not a woman. Obviously, I guess. Yours from Yorktown?"

"NYPD."

"All the way up here?"

"I don't live in Westchester," Connor said.

"Still."

Connor shrugged.

"Do you think they know about each other's case?"

"Different departments. I don't know."

"We should tell them."

"We probably should." Connor finally took a sip of the scotch. He set the glass down, got to his feet, started a slow pace to one end of the kitchen and back. On the drive over, he had weighed whether he should tell Olin about the email he'd found, the text he'd sent. He had been unable to come to a decision. He had told himself he would know what to do when he arrived, but standing here, listening to Olin talk about turning everything over to the police, he still wasn't sure.

Just then, his father's phone vibrated in his pocket. He pulled it out to have a look. There was a message from Roland: *See you then.*

To hell with it, Connor thought. He needed an ally, and Olin had every right to know what was going on. He placed the phone down on the table, with the screen still lit up and the message visible.

"I'm going to tell you something, but I want you to keep this to yourself for now, okay?"

"What is it?"

"I've been doing some digging on my own. The day my parents were abducted, my dad met with someone. I don't know why, so it's probably nothing, but I want to find out for sure. I sent him a message from my dad's phone asking to meet tomorrow. He just responded." Connor gestured toward his father's phone, and Olin read the message.

"I could use some backup, you know, just in case."

Olin's expression shifted to something that was both doubtful and intense. "Why don't you tell the detective about it? They should have all the information we can give them, right?"

Connor wasn't sure why, but he didn't want to tell Olin he thought Olivia had dropped the ball with the first lead she'd had. Maybe it was because he didn't want to undermine Olin's trust in his own detective. Even though the guy's parents were likely dead, there was no reason for Connor to chip away at Olin's hope. So he said instead, "I will. If it's something. I just want to check it out myself first. Like I said, it's probably nothing. And I don't want the police wasting resources when every second matters."

Olin leaned forward, resting his elbows on his knees, and looked down at the floor. He stayed like that for a long time. When he looked back up at Connor, his eyes were glassy. "Okay, I'll help you. You're right, we don't need them wasting resources if it's nothing. But if it isn't nothing—"

"We'll tell them."

CHAPTER 18

CONNOR AND OLIN agreed to meet the next day at Deerfield Park an hour before Roland was scheduled to arrive. There was nothing else for Connor to do now but wait. He paced the first floor of his house, nervous energy catapulting him from room to room in an endless loop. Living room to dining room to kitchen to foyer. Living room to dining room to kitchen to foyer.

The days he spent alone in the house weren't too bad, but the nights were still hard. Perhaps it was because, no matter what he told himself, he still worried the killer might come back.

He looked out the window. The cul-de-sac was empty.

The TV was on for company, blasting a rerun of *Modern Family* loud enough that the neighbors could probably hear it.

He checked the wall clock. It was ten p.m.

He thought about taking another Ambien—he was still taking them most nights—but was doing his best to resist the urge. Although they helped him sleep, they also left him feeling groggy the next day. And even when that passed, there seemed to be a fog that hung over his thoughts, left him feeling not quite as sharp as he normally did.

That wouldn't do tomorrow. He had to be on his A-game when he confronted Roland. Earlier, he had reasoned that if Roland agreed to meet, he wasn't involved in his parents' abduction. But since getting the text from him, Connor had realized the flaw in that logic. Roland might just want to see who was using Frank's phone. If that was the case, the meeting could be even more dangerous than he had imagined.

He willed himself to sit on the sofa, to try to calm the nervous energy. He tried to focus on the sitcom, tried not to think about the killer coming back or the meeting tomorrow. He hoped that if he could just clear his mind, relax, he could get some good, natural sleep. But it was useless. His mind just kept spinning. As long as he stayed in this house, the Ambien was the only way he was going to get any rest.

He did have another option though, didn't he? Austin had insisted twice now Connor stay with him. Maybe it wasn't such a bad idea.

He muted the TV, pulled his cellphone out of his pocket, and placed the call. As it rang, he looked again at the wall clock, which now read 10:30, and wondered if it might be too late. But Austin sounded wide awake when he answered.

"What's up, Connor?"

"I think I would like to take you up on that offer. To stay at your place."

"Sure. Like I said, *mi casa, su casa*. I think it's a good idea, really. Just bring some stuff with you to work tomorrow so you can come straight here afterward."

"Actually, if it's all the same to you, I'd just as soon come over tonight. I can't sleep in this house anymore."

There was a rustling on the other end of the line. "Hey! Get down!" Austin said, the phone clearly away from his mouth. Then he was back. "Sorry. Damn cat won't stay off the kitchen counter. Yeah, sure. If that's what you want, come on over. I just got to put some sheets on the bed. It'll be ready for you when you get here."

Connor thanked Austin and hung up. He had refused the offer originally because he had thought it would be awkward—staying with his boss. But now that he had accepted it, it didn't feel strange at all, and he realized that somewhere along the way they had actually become friends. Perhaps it was inevitable, working side by side like they had fixing up that house.

Connor grabbed a backpack and a carry-on suitcase. In the backpack, he stored his laptop, power cord, cellphone charger, headphones, and an assortment of other electronics he deemed essential. In the carry-on, he packed enough clothes for a week and his toiletries.

After he zipped up both bags, he went through a mental checklist to make sure he wasn't forgetting anything, and decided he should take the Ambien, as well. Although he was hoping for natural sleep, he couldn't take the risk that he wouldn't get any at all.

Austin's apartment was in a gentrified area of the Bronx, with a sushi restaurant on the corner and a twenty-four-hour mini-market that sold organic vegetables across the street.

He had told Connor it might be hard to get parking, so Connor considered himself lucky when he found a spot along the curb on his first pass around the block.

It was a tight fit. But with numerous turns, inching the car back and forth, he squeezed his Ford Fiesta in behind a new Mercedes and in front of a rusted-out Suzuki. *Such is the nature of the Bronx*, he thought.

Austin buzzed him into the walk-up, and Connor climbed the black-and-white checkered stairs to the fourth floor. Connor had never been in a walk-up before, and he stopped to look down only once. Between the flights of stairs, he could see all the way to the lobby. It was dizzying. He felt like he might fall, like somehow, simply by standing where he was, he might just tip over the edge and tumble to the ground. He grabbed the handrail for stability, closed his eyes.

As far as Connor knew, he wasn't afraid of heights. He had been in his share of tall buildings over the years—in both New York and California. Until today, it had never bothered him.

But he also remembered reading somewhere once that such a phobia can develop suddenly as a reaction to trauma, that it sometimes stemmed from a fear, conscious or not, of being injured by things beyond one's control.

He wasn't sure that was true, or if it was the case here. Maybe he was suffering from low blood sugar. Whatever the cause, he was *not* looking down that stairwell again.

"Hey, you coming or what?" Austin shouted.

Without answering, Connor opened his eyes, kept his gaze aimed straight ahead, and climbed the last of the stairs.

"Man, you're slow," Austin said with a smile, as Connor stepped into his apartment.

The space was warm and inviting, with a lot of soft colors, and everything just so. Throw pillows arranged on the sofa in colors that complemented the drapes. Built-in bookshelves framing the window opposite the door. Sometimes, when deep in the muck and mess of the remodel, Connor wondered if it was really going to turn out okay. The look of the apartment did a lot to assuage his concerns. Although decorating wasn't remodeling, Austin seemed to have an eye. But instead of saying all that, Connor summed it up with simply a "Nice place."

Austin glanced over his shoulder at the apartment. "It's home." He closed the door, pointed to a hall that led off the living room. "Your room's over there."

Connor hauled his luggage down the hall. Austin's cat scurried out of the bathroom and, at the sight of a stranger, took shelter under the sofa.

"Name's Biscuit. True definition of a scaredy-cat. She'll warm up to you."

The bedroom was small and, because of that, the bed had been pushed against the wall. But the space had received as much attention to detail as the rest of the apartment had. The bed was dressed in white linens with military corners. A furry white throw rug had been placed in front of it. There was a small desk and a bedside table, both mahogany, and a floor lamp that seemed to cast just the right amount of light for the room.

Connor put his carry-on in one corner and his backpack by the desk.

"Can I get you anything?" Austin said from behind him.

Connor turned around. "No, thanks. I just want to get some sleep."

And he meant it. Because, he'd realized, he could sleep here. The constant anxiety he had felt since his parents were taken, the fear that they might never come back—none of these were gone. They would be with him until his parents returned. But being out of his house, away from the reminders of that horrible night, and no less being here, in a room that practically told you to sleep—it was exactly what he needed.

CHAPTER 19

CONNOR DIDN'T REMEMBER falling asleep, didn't remember dreaming, and didn't wake up until Austin knocked on the bedroom door.

"Rise and shine, sleepyhead. Coffee's in the kitchen. We got to get moving. Today's going to be a short day. I've got stuff to do up at the cabin in the afternoon."

Connor had been planning to bow out early, claiming he had a doctor's appointment. But he was glad he wouldn't have to. He didn't like to lie. He especially didn't want to lie to Austin. The man was as much of a friend as he had in New York anymore, and you didn't lie to friends.

Which was why, he decided, he should tell Austin about *Uncovered*.

He waited until after Austin had used the electric saw to cut the smooth lines in the drywall that would frame the opening between the living room and the kitchen. Then, once they had taken measurements and cut a series of two-by-fours for the extension jamb, Connor made his move.

"Listen," he said as he held two of the boards together, end to end and at a ninety-degree angle, "I need to tell you something."

Austin took the nail gun, positioned it over the joint, and fired. "What is it?"

"That show I told you about. *Uncovered*. Remember how I said they came to me, asked if I would be interested in being a part of it?"

"Sure. You said it would be a bad idea."

"So, I changed my mind."

Austin fired a second nail into the joint, and the two men moved as one to line up the next board at the other end.

"You're going to do it?"

"That's the thing. They filmed yesterday."

"Okay."

"You're not upset?"

"Why would I be? It was your choice. I don't think anything will come of it except a bunch of nut-jobs phoning in garbage leads. But you have to do what you think is best. Maybe I would have done the same thing in your position." He aimed the nail gun over the second joint and fired. This time, though, nothing happened. "Shit." He tried again. It still didn't fire.

"What's wrong with it?"

"Hell if I know. I've got a hammer in the truck. Go grab it, would you?"

Connor patted his hands together to shake off the dust and went outside. He felt a little foolish for thinking Austin would care whether he did the show, but he was still glad he'd told him.

He searched the toolbox in the bed of the truck. No hammer. He checked the cab, and it wasn't there either. Maybe Austin had left it at the apartment.

Connor looked over at the shed and thought it wasn't unreasonable he would find one in there. The double doors on the shed, however, were secured with a padlock. So much for that.

"No hammer," he told Austin, when he went back inside.

"You sure?"

Connor nodded.

"All right." Austin looked around the dusty room. "Let's get all this swept up, and we'll call it a day. Start back early tomorrow."

CHAPTER 20

DEERFIELD PARK WAS on a small plot of land about a mile from Connor's house. It had a jungle gym and swings, benches for parents to sit on while they watched their children play. Other than a narrow stretch of grass big enough to picnic on, that was it. Across the street were a series of tennis courts. But they went by the name Deerfield Courts, so Connor discounted them as a likely place for the meet.

He texted Olin when he arrived and Olin, who had been sitting with his back to Connor on one of the benches, stood up and waved. He was wearing a blue button-down, tucked into a pair of khakis.

Connor went over to join him.

"Where do you think we should be looking?" Olin asked.

Connor gave a half-shrug. "He'll probably come sit down on one of these benches, that would be my guess."

"Okay."

"Just watch for anything."

"Got it."

Then Connor and Olin sat in silence for a while. They had already discussed the plan, so there was no need to go over it again. Connor watched half a dozen children play around the jungle gym. Four of them seemed to be engaged in a game of tag. He glanced at the parents. All but two were women.

One of those men could be Roland, he thought. There was no way to tell by looking at them. He would just have to watch, wait, see what happened.

At some point, Olin asked how Connor had slept, then how he was holding up and whether he really thought confronting Roland would amount to anything. Connor didn't have much in the way of answers. But he also suspected Olin wasn't looking for any.

Eventually, both of the men left with children, which cleared the deck, Connor thought. Odds were good now any man who showed up without a child was their guy.

"Which one's yours?"

The voice came from Connor's left. He turned, saw a woman not much older than he was in a floral-print dress. Her hair was pulled back in a ponytail. She was striking.

Connor wasn't sure what to say. He didn't do well talking to women, especially not those he found attractive, and *especially* not now, when any answer he gave would have to be a lie. He licked his lips. "Umm . . ."

"We're just taking in some fresh air," Olin said, getting to his feet and smiling in a way that seemed both charming and practiced.

The woman's own smile faltered. She did her best to recover, wished them both a good day, and went to sit on another bench.

"Good job," Olin said. "Now she's going to think we're some kind of pervs or something."

Connor would have told Olin he didn't care what that woman thought of him if he had been listening, but he wasn't, because on the other side of the park, at the edge of that strip of grass that masqueraded as a lawn, was a man. He hadn't been there before. He was tall, heavyset. He had a goatee and was wearing a red bowling shirt. Under one arm, he was carrying a newspaper, but he didn't seem interested in finding a place to read it. Instead, he looked around—left, right, over his shoulder twice.

Connor tapped Olin's arm and nodded toward the man. "That's him."

"You sure?"

No. Not completely. He made for a likely candidate, though. "You know what to do. I'm going in," Connor said, already on the move.

He took his time crossing the park, meandering around the jungle gym and the swings. He didn't want to spook the man, and Olin needed time to get into position.

Roland—*this has to be him*—glanced at Connor more than once, but not in a way that was meaningful. He was looking at everyone. He pulled his phone out of a holster on his belt and typed something into it.

A second later, Connor felt a vibration in his pocket. It was his father's phone. Roland had sent a message: *I'm here. How far away are you?*

Connor put the phone back in his pocket. *Got you.*

He continued his slow approach until he saw Olin in the distance, blocking Roland's path if he tried to run, or worse—tried to drag Connor away with him. Roland was too big to be the man who had abducted Connor's parents, but he could still be dangerous if he was involved. Frankly, since Connor didn't know the nature of Roland's meeting with his father, he might be dangerous even if he wasn't.

"Excuse me," Connor said, once he was only feet away. "You're Roland, right?"

Roland's nervous gaze focused in on Connor. "What is this? Who are you?"

"You're looking for Frank Callahan. I'm his son."

"Oh, this is bullshit." Roland turned, started to walk away. "I don't know what Frank thinks he's doing sending you here. That's insane. If he has something to say to me, tell him he'd better do it himself."

Okay, so he definitely wasn't involved in the abduction. Knowing that made Connor braver. He grabbed Roland's arm. "Wait. Listen—"

Roland shook him off, dropping the newspaper as he did so. "Don't touch me! Frank and I had a deal. If he's thinking about doing anything to undercut that, he's going to regret it. You tell him that, too."

Connor saw Olin closing in on them. Not quite running, but moving fast, for sure.

"What are you talking about?"

Roland stopped, looked at Connor. "You don't know? He sent you here to talk to me, and you don't even know what you came to talk to me about?" He blinked, looked like he was trying to process information his mind couldn't accept. It was probably how he would look if Connor had just presented him with evidence that aliens existed. "What did he want you to tell me?"

"He didn't send me to tell you anything. That's why I'm here. He's—"

Roland turned, ready to start moving again. This time, instead of Connor stopping him, Olin did.

Olin held out his hands. "Hey, big man. We just want to talk to you, okay? Tell us what you know about Connor's dad, and we'll leave you alone."

Roland could have looked from one of them to the other by simply shifting his eyes, but he turned his whole head instead. Back and forth, like he was watching a tennis match. "Oh, you two are batshit crazy." He tried to push past Olin, and Olin grabbed him, wrapping him in a bear hug.

"Let go of me!"

Then another voice joined the conversation. "Hey! You two!" It was a cop, coming up from behind Roland.

"You can tell us or you can tell the cop," Connor said. "Your choice."

Roland was still struggling to get free. But Olin was lean, wiry, strong, and he wasn't letting go.

Roland's face turned a bright red. He huffed and puffed so much Connor wondered if he might pass out.

"Just tell us," Connor said.

"Let go of him!" the cop shouted.

"I'm not letting go until you tell us what we want to know," Olin said. "We can all go to jail for all I care."

Roland expelled a breath in Connor's direction that smelled like tuna and garlic. He stopped struggling, then calmly said, "Fine with me. We'll see how your father likes it when Lee—"

"Hey!" It was the cop again, only now he was almost on top of them.

"Forget it. Let's go," Connor said, already starting to move. Olin followed his lead, and Roland took off in the other direction. The whole thing lasted less than a minute but seemed to Connor like much longer.

"Stay where you are. I need to talk to you two!"

CHAPTER 21

WHEN THE HACKER had bought this house, there was no cell coverage, no hope of internet access. Which, in those days, was okay with him. Years had passed, though, since he had been to the property. A lot of bad things had happened.

One good thing that had happened—at least, right now, he considered it good—was the proliferation of cellular service and the wi-fi speeds that had come along with it. There were very few places anymore where you couldn't get a signal.

He set up his laptop on a rustic dining room table and connected to his cellphone. Then, before he got down to business, he made a pot of coffee. He always drank coffee when he worked, usually one cup after another until he was so wired up his fingers would shake and he felt like he couldn't hold onto his thoughts.

Out here, he also made the coffee for the smell.

The place had been unoccupied for so long, it had an odor to it that wouldn't go away. He had tried opening all the windows, burning candles, lighting a fire. Still, that stale, musty stench remained. The house probably just needed a good cleaning. When all this was over, he would hire someone to come in and do that.

The hacker downed cup number one in a single long drink. It burned a little, which he didn't mind. Then he poured a second cup and got to work.

It will all be over tomorrow, he thought. And while his life would never be what it once was, after the job was done, it could return to something close. Or so he told himself.

But breaking into this particular computer system was not as easy as he'd thought it would be. The back door he had been counting on had been sealed up. He would not be beaten that easily, though. His freedom, maybe even his life, depended on his success.

He tried another method, and then another. Hours passed. He finished his first pot of coffee and brewed a second. Finally, when he had reached the point where the caffeine was keeping him from thinking straight, he got in.

The hacker familiarized himself with the systems but changed nothing. Most things worked the way he thought they did. When he was finished, he left a back door of his own behind so that when he returned tomorrow, he could hop right in.

He shut down his laptop and returned it to his computer bag. He opened a bottle of wine, poured a glass. In part, he was celebrating his success. It felt good to have pulled off the hack, to have gotten in and out undetected.

But there was also a sadness in his drinking because, the truth was, he didn't want to do what he would have to do tomorrow.

Don't think about that. It's the deal you made. Just do it and don't think about it.

He finished the glass of wine and resisted the urge to have another. He still had an hour's drive ahead of him. He was sure a second glass wouldn't put him over the limit, but he didn't even want to get close.

The hacker went down to the cellar to tend to one last piece of business. Then he locked up the house, tossed the laptop bag into his truck, and, with hands still shaking from the caffeine, fumbled with the car key until he got it into the ignition.

One. More. Day.

CHAPTER 22

LIKE ROLAND, CONNOR and Olin ran. The cop shouted for them to stop. *Yeah, right.* Connor didn't know where Olin was parked, but Olin seemed to be veering off to the left. The closest lot in that direction was behind the tennis courts.

Connor, on the other hand, was parked on the street, which meant his car was quite a bit closer. His little piece of shit Ford Fiesta might not be fast, but it would be fast enough to get them out of there.

"This way!" he said to Olin. "Stay with me."

Olin fell back in line. They reached the Fiesta seconds later. "Get in," Connor instructed, right before he attempted to slide across the hood. He had seen it done enough times in movies, imagined it would be faster than circling around the vehicle. But an action star he was not. The slide turned into a roll and he tumbled to the cement on the other side.

Olin gave him a look when he got in the car but didn't say anything.

Connor threw the gearshift into drive and took off. There was no one parked in front of him, thank goodness.

For the first two blocks, neither of them said a word. Connor wasn't even sure he took a breath. He kept glancing at the rearview mirror. He didn't know what he was looking for. It was foolish to think they were suddenly going to find themselves in a police chase. Especially when there hadn't been a crime committed. (Well, maybe grabbing Roland like Olin had would count as assault, but Roland wouldn't be pressing any charges.)

Squat brick buildings and storefronts swallowed the park almost immediately.

Olin spoke first. "Did you see how red his face got?"

Connor could hear the amusement in his voice. He looked at Olin, couldn't believe he found any of this funny.

Olin's grin stretched wider and he added, "I thought his head was going to explode," as he started laughing.

Then, for some reason, Connor pictured Roland's head exploding and he laughed, too. There still wasn't anything funny about their situation. Maybe it was just a subconscious effort to break the tension. Whatever the reason, once the laughter had passed, things got serious again.

"We still don't have any idea what he was up to," Connor said.

"Yeah, I know."

"But at least we know he wasn't involved, and I guess that's something."

"What makes you so sure of that?"

"What he said. He sincerely wanted to know what Dad had asked me to tell him. He wouldn't have asked that if he already knew they were missing."

"So what now?"

It was a fair question. As much as Connor had been glad to discover that Roland wasn't involved in the abduction, he had been hoping (almost certain, actually) that he would get something out of their meeting.

A part of him even felt like he had. But if that was so, what was it? Roland had been evasive throughout their entire conversation. Had he slipped up somewhere? Connor tried to remember.

And then, all at once, he did. It had happened when Olin had Roland in a bear hug and the cop was only feet away. Connor had almost missed the comment entirely. In his mind, he was already running back to the car, even though his feet were not yet in motion.

"We'll see how your father likes it when Lee—"

There was only one thing that came to mind when he replayed Roland's comment in his head, and that was Leewood Construction. His father's employer.

"Maybe," Olin said, when Connor made the connection for him.

"Maybe?"

"It could also have been 'Leroy.' Or, hell, maybe he didn't say 'Lee' at all. Maybe he said 'he.' As in, 'We'll see how your father likes it when *he* has to bail you out.' Or 'the.' As in, 'We'll see how your father likes it when *the* police call to tell him his son is in jail.'"

Connor had to admit that seemed plausible. But: "I still think he was talking about Leewood Construction."

Olin, whose knees were pressed up against the dashboard, fished around under the seat until he found the lever to push the seat back. "Okay. You could be right. So what's next? Should we call Olivia and tell her what we've got? You want me to call my guy?"

"Not yet. We still don't know this is anything."

"The deal was—"

"Like I said before, let's make sure there's something to this first. You saw how Roland reacted. Do you want to waste the police's time with this if it turns out to be nothing?"

Olin crossed his arms over his chest, looked out the passenger window. After a while, he said, "I just want my parents back."

Connor felt a pang of guilt for keeping the story about the parking garage fire to himself. But he liked having a partner work the case with him, and, as far as he was concerned, they would get farther together than Olivia would. Besides, he couldn't say for sure Olin's parents were dead. Maybe there was a third couple who had been taken.

"I know," he said. "Me, too." Then he remembered what Frank's boss had said to him when he called: *You'll let me know if there's anything I can do to help, okay?* "Let's go by my dad's office. See if there's anything there."

Leewood Construction occupied a converted warehouse, complete with a large parking lot and a chain link fence. Connor had been here only once before. It had been a Saturday and the building, which was quiet on the weekend and surrounded by other warehouses that were equally quiet, had struck him as eerie. Frank had forgotten his laptop, he had explained, and said he needed to review a proposal before it went out on Monday morning. Some sort of big government job. Worth millions, if they got it.

Connor had been twelve at the time, and couldn't understand the value of a multi-million-dollar contract. He just remembered complaining about being hungry and his father assuring him he wouldn't be long.

Today, there was activity at all of the warehouses, and the lot at Leewood Construction was mostly full. Connor took a ticket from an automatic dispenser at the gate and found a parking spot for guests near the door.

The lobby was all old beige carpet and wood paneling. A receptionist, clacking away at her computer, asked how she could help without looking up.

"Is Victor in?"

Victor, aka Victor Leewood, owned Leewood Construction.

Perhaps it was invoking his name that got the receptionist to pay more attention to them than to her computer. Either way, she stopped the two-fingered hunt-and-peck clacking and looked Connor straight in the eye. "Who are you?"

He realized, now that he could see her face, she was older than he'd first thought. She had silvery white hair brushed back from her forehead and a coat of foundation thick enough to mask most of the wrinkles.

"Connor. Frank's son."

She placed a call from her desk and told them to wait. But with nowhere to sit, waiting meant standing.

There were no windows. On the wall behind them were a series of architectural photographs. Most were of tall glass buildings. There were also a few restaurants and retail locations. Connor recognized one— The Benchmark Diner—as a project his father had talked a lot about and assumed they were all Leewood Construction projects.

Fortunately, it didn't take but a minute before Victor emerged from the hallway behind the receptionist. He was wearing a plaid shirt and cowboy boots. Connor half-expected a "Howdy-doody" when he saw the man. What he got instead was "Which one of you's Frank's son?" delivered in that same Brooklyn accent he had heard on the phone.

"I am," Connor said.

Victor's face crumpled in. He looked as if he was about to well up. He hugged Connor without asking or waiting for a cue that it would be welcome. Connor imagined this must be how Roland had felt when Olin had him locked in a bear hug. To avoid making it awkward, Connor hugged him back.

"I'm sorry," Victor said. He let go, wiped his eyes with one knuckle.

At least he didn't throw out a bunch of empty platitudes, Connor thought. He appreciated that.

"What can I do for you?"

"Do you mind if we check out my dad's desk?"

"Sure. No problem," Victor said, looking a little confused. "May I ask why?"

"It's stupid, I'm sure. I just want to see if there's anything there that could help us understand what's going on."

"I can't imagine there would be, but . . ." Victor nodded. "If I was in your position, I'd want to look, too." He turned around. "Come this way."

Victor led them down a hallway lighted by buzzing fluorescents overhead. Every so often, one of them flickered like it needed to be replaced.

He turned a corner, silently passed a series of cubicles, then opened a door that Connor at first thought must be a closet. It wasn't. The door Victor opened led to an office as big as Connor's bedroom. It was furnished with an L-shaped walnut desk that faced the door, a small circular table with three chairs, a whiteboard mounted to the opposite wall, and a bookcase filled with unlabeled black binders.

"This is it," Victor said. "Take all the time you need." Then he left Connor and Olin alone and the door open.

Connor looked around the space. This was where his dad worked. It was a big part of his life, and there were little things everywhere that Connor could tell made this space uniquely his father's. There were pictures of Connor and his mother on Frank's desk. A collection of numbered and colored building blocks that were stacked on the bookshelf to make a pyramid (Frank had kept them since he was a boy and Connor remembered playing with them, as well). An anniversary card from Connor's mom celebrating their first year together with "Two hearts, forever one" scrawled across the front in cursive.

It seemed like everywhere Connor looked, there was another reminder of his family and the love Frank had for them. Now he, too, wanted to cry. He pushed the emotion down. "Go through the binders. I'll check the desk."

"What are we looking for?" Olin said.

"I don't know. Anything that seems out of the ordinary, I guess. Especially anything that's got Roland's name on it."

"This seems like a long shot."

Connor agreed, but he was going to look anyway. It couldn't be a coincidence that Frank had met with Roland the same day he was abducted. *Are you sure?* asked a little voice from the back of his head. *I'm sure*, he answered, because whatever the two men had been up to, it couldn't have been good if they didn't want anyone to know about it. And just like one conspiracy theory makes it easier to believe another, bad things tend to follow bad things.

Sitting in the desk chair, Connor went through all four drawers, starting at the top left and working his way to the bottom right. In the first drawer, he found red and black pens, a roll of stamps, and a stack of small bills under a paperweight Frank had carved in the garage. The one underneath it had a box of Ritz crackers and a big jar of M&Ms. Top right: empty. Bottom right: a collection of manila folders that were named by project and included an assortment of blueprints, spreadsheets, and handwritten notes.

Then Connor moved the mouse to bring the computer to life, and found himself confronted by a request to log in. "Rickety Rat" wasn't going to work here.

"What have you got?" he asked Olin.

"I'm not really sure," Olin said as he flipped through one of the binders. "But nothing with Roland's name on it."

Connor got up to have a look. The binder contained the same sort of information the folders had, and he assumed that the binders were likely composed of completed bids whereas the folders represented those that were still in process.

"How about you?" Olin asked.

"Nothing."

"Did you check the computer?"

"It's locked."

"Can't you get in anyway? Aren't you supposed to be a hacker or something?"

Connor had told Olin about his extracurricular activities on the drive over. "It doesn't work that way."

"Can't you try something?"

Without answering, Connor returned to the computer and did his best to guess his father's password. After three attempts, the computer locked him out.

"Finish going through those binders," he told Olin. "I'm going to see if Victor has a way to get us around the login."

CHAPTER 23

OLIN FOUND NOTHING suspicious in the binders, and Connor didn't do much better getting his father's password. Victor had said he would be happy to help, but their only IT person was out of the office and wouldn't be back for a couple of hours.

A couple of hours seemed like an eternity right now. Maybe they would come back later.

"You said you found the information about Roland on the computer at home, right?" Olin said when they were back in the car.

"Yeah. And his phone."

"Maybe there's more."

"I checked that computer. If there was anything else there, I would have found it."

Olin shook his head. "Not on the computer. In the house."

Connor thought about the money he had stashed in the back of his sock drawer. Was it possible there was more information about Roland offline? Connor doubted it. He and Frank had been careful. Then again, he also had nothing to lose by looking.

For a brief moment after they stepped through the front door, Connor worried Olin would judge the house as being inferior to his own. He wasn't sure why he cared. This house had been more than enough for him growing up. Still, when Olin said nothing, he was glad.

They went through every room methodically. They looked under the furniture, examined every item in every closet, looked in every drawer.

By the time they were done, they had found exactly what Connor had expected to find: nothing.

They sat down at the dining room table. It was still littered with the items Connor had found in the box in his parents' closet.

"What's all this?" Olin said, leaning in to get a closer look.

"Pictures, mostly. Mom kept saying she would get around to framing them."

Olin sifted through the items with one finger, sliding them around so he could see everything without moving much. "I take it you went through all this already?"

Connor nodded.

When Olin got to the plane tickets, his brow furrowed and he leaned in closer. Then he picked them up so he could get a better look. "Your parents went to the Czech Republic?"

"My mom's family comes from there. She wanted to see it."

"So did mine."

"Your parents are from the Czech Republic?"

"No, but they went there." Olin looked from one ticket to the other. "Right about the same time, too, if I remember correctly." Then he looked at Connor. "Do you think they went together?"

Connor thought it was almost inevitable. The Czech Republic wasn't exactly on the list of the top ten tourist destinations. Was that what tied these abductions together? Connor had his doubts. That trip had been so long ago, and his parents had never gone back. But it might mean his parents knew Olin's parents. And that, like Frank's relationship to Roland, would be something to look into.

"June 12, 2005," Olin mumbled, his attention again on the tickets. "Yeah, I'm sure that's when they went."

"Wait. What was that date?"

"June 12, 2005. Why?"

Connor snatched the ticket out of Olin's hand to see the date for himself. "I would have been four years old then."

"So what?" Olin said, now looking more carefully through the pictures. "I would have been five."

"Look at my mom's last name." He pointed to it. "It's Jones." He grabbed the other ticket off the table. "And here. This one. This is my dad. Frank Callahan."

"What's your point?"

"They weren't married. I thought this whole time they had gone before I was born, but that's not what happened."

"That's your big revelation? You do know you aren't the first person who was born before his parents got married, don't you?"

Connor was too wrapped up in his own thoughts to catch the sarcasm. "Of course. But she was married before. Maybe . . ." He trailed off, trying to make sense of the possibilities.

"You're thinking she had an affair?"

"Maybe. But maybe I'm not Frank's son. Maybe the guy who runs that website—TruthSeekers—maybe he was right. What if I'm Matt's son?"

"But your last name is Callahan, isn't it?"

"It is." Connor leaned back in the chair, let the tickets fall onto the table. It didn't make sense. He wished his mom was here so he could ask her to explain.

"Well, they definitely knew each other," Olin said. Connor gave him a look, and Olin tapped one of the pictures. "Those are my parents. They're younger here, but that's them, all right."

Connor leaned in to get a better look at the picture. There were six people in it, all standing together. "And those are mine," he said, directing Olin's attention to a different couple.

CHAPTER 24

OLIN AND CONNOR moved from room to room, pitching theories but accomplishing little, until they worked their way up to Connor's bedroom, where Connor took a seat at his desk and Olin perched himself on the edge of Connor's bed.

"I was thinking about that guy from the website," Olin said.

Connor looked confused.

"The TruthSeekers guy?"

"Dylan? What about him?"

"Do you think he could be involved in this?"

"I did in the beginning. But not anymore."

"Why not?"

"I've been to his house. It doesn't seem like—"

"What? You know where he lives?"

"Yes, but—"

"And you told the police about all this, right?"

Connor shook his head. "No."

"Why not?"

"Same reason I didn't tell them about Roland right away. I wasn't sure there was anything to it. Besides, the whole thing—hacking into his site—wasn't exactly legal."

"But we're going to tell them about Roland now. I mean—there was nothing at your dad's office, so now we have to, right?"

Connor considered that. He still didn't think Roland was involved in the abduction. But he also knew the evidence he had used to reach that conclusion was weak. And since he had gone as far as he could with that lead on his own, there was only one answer. "Yes."

"And TruthSeekers. We're going to tell the police about that, too."

"Listen, I'll admit the thing with Roland is strange. But TruthSeekers—I found Dylan. I started that. Even if I still thought he might have been crazy enough to take my parents, why would he take yours?"

"I don't know. I mean—who's to say there's a connection at all between the abductions? Whoever it was took my parents. He took your parents. Maybe there were others."

Connor looked at the photograph again. "Our parents knew each other. Seems like a hell of a coincidence if the abductions aren't related."

"Not necessarily," Olin said. "For all we know, our parents haven't seen each other since that trip fifteen years ago. I mean, my parents have never talked about you guys. Have yours ever talked about us?"

Connor didn't respond. He didn't need to. Olin already knew the answer, and didn't even pause long enough for Connor to speak, had he tried.

"Maybe my parents were on his radar because . . ."

Because they're rich, Connor thought. It was probably exactly what Olin was going to say, too, but he seemed to catch himself and said instead, ". . . because of what my father does for a living. For all we know, you just poked the bear. Just unlucky. If you hadn't gone snooping around his website, your parents might not have been taken at all."

Connor still thought it was too much of a coincidence to be true.

"How about this?" Olin said. "We'll go talk to him. Just like with Roland. Then we'll take it from there."

Connor didn't like that idea. A man who put up a website like TruthSeekers was probably unstable, even if he wasn't a kidnapper. But he could also tell Olin wasn't going to let go of it. If Connor didn't help, Olin would definitely take it straight to the police. And then, even if Olin was wrong, Connor would still have to explain why he was hacking into the TruthSeekers website and why he hadn't told the police about it before. He doubted any answer he gave them would make them happy.

But, while confronting Roland had been their only option for getting information from him, it wasn't their only option for getting information on Dylan.

"I have a better idea."

CHAPTER 25

OLIVIA WAS STILL annoyed with her captain. She was just starting to scratch the surface with Aden when he had knocked on the interrogation room door and then poked his head in. "Can I have a word with you?"

The captain, Lucas Flemmings, was a slim man and shorter than average. He made up for it a little by always standing with his shoulders back and chest out. Olivia had gathered it was something the Navy had drilled into him and suspected he made a point of standing that way for the extra inch it gave him. His suit jacket was buttoned. His tie was perfectly knotted and positioned. He was the epitome of military precision.

Olivia followed him out of the room.

He waited until the door was closed before he spoke. "You're done with him."

"What? But, Captain—"

"The FBI and ATF are taking over."

Olivia noticed a small group of men and women huddled together a little farther down the hall. She didn't know any of them. But something about the way they looked, dressed, and stood was enough for her to know those were the agents Lucas was referring to.

She thought about pleading her case, reminding him that she had found the bomb, she had made the arrest. She at least deserved a chance to finish questioning Aden. But she knew it wouldn't do any good. Lucas was inflexible. Even if he wasn't, she doubted the agents beyond him would allow it.

She turned and headed toward the exit without a word.

"It's for the best," he called after her. "You've got your hands full, anyway, with that murder case, don't you?"

Suddenly, the pieces fell into place. The only way the FBI or ATF would have known about Aden would have been if someone had told them. And the only person besides Olivia who had known what Aden had been up to was Lucas. It wasn't even a mystery how they had gotten to the station so fast. Olivia had called Lucas as soon as she had made the arrest. He must have turned around and called the federal agencies as soon as she was off the phone.

The implication was clear: Solve the damn murder.

She rerouted to the coffee maker and poured coffee into a Styrofoam cup. To hell with giving it up. If the only vice she had was coffee, she was doing all right. She went back to her desk, called the babysitter to say she would be even later, and pulled out the Callahan file.

Olivia was determined to find something she had missed. On some level, she knew Lucas was manipulating her, that this was exactly what he wanted her to do. But since it was also what she wanted to do, she didn't mind. She knew they were going to have to hand Aden over to the federal authorities sooner or later. What did it matter if she got the information out of him or they did?

Besides, she had only started looking into Aden because she was feeling bad about her lack of progress with the Callahan murders. But, really, when you're stuck on a problem—any problem—the key isn't to go work on something else. It's to dig deeper.

So that's what she did.

Olivia stayed at her desk studying the file until the babysitter called to say she had to leave. Then she took the file home with her and continued to study it there. After she checked in on her daughter to make sure she was sleeping soundly, Olivia propped herself up against a stack of pillows on her bed and spread the file's contents out in front of her. There were copies of the reports filed by the officers who had first arrived at Connor's house. Notes from her conversations with him. Photos of the disarray the kidnapper had left behind. More photos of the fire at the parking garage. And on and on it went.

She must have gone through every item more than twenty times before she finally saw it. Actually, she didn't exactly "see" it, since there was nothing to see. It was more of an idea—maybe even a wish. But it was enough of a possibility to be worth a follow-up. Olivia was disappointed in herself for not thinking of it sooner.

Olivia didn't sleep well. She was anxious to get up and get moving. After she dropped Erin off at preschool, she went back to the 7-Eleven that had sold the cellphone to the killer.

The manager had a patchy beard Olivia suspected he had grown to make himself look older than he was. It didn't. Instead, he looked like a kid who couldn't grow a beard.

She showed him her badge. "Remember me?"

His name was Howard, and he was the same man who had given her the information about the cellphone the first time. He grunted, which she had gathered from their last interaction was as close as he got to a yes.

"You guys have CCTV here?" Olivia had looked around the store when she had arrived and hadn't seen any cameras, but sometimes they were hard to spot.

Another grunt. This one a no.

The wish evaporated.

"Not inside."

"What do you mean?"

Then he strung together the single longest sentence Olivia had heard from him. "We have a camera facing the parking lot."

"Can I see the footage?"

Howard shrugged. What did he care? He took her to the office at the back of the store, showed her to the computer, and logged in. Then, he mumbled something unintelligible about customers and, before she realized it, he was gone. That was fine with her. He creeped her out. She was glad she wouldn't have to go through the footage with him looking over her shoulder.

Olivia did her best to line up the time of the purchase with the time on the video. Fortunately, there weren't a lot of customers that day. It wasn't hard to figure out who had bought the cellphone.

Unfortunately, she could only see him from the back. He was in his forties, she guessed, from his build. But if she was honest with herself, she had to admit that he could just as easily be thirty as sixty. It was hard to tell a lot about a person's age from behind.

Then he got into a Mustang and drove off, giving her a clear view of his license plate in the process, and she thanked her lucky stars that the ping-pong game of fortune had ended in her favor.

Olivia stopped the tape and called in the plate number. A minute later, she knew who the car was registered to and where she could find him. She hurried out of the store with barely a thank you. Howard responded with even less.

CHAPTER 26

CONNOR DROVE OLIN to 121 Forrest Creek Drive. Dylan Naese's house. "Truth seeker extraordinaire," as he called himself on the website. Connor pulled up to the gate.

"What if this doesn't work?" Olin said.

"Then we'll come back in the morning and try again." He pressed the button on the callbox and waited. When no one answered, he pressed it again. For ten minutes, he kept pressing that button. Long enough to annoy anyone if they were at home. Then he pulled up to the next street, made a left, and parked along the curb. His was not the only car on the side of the street, and he hoped, even though it had seen more wear than the others, it would not stand out.

"Let's go," Connor said, opening his door.

Olin was slow to move. He looked to Connor like his nerves might get the best of him.

"Let's *go*," Connor repeated.

Then Olin nodded his head with a little too much vigor and got out of the car.

Connor made a "come here" gesture as he closed in on the back of the property. He slipped between the brick wall and the fence like he had last time.

Olin slid in beside him. "Are you sure this is a good idea?"

Connor was already on the move. Ten feet in, he stopped, kneeled down, interlaced the fingers of both hands. Olin reluctantly stepped onto them, and Connor lifted him to the top of the wall. He watched as Olin got one leg over, stabilized himself.

"Come on," he whispered, reaching down to offer Connor his hand.

Seconds later, they were over the wall.

The backyard was an expansive manicured lawn. An assortment of bushes and flowers were strategically placed. There was a fire pit and a swing close to the house, accessible via a pair of French doors that seemed to lead into the kitchen.

"I don't know what you think we're going to find out just by looking through the windows," Olin said as they crossed the lawn, because that was what Connor had told him they were going to do.

Connor had insisted they might see something that could help them figure out who they were dealing with. It sounded ridiculous to him as he was saying it. He had no intention of merely looking through the windows. But it was the pretext Olin needed to come with him.

At least that was what Connor had assumed until he grabbed one of the door handles on the French doors.

"What are you doing?" Olin whispered.

"What do you mean?"

"You said we were just going to look through the windows."

Connor took a deep breath, exhaled loudly. "I lied. If we want to know what's going on, we've got to go in. We're not going to touch anything. He'll never even know we were here."

"And I'm supposed to trust you now?"

"Stay out here if you want." Connor pressed down on the handle. He didn't expect it to turn. Getting in wouldn't be that easy, he was sure. But it did turn. Perhaps someone had left it open by accident, or perhaps, with the house ensconced by tall brick walls, Dylan didn't feel any need to ensure all of the doors were locked when he left.

Whatever flavor of crazy he was, an unlocked door was more proof in Connor's mind that he wasn't the kidnapper. Still, they had come this far. It was worth seeing what they could find out.

Olin held out his hands. "Wait! What if they have an alarm?"

"Then we'll run like crazy," Connor said, and yanked the door open. They both froze. Listened.

"No alarm," Connor said. He went in.

Olin looked around, cursed under his breath, and followed him.

"Close the door," Connor said, and Olin did.

"What are we looking for?"

"I guess we'll know it when we find it."

Connor looked left, then right. The kitchen was huge—custom cabinets, stainless steel appliances, marble countertops—and led off to other rooms in both directions. They had to prioritize their search, he realized. Otherwise, they could be here for hours, and who knew when Dylan would get home?

"Look for a basement or an attic. Let's start there."

"Why?"

"Where would you hide things you wanted to keep secret?" Connor said, already moving toward a door just beyond the kitchen. Something about it reminded him of the one that led to the attic in his own house. Here, though, it opened into a pantry.

They followed the adjoining hall to the living room. The space was furnished with leather sofas, antique bookcases, an Oriental throw rug, and a velvet fainting couch near the windows. There was only one door within sight, and it led to a half-bath.

When Connor had first visited this house, he had been surprised by the grand nature of the exterior. It did not seem like the kind of place where he would expect to find a man as unstable as the one behind the TruthSeekers website. Now that he had made it inside, it seemed even less so. But this was the registered address for the domain, so they would keep looking.

The only other doors on the first floor led to a coat closet and garage. Apparently, the house had no basement. Just as well. Although Olin hadn't commented on the trespassing since he had followed Connor inside, he looked nervous.

From the pictures Connor had seen of Olin online and around his house—playing soccer, sailing, posing on hiking trails with his friends—he had expected his confidence to translate into courage. It had not. At least, not when it came to something like this. Maybe the risks associated with hacking into strangers' websites had made Connor better suited for this task.

"Let's go upstairs," Connor said, already leading the way.

At the top of the stairs were a small sitting room that overlooked the foyer and a hallway that forked at the far end. They moved together to that fork, opening doors that led to a laundry room and a linen closet along the way. Connor gestured toward one of the hallways. "You go right. I'll go left."

Olin nodded. "Let's get this over with."

The first door Connor came upon led to the master bedroom. It looked like it was right out of a magazine, with a four-poster bed and a tray ceiling. And just like the rest of the house, everything seemed to be in its place.

The idea that this room, and all the rest of the rooms, looked like they were straight out of a magazine tickled something in the back of Connor's brain, and he had only one conscious thought: *Is that what's happening here?* The underlying idea that had formed all at once and without words was that the entire house was staged to simulate Dylan's idea of normality. It suggested a degree of self-awareness Connor had not expected from someone who ran a site like TruthSeekers.

"Hey, Connor."

"Yeah?"

"Come here."

Connor stepped out of the bedroom, saw Olin at the other end of the hall, looking through another open door. "What is it?"

Olin pointed at the doorway in front of him. "I think you should have a look."

CHAPTER 27

OLIVIA PULLED UP to the house where the license plate was registered, with two black-and-whites behind her. She noted the old Ford pickup at the top of the driveway and a car of some sort covered by a tarp at the bottom. Olivia intentionally parked in front of the driveway to seal off any chance for escape. The cruisers parked behind her.

The neighborhood was poor, with small, ramshackle houses and weed-infested lawns.

She started moving toward the front door as soon as she was out of the car. The four uniformed officers who had followed her here fell in behind her.

She looked over her shoulder. "You two take the back." There was no way this guy was going to escape.

Olivia stepped onto a porch that badly needed a fresh coat of paint. Rusty wind chimes hung from the ceiling. Olivia knocked. Her mouth went dry. Her jaw tightened. She was on edge. But it was the kind of edge she liked being on. These were the adrenaline-fueled moments that made the job worth doing, right up there with sweating a suspect in the interrogation room.

There was also a part of her that hated it. That part of her worried every day she might not come home, and it worried her on days like this more than most. She worried what her daughter would do without her, whether

her ex would buck up and be a real father. As things stood, it didn't seem like he could be a father at all—just missing the gene, her mom said—and she hoped that at tomorrow's custody hearing the judge would agree.

She pounded on the door, announced herself as police. Unconsciously, her right hand went to the gun holstered at her waist. She snapped open the strap that secured the weapon in place. Normally she kept her gun in a shoulder holster, but that wasn't convenient when she was also wearing a bulletproof vest. Which was just as well, since it was harder to get to, and if Broderick Hansen—that was the name associated with the license plate—came out shooting, the time it took her to pull her gun might make the difference in whether or not she lived.

She heard the deadbolt turn. Her fingers closed around the gun's handle. The door opened. Before Olivia could even see who it was, she was demanding to speak with Broderick.

"Hold your horses," said the man who had opened it. He was wearing just a robe and had to be seventy, at least, Olivia thought. His eyes darted between her and the two uniformed officers. "What is this about?"

"Sir, we need to speak with Broderick—"

"I heard you. I'm not deaf."

"Yet," said a woman as she came up behind him. She was wearing a faded blue nightgown and looked just as old.

Olivia could tell she thought she was being funny and had no patience for it. "Sir!"

"I'm Broderick Hansen."

This was not the man on the CCTV footage. Even though she had only seen him from the back, Olivia was sure of that. This man had the wrong build, the wrong posture, the wrong hair. She doubted they were even the same height.

"Sir, do you have an ID on you?"

"Sure." He reached toward his back pocket. Olivia imagined he had a gun of his own. She could see him pulling it in her mind's eye, braced for the chaos that would follow. Her fingers, which were still wrapped around the handle of her own weapon, moved slightly so that her pointer was on the trigger.

She was about to tell him to slow down, even though he was already moving slowly, when she saw the leather corner of a wallet appear from behind him. He opened it, took out his license, and held it up so she could see.

The name on the license was indeed Broderick Hansen.

Olivia relaxed a little. She let go of her gun, let her hand fall to her side. "Has anybody borrowed your car recently?"

"No."

"I wish they would," the woman said. "Borrow it and keep it as far as I'm concerned."

"So the Mustang has been in your possession the whole time? You're sure?"

"What Mustang?" the woman said, first to Olivia and then to Broderick. "Did you go buy a Mustang without telling me? Are you some kind of dummy? We can't afford a car payment right now. Maybe if you got a job—"

"Who's going to hire me at my age?"

"Mr. Hansen," Olivia said, to direct the couple's attention back to her. "Are you telling me you don't have a Mustang?"

"I wish."

Olivia recited the car's license plate number.

"What about it?"

"That's not your license plate?"

"That's my license plate. One of them. So what?"

"So, you just told me you don't own a Mustang."

Broderick almost laughed. He waved dismissively at Olivia. "That's no Mustang."

"Excuse me?"

Broderick turned to the woman next to him. She hadn't stopped glaring at him since the Mustang had first been mentioned. He didn't seem to notice. "She's talking about that old Honda we got under the tarp." Back to Olivia: "Lady, those glasses you're wearing might not be thick enough."

Suddenly, Olivia realized what should have been obvious all along. But she wasn't going to leave without being certain. "Show me."

"What?"

"You say that's no Mustang. Let's go have a look."

Broderick shrugged.

Olivia and the uniformed officers made room for him to step outside. They followed him around to the driveway. He grabbed one corner of the tarp and pulled. It slid off the vehicle all at once, landing in a crumpled heap beside the front tire.

The Honda Civic that had been underneath was a good twenty years old, and looked every bit of it.

"See. Like I said. No Mustang. I'm not even sure this thing drives anymore."

Olivia walked from the front of the vehicle to the back. No license plate on either end. *Shit.*

"Stay right here," she said to both the officers and Broderick. Then she went up the street for some privacy. She called the DMV again, gave them the license plate again. This time, though, instead of asking who owned the vehicle, she asked for the make and model.

They told her exactly what she feared they might: The vehicle associated with that plate number was a 1984 Honda Civic.

The plates had been stolen. She wondered if the Mustang had been stolen, too.

CHAPTER 28

THERE WAS SOMETHING in Olin's voice that Connor didn't like. He quickly made his way to the other end of the hall, trying not to think about all the horrible things he might find beyond that door. But his mind went there anyway. Decaying corpses. Maybe his parents. Maybe Olin's. Maybe weapons or torture devices or cages—God, what if there were cages? Or—and this scared him even more—what if it was something worse? (Because even though Connor didn't think it was Dylan who had targeted both of their parents, Olin had gotten inside of his head, and he couldn't dismiss the possibility entirely.)

But that wasn't what he found. What he found was another bedroom. At first, all he saw was the mess. Clothes littered the floor and hung over the furniture. The bed was unmade and slightly askew. The walls were covered with posters of bands Connor didn't know: The Mowgli's, Jukebox the Ghost, Billie Eilish. There was a simple white desk with a stack of notebooks on it and, perhaps most importantly, a laptop.

Connor had not considered until now that this was the first computer he had seen in the house. He knew immediately this had to be the madness behind the TruthSeekers website, the secret self the rest of the house tried so hard to hide.

He stepped into the room and flipped through the notebook closest to him. It contained a series of math equations—they reminded him of the notes he had made in his college algebra class—and a name on the back of the cover. Spelled out in all capital letters, it read: D-Y-L-A-N.

Strange, he thought. Something about that didn't seem right.

He turned around, saw the posters weren't the only things stuck to the walls. There were also photos. Lots of them. Most were of happy young women posing together. Some silly, some less so. They posed in front of a Starbucks, with animals at a petting zoo, in various bars and shopping malls. Unlike the photos in Olin's house, there seemed no rhyme or reason to them. Well, except for one thing. One important detail Connor didn't notice until he had looked at enough of them up close. Of all the people, there was one who came up more than any of the others. A woman with red hair and freckles. She looked to be about twenty-one.

Suddenly, it all came together.

Dylan wasn't an unstable man capable of kidnapping. He wasn't a man, at all. He—*she*—was just a college student.

Olin grabbed Connor's arm. "What's that?" he whispered. He was looking straight ahead, but didn't seem to be focused on anything in particular.

"What?" Connor responded, also whispering. He felt a little foolish about it, since they were the only ones in the house.

"Sounds like a car."

"It's just your nerves."

Olin moved to the bedroom window, trying not to step on Dylan's clothes as he went. It was a futile effort.

"Do you see anything?" Connor asked. Even from where he was, he could make out part of the driveway, so he knew the window faced the front of the house.

"No."

"Like I told you. It's just your nerves."

Then there was a much louder sound—a mechanical rumble. It lasted only five or six seconds. Connor and Olin stood frozen in place until it was over, then simultaneously looked at each other. Connor knew what it was and suspected Olin did, too. Still, he said it out loud just to make sure they were on the same page. "That was a garage door," he whispered. Only now, whispering seemed to make sense.

"I told you," Olin said.

The mechanical rumble started up again. It lasted another five or six seconds.

Door open. Door closed.

Olin looked left and right as if assessing an unseen enemy. "I *knew* this was a bad idea."

"Relax. We'll get out of here."

"How?"

It was a fair question. There was no climbing out a window from this height. Then Connor had an idea. He peeked into the hall, heard a door open downstairs. Presumably, it was the one that led to the garage. "This way," he hissed, as he hurried from the bedroom to the laundry room.

Olin cursed and followed him. "This is your plan?" he said, once they had crossed the hall.

Connor remembered the laundry room door had been closed when they had come upstairs, and he kept it open only a crack now. "Shhhh." He had his ear pressed to that crack, trying to hear what was happening.

Someone treaded across the hardwood floors downstairs. The sound faded and transformed as that someone stepped into the kitchen, then disappeared completely for a minute. No one spoke—upstairs or down.

"I think, whoever it is, they're alone," Connor said.

The footsteps returned, moved somewhere else on the first floor.

"What's the plan?" Olin said.

Connor had been hoping that whoever it was would come upstairs, disappear into one of the bedrooms for a while, giving them enough time for an easy escape. It no longer seemed like that was going to happen.

But then he heard a much softer sound. A *rat-a-tat-tat* he recognized. And at least he knew where in the house the person was.

When Connor and Olin had searched the first floor, Connor had come across a room to the left of the front door that, it seemed to him, had been converted from a formal living room into a library. Built-in bookshelves lined every wall, and every shelf was packed with books. There was also a desk dead center that looked out onto the foyer, but was bare save a Georgetown brass-finish desk lamp.

At the time, he had thought the room was mostly for show. But with the whole house maintained in pristine condition, he now knew better. That *rat-a-tat-tat* was the sound of a keyboard, and that desk was likely where Dylan's parents sat when they worked from home. It was easy enough to imagine her father or her mother coming in with a laptop, stopping by the kitchen for snack, and then setting up at that desk for the remainder of the day.

They probably wouldn't be moving anytime soon.

"This is our chance," he told Olin, and explained what was happening. "If we go back down the stairs and out the way we came in, they won't see us."

"Are you sure?"

"I'm open to better ideas," Connor said.

Olin looked to the side, bit his lower lip, then nodded.

They crept out of the laundry room to the staircase and then started down, one stair at a time. Slowly. Carefully. Making sure every footfall was nearly silent.

Connor kept his ears open. More *rat-a-tat-tat*. The sound of the chair squeaking. Caster wheels rolling. He briefly detoured to the library to peek in, just to be sure he was correct in assuming the person at that desk was not, in fact, the woman they were looking for. It was not. The man sitting there had a thick mane of black hair brushed away from his face and looked a good thirty years older than Dylan.

Has to be her father, Connor thought.

Like with Roland, Connor could tell from his build that he was not the man who had entered his house. Not that he thought he would be. After Connor saw Dylan's room, he was all but certain she was not involved in the abduction.

He and Olin moved carefully across the living room, back to the hall that would take them to the kitchen. Then Connor heard glass break behind him and whipped his head around. Olin was standing next to a half-moon table, his mouth and eyes wide with alarm. (They would have been comically wide if the situation wasn't so serious.) By his feet lay shattered glass that had formerly been a vase.

Olin immediately began apologizing in a strangled whisper.

At the same time, Connor heard the *rat-a-tat-tat* stop, the caster wheels roll, the squeak of the seat as the man who had been sitting in it got to his feet. Connor didn't bother to whisper. "Run!"

Olin did as instructed. They reached the back door, fled into the yard. They just had to get over that wall and they would be all right. Just like last time, Connor hoisted Olin up onto it.

"Oh, shit," Olin said, looking toward the house.

"Give me your hand!"

Then there was the sound of a gunshot. The bullet drilled into the brick wall not a foot away. "You think you can steal from me?"

Connor instinctively turned.

The man was holding a shotgun and had it aimed in Connor's direction. "Stay right there! I'm calling the police!"

Connor reached up, and Olin grabbed his hand. He scrambled up the wall as Dylan's father fired another shot. Then he and Olin fell over the top and crashed onto the ground behind the property.

They scurried back to the street as fast as they could and ran to the car. Connor hoped Dylan's dad wouldn't come out his front door shooting. Later, he would realize how crazy that idea was. The man was most likely on the phone with the police or checking his wife's jewelry box to see if anything had been taken.

Once they were a safe distance away, Olin turned in his seat. "Why is it every time we follow your advice, we end up nearly getting arrested or shot?" He sounded winded.

"That's only happened twice," Connor said, and realized the absurdity of his response.

"I'm just saying—maybe we should start doing things my way."

Connor got the message. He pulled his cellphone out of his pocket at a red light and scrolled through his call log until he found Olivia's number.

CHAPTER 29

OLIVIA WAS PULLING out of the pickup line at Lancelot Academy with her daughter in the back seat when her phone rang. Erin, who was only five years old, didn't seem to notice. She was telling Olivia about the turtle her teacher had brought in today, and could barely stop long enough to take a breath, let alone for her mother to take a phone call.

"Honey. Honey, please. It will only be a minute."

"But—"

"Please. Just a minute. I promise." Then she answered before her daughter could say anything else.

"Detective Forbes. Hi. Listen, there's something you need to know." She recognized Connor's voice. Another voice she didn't know said something in the background. "All right, there are a couple of things you need to know. They're about my parents' abduction."

She noticed he wasn't using the word "murder" yet. She wasn't surprised. It took some people a long time to come to terms with that. "What is it?"

"First. It's about, um . . . It's about my dad. There's a guy named Roland Cooper. I don't know what their connection is, but I found his name in my dad's email and I tried to talk to him. You know, just to see if he knew anything that might help."

Olivia wished he hadn't done that. Connor should have come to her with the name and let her handle it. But she wasn't going to interrupt, either. She wanted to hear what he had to say.

And, she realized, she had better take some notes. Just to be safe.

There was a Dunkin' Donuts immediately in front of her. She pulled into the parking lot. Erin threw her hands up and cheered.

"Not yet, honey. You be good and we'll get you a treat when Mommy's done, okay?" Back to the phone. "Go on," she said as she fished a notepad and pen out of her glovebox.

"Well, I don't know. There might be nothing to it. But it seemed strange. He was being all covert-like. Didn't want to talk to me. I thought, you know, maybe you would have more luck."

"Is that it?"

"No. There's something else, too. And this one seems pretty important. The guy who kidnapped my parents. He took someone else's parents also. His name is Olin. . . . What's your last name?" More mumbling in the background. "Wilson. His parents are Mark and Hillary."

Olivia could hardly believe what she was hearing. "Slow down. There was another abduction? How do you know?"

"Same M.O. Van. Ski mask. Taser."

"And he's there with you now?"

"Yes."

"Can I speak to him?"

There was a moment of silence, then another voice. "Ma'am?"

"Are you Mr. Wilson?"

"Yes, ma'am."

"Your parents were taken, too?"

"Yes, ma'am."

Olivia was furious. She couldn't believe she was just hearing about this now. "Who's the detective working your case?"

There was a pause, and then Olin gave her a name. She wrote it down underneath Roland's.

"NYPD?"

"Yorktown."

"But there's more." Connor again. "These abductions—they're not random. My parents. His parents. They knew each other."

"So you two—"

"No, we had never met." Connor seemed to have correctly guessed where she was going with her question.

"How did you find out about Olin's parents? Or is he the one who found out first?"

Connor told her about the spot that would air on *Uncovered* soon, how the producer had told him about Olin's parents, and she wished he had talked to her about that, too. Most shows like it stuck to cold cases. *Uncovered* was one of the few that went after crimes still actively being worked. Sure, she would have a lot of leads to follow up on after it aired, but most of them (probably all of them) would be garbage. In cold cases, that was okay. Any lead was better than no lead. But even though Connor's case was at a dead end right now, it was still active, still being worked, and the time she spent following up on garbage leads could be better spent in other ways. Shows like *Uncovered* brought out a lot of crazies.

"How do you know they know each other?"

"We found a picture in my house with all of them in it. But that's not the important part. My parents took a trip to Prague some fifteen years ago. So did his. Right about the same time. We're thinking they might have gone together."

"Connor—"

"I know. I'm sure they're not the only people in New York who went to the Czech Republic around that time. But they all went, and they were all abducted. I'm not saying it has anything to do with the trip. That was a long time ago. But it seems like something to look into, doesn't it?"

Fair point, Olivia thought. There had never been a ransom call. If the killer was abducting people who knew each other, it might be about something other than money. It was also likely the reason he hadn't taken Connor. There was a purpose behind this. She felt a small rush of adrenaline, a renewed hope that she could solve this crime. In a normal abduction case, you worked it the best you could, but there was often not much you could do other than wait for a call. If there was a reason behind it, though, you just had to find the reason.

"Anything else?"

Connor seemed to hesitate. "No, that's it."

"You're sure?"

"I'm sure."

"All right. Thanks for filling me in. I'll sync up with the Yorktown PD, and we'll check this out."

Connor thanked her as well, and she hung up.

"That took *forever*," Erin whined from the backseat, stretching out the word "forever" until she ran out of breath. "*Now* can we get a treat?"

Olivia glanced at her daughter via the review mirror and smiled. "Sure."

Erin could be a handful. Even plopped in front of the TV, she didn't stay still long, so Olivia didn't get a chance to place any more work calls until after her daughter was in bed. She left a message for the Yorktown detective, asking him to reach out to her in the morning. Then she pulled out her laptop, connected to the NYPD's VPN, and went to work.

There wasn't much on Roland Cooper. Just the basics, the sort of public record everyone leaves behind: birth certificate, marriage certificate, credit report (he had four cards and thirty-two thousand dollars in debt between them, not to mention loans for his car and his house). Some traffic tickets, but nothing unusual. She doubted he had anything to do with the abduction, but she would follow up with him tomorrow anyway.

In the meantime, she shifted her attention to Olin's parents. Mark and Hillary Wilson. Married in 1992. Mark was a money manager for Fidelity. Hillary had worked a few odd jobs over the years—she had spent three months as a receptionist at Save the Oceans, another three months as a frontline activist (whatever that was) for Save the Rainforests—but was, by all accounts, a housewife.

They lived in an affluent Westchester neighborhood in a big house that Mark had inherited from his parents. They were both lifelong New Yorkers and both had attended Columbia University.

Olivia turned her attention to Connor's parents. She knew a lot about them already, but only the recent stuff. As she dug further into their backgrounds, she learned that while Frank had moved to New York from Alabama when he was twenty-six, Kim had, like Mark and Hillary, grown up in New York and been a student at Columbia. The three had even graduated the same year.

And further digging did indeed reveal all four had traveled to the Czech Republic. The US Customs and Border Protection agency had records for them leaving and returning together. But there had been at least one other person with them.

Before marrying Frank, Kim had been married to a Matthew Jones.

She had still been married to him on the date of the trip, and the US Customs and Border Protection agency had a record for him leaving the US on the same day as everyone else.

The only thing was, they had no record of him coming back. Ever.

That had to be a mistake, Olivia thought.

CHAPTER 30

ADEN WAS DENIED bail. He hadn't expected the hearing to go any other way.

He was transferred to the Metropolitan Correctional Center and put in a cell by himself on a high-security wing. He spent little time in it, though. Federal agents of all stripes questioned him for hours on end. They wanted to know the basics, of course: what his plan was, whether he was working alone.

But they also asked other questions. A lot of them.

He said not a word. Not to anyone. Not ever. Even when he was allowed out of his cell for short periods of time, he didn't speak to the guards or other inmates.

Not until tonight, anyway. Tonight, he asked the guards if he could make a phone call.

The hacker was watching a baseball game when his cellphone rang. The Yankees versus the Bears. The score was three to one, in favor of the Yankees. Seventh inning. It seemed inevitable at this point the Yankees would win. Somehow, that made the world seem a little better.

He glanced down at the cellphone sitting on the sofa beside him. It was a burner. Only one person had the number.

He picked it up.

"You have a collect call from the Metropolitan Correctional Center. Will you accept the charges?"

The hacker hadn't heard about Aden's arrest, but that had to be who was calling. Did this mean the plan was off? He hoped so.

"Yes, I'll accept the charges."

There was a click and then silence.

The hacker stood up, walked to the window, and looked out at the city while he waited to be connected to Aden. His heart sank as he realized he had probably already been connected, that Aden was sitting there quietly on the other end, and he followed the protocol.

"Betty, is that you?"

Another five seconds of silence. Then there was a single long beep, so loud he had to hold the phone away from his ear. It was the sound of someone holding down a key on the phone's keypad. And that was followed by more silence.

"I think you have the wrong number," the hacker said, and then hung up.

So much for the possibility that Aden's arrest had put a stop to his plan. They were still on.

Just do what you have to do. It's the deal you made.

CHAPTER 31

"WHY DIDN'T YOU tell Olivia about Dylan?" Olin said, when Connor hung up the phone.

Connor stared at him incredulously. "Dylan's dad just saw us breaking and entering. The police are probably at his house right now taking a statement."

"But we didn't steal anything."

Connor shrugged, keeping his eyes on the road. "If we told Olivia, she would have to go and talk to her," he said flatly. "My name would inevitably come up. Maybe yours would, too. And if her dad figured out who we were, maybe looked us up online or something, we'd be fucked." He turned quickly to Olin and then back to the road. "Besides, what good would it do? She's not the person we're looking for."

He could tell from Olin's expression that Olin didn't like the idea of keeping anything from the police. But Olin had to know he was right.

Neither of them said much else until they pulled into the parking lot across the street from Deerfield Park. Olin's car was still there.

"I'll talk to you soon," Olin said as he got out.

"Sure," Connor agreed. But he wasn't sure Olin meant it, and he wasn't sure he did, either. Having handed everything over to the police that they could, what more was there for them to do? What reason did they have to meet again? At first, their shared pain had seemed like the kind of thing that might bind them together as friends for life. But maybe that was just because they had a common goal. A quest, as it were.

For a little while there, Connor had felt like he might be in control of his destiny (and, by extension, his parents'). Olin had certainly felt the same way.

Now, as he watched Olin get into his BMW and pull away, he was starting to think the whole thing might have just been a way to distract himself from the possibility that he would never see his parents again.

He drove back to Austin's building, barely going the speed limit. He was in no hurry to be anywhere, and felt like even the simple act of turning the steering wheel took all the will he could muster. At one point, coming up to a red light, he thought about not stopping at all. It was a busy intersection. Cars crossed at forty-five, maybe fifty, miles an hour. With no one in front of him, he could sail straight into it, and there was a decent chance he wouldn't make it out.

But he could also end up paralyzed, and his situation would immediately become worse than it was now. Dead parents. Dead body. All he would have left would be his brain—and all he would be able to do then would be to mourn the loss of both.

Besides, his parents wouldn't want him to do that. They would be disappointed in him if they knew what he was thinking. You don't give up on life just because things are hard.

Austin picked up on the change in his mood almost as soon as Connor walked through the door. "It's going to be all right," he said. Then, perhaps because he didn't know what else to do, he ordered them a pizza, calling it comfort food, and put on a movie titled *Get Him to the Greek.*

It was the type of comedy that might have made Connor laugh a month ago. Tonight he could barely focus on it, and halfway through, he simply stopped trying.

"I'm going to bed," he told Austin.

Austin seemed disappointed but didn't put up much of a fight.

CHAPTER 32

OLIVIA COULDN'T SLEEP. Not well, anyway. She woke up every hour or so and checked the alarm clock to see how close she was to morning. At four a.m., she decided she had slept as much as she was going to. She got up, took a shower. She was anxious to get started.

The US Customs and Border Protection agency still wouldn't be open for several hours. She was stuck unless she wanted to skip straight to calling the Czech police to see if they knew anything about Matthew Jones. What the hell? Why not?

These days, the US Customs and Border Protection agency digitally logged travel to and from the county. That wasn't being done when Matthew had gone to the Czech Republic, so it was possible his return trip had been overlooked when the staff was transferring paper records into the computer. As far as she knew, the paper records still existed for just such an occasion. But how long would it take to dig them up? Would she be waiting another day for an answer? Two? And if he had come back, why couldn't she find an address for him online? Or anything at all, for that matter?

The Czech Republic's international airport was located in Prague, the country's capital. She figured it made sense to start with the police there and fan out to smaller cities if she needed to. Since the Czech Republic was five hours ahead of New York, she could start placing her calls now.

She looked the force up online. The first listing she came across was *Policie České republiky*. It sounded promising.

Olivia dialed the number, then spent half an hour getting routed through officers who spoke varying degrees of English until she finally ended up with Oldrich Kozar. From what she could gather, he had been on the force for some thirty years and, as luck would have it, spoke English well.

"I think I remember this Matthew Jones," he said. "Hold on while I check something."

That sounded promising. Olivia was glad she hadn't waited to speak with the US Customs and Border Protection agency first.

"Yes," he said. "Here it is. Matthew Jones. Arrested and charged with . . . How you call it? First degree murder, correct?"

Of all the things Oldrich could have told her, she would have never guessed this. "Are you sure?"

"Oh, yes. Very sure. I remember this case. Matthew Jones killed a woman . . . What was her name?" Olivia heard the detective flipping through pieces of paper. "Heather Callahan."

"Related to Frank Callahan?"

More flipping pages. "She was his wife."

"Are you sure about that?"

"Detective Forbes, I can assure you we have our facts correct."

"I'm sorry. I hadn't meant—"

"It's okay."

"Do you know why he killed her?"

"It says here they were having an affair. She wanted to break it off, and he did not. This is . . . common."

"Excuse me?"

"I mean, sometimes, these things . . . they happen."

"What things happen?"

"Things."

"Murder?"

"Not usually. But, you know, things."

Olivia suspected he meant assault, and unfortunately things like that did sometimes happen when couples broke up. "Is he still in jail?"

"But yes. Tell me, why are you calling all the way from America about this old case?"

Olivia filled him in on the abductions and subsequent murders.

He grunted. "That's quite a thing."

"I know it's a long shot, but could you review your case files? See if there's anything in them that might help us figure out what's happening now?"

"Why do you think that case has anything to do with this?"

Olivia was still in her robe, propped up on the bed, legs crossed. "I'm not sure it does." She looked at the clock. It was almost six now. Erin would get up soon. "But something ties these abductions together."

"Okay. I will look. But—how you say?—don't get your hopes high."

CHAPTER 33

LIKE OLIVIA, CONNOR woke up almost every hour on the hour. Was he actually at a dead end? Certainly there was something he could do, some clue he had missed. There had to be.

Well, there was one thing.

Dylan.

He could still talk to her, he thought, staring up at the ceiling. He didn't expect it to bring him any insight. But at least it would focus his mind, give him something to do. Besides, Dylan knew something about his real father. And maybe his mother. Hoping it might have anything to do with their kidnapping seemed like a stretch, but he should still find out what it was.

But how? After the encounter with Dylan's father, he couldn't exactly walk right up to the front door and ask to speak with her.

He would have to do it somewhere else.

That would mean following her. Waking up early (done), driving to her house, trailing her until she was alone. But that all sounded like a terrible idea.

Maybe there was a better way.

Connor sat down at the small mahogany desk in the bedroom and opened his laptop. He didn't bother to turn on the lamp. He knew his way around a computer almost well enough to work it blindfolded, and the screen cast enough light for him to see the keyboard on the rare occasion he needed to look.

He got the IP address from Dylan's email (the same IP address he had used earlier to find her house) and employed a technique called banner grabbing to search for open ports. From there, it was just a matter of exploiting the applications that used those ports to find a way in. It took a while. Hacking his way into a stranger's machine always did. Soon enough, though, he found himself looking at Dylan's computer just as if he were actually in her bedroom.

He checked her Outlook calendar, hoping for a list of appointments, and found it blank. He wasn't surprised. That was a long shot anyway. Then he had a better idea, and a little bit of Googling confirmed his suspicion.

When he was done doing what he'd logged in to do, he closed down his computer and slid it back into the bag beside the desk.

Olin would want to be a part of this, Connor thought. He no doubt needed the distraction, as well. But Connor wasn't going to call. It was too early. Besides, this was the kind of information that should be delivered in person. He had no reason to think the police were listening to every call he made. They might not be listening to any at all. But they had installed software on his phone that would let them.

Sure, they had told him he would have to activate the application if he wanted them to hear the call. And at the time, he had taken that statement at face value. But now he had his doubts. For all he knew, they considered him a suspect in his parents' abductions, and the application was a clever way of capturing not just calls from the kidnapper, but any calls they wanted. Maybe texts, too.

As he pulled a clean pair of jeans and a Ramones tee shirt out of his suitcase, he told himself that was unlikely. If Olivia was monitoring the calls and texts on his phone, she would also be monitoring the ones on his dad's. She would have already known about Roland.

But then he reminded himself that one could never be too careful.

Connor opened the bedroom door and crept through the dark apartment. His foot brushed against something soft, and he jerked back, his heart hammering, as Austin's cat bolted into the living room, likely taking shelter under the sofa again.

Once he caught his breath, he continued on to the kitchen. Austin had a spiral notepad and pencil that he used for his shopping lists in a drawer by the stove. Connor took them out, hastily scrawled out a brief note that said he would not be able to come to work today and that he would circle up with Austin later. He had some personal business to attend to.

He used a magnet that read "Summertime's funner time" to stick it to the fridge.

Connor was halfway to Olin's house when Austin called. He'd expected it. Austin was probably worried about him—taking off before sunrise and leaving a cryptic note like he had.

"You're up early," Austin said, when Connor answered. "Where are you?"

"I've got something I have to do. I left you a note on the fridge."

"I saw it. You're not coming in today?" He sounded annoyed.

"I will if I can."

"What is this about? Did the police call you? Did they find something?"

"Nothing like that."

"Then what? Is something else going on?"

Connor wasn't sure what to say, so he said nothing. He didn't want

Austin to know that he had hacked into Dylan's website, broken into her house, and remotely taken control of her computer. He didn't want *anyone* to know all that. Well, no one but Olin, who had been a part of the break-in and would be a part of what came next.

"Is it something I can help with?"

"I found something out yesterday," Connor said, finally realizing he had a story to tell Austin that might put an end to the questions. "My dad met with some guy named Roland. I mean—it could be nothing, right? But the whole thing seemed strange. I thought I would have a look around my house. Maybe I'll find something that will tell me why they met. It probably has nothing to do with his kidnapping. But I . . . I just have to do something, if I can." At least that much was true. He did have to do something. Trying to figure out why his father had met with Roland wasn't it, though. He had gone as far as he could with that. It was in Olivia's hands now.

Austin sighed. "I guess I get it. Do what you have to do. But I want you home early tonight. I have something I need to talk to you about."

"What is it?"

"Better we talk in person."

CHAPTER 34

OLIN DIDN'T COME to the door right away. Connor figured he might still be asleep. No matter. He wasn't giving up. Employing the same strategy he had at Adriana's and again at Dylan's, he rang the doorbell again, and this time kept ringing it—one *ding-dong* after another—for a minute or more, before finally sitting down on the brick stoop with a sigh of frustration, his legs hanging over the edge and splayed out across the walkway.

Olin might be ignoring the doorbell because he didn't want to see him. After what had happened last time, Connor wouldn't blame him if that was the case.

Maybe the best thing to do was to leave him alone. Connor had likely been projecting his own emotions onto Olin when he had thought Olin would want to confront Dylan with him. Not everyone handled pain the same way. Some people, like Connor, felt compelled to act. Sometimes that action was meaningful. Sometimes it was not. But in all cases, it buried the pain for a while, dulled its edge.

Olin had been a man of action only because Connor had pushed him into it. He had wanted to turn everything over to the police from the moment they had met. And then what? Wallow in his misery? Maybe. Some people, Connor had gathered, liked to feel every second of their pain.

And who was he to judge? Who was he to say one way of healing was better than another?

Although he liked Olin, liked having a partner in this investigation, it had been selfish of him to come here, he decided. He could handle this on his own.

Connor stood up, dusted off the back of his jeans, and had just started toward the car when he heard the door open behind him. He turned around.

Olin was standing in the foyer, yawning and with deep bags under his eyes. He was wearing flip-flips, shorts, and a gray tee—a combination, Connor noted, that looked more like something he himself would be wearing.

"What are you doing here?" Olin said, and glanced to his left. Connor remembered from his last visit there was a pendulum clock on the wall, just out sight. "It's really early."

"I didn't want to wait. I had an idea."

"Great. Keep it to yourself."

Connor stepped forward. "No, wait. Listen, yesterday was a mistake. It was a terrible idea to break into Dylan's house."

"You think?"

"But I still want to talk to her. I mean, she might still know something, right? After all, she knew about Matt. So what else does she know?"

"Leave it alone. We're not going back to that house."

Connor noticed he used the word "we." It gave him hope Olin was interested in hearing what he had to say. He took another step forward. "Of course not. I have a better idea." He looked around. Although there was nobody within sight, he still didn't like discussing his plan where, in theory, anybody could hear him. "Can I come in?"

Olin moved out of the doorway.

Connor followed him in and closed the door. "All right," he said as soon as he turned around. "Here's what I'm thinking. Remember how I told you I found Dylan's house using her IP address? I used it again to get on to her computer." Connor had explicitly avoided the phrases "break in to her computer" and "hack into her computer" because they both had a ring of criminality that wouldn't sit well with Olin.

Apparently, though, his word choice didn't make any difference. "What?" Olin threw his hands up in the air. As they came down, he grabbed handfuls of his hair and pulled his head forward with frustration. "If they find out what you did—"

"They won't."

"—and they figure out you're the one who did it . . ." He let go of his hair, looked back up. "It's not going to be hard to link that to the break-in, and then . . ."

He didn't finish his thought. He didn't have to. Connor got the idea. "They're not going to figure it out. I know what I'm doing."

"Really? Dylan already traced your last hack back to you."

Connor ignored the commentary. "I did some searching online and found Dylan's cellphone number. Then I traced that back to AT&T, and from there to a device. A Samsung Galaxy, to be precise, which was exactly what I was hoping I would find. There's a lot of stuff out there about hacking Androids. I normally stay away from all that. But this— it seemed like it might be worth making an exception for. Anyway, to make a long story short . . ." He pulled out his iPhone, browsed to a website, entered some information, and turned the phone around so Olin could see the screen.

On it, there was a map. Pale yellow background. White lines for streets and gray boxes for buildings. And a single blue dot.

"You see that dot? That's Dylan's cellphone. As long as we know where her phone is, we know where she is."

"What if she leaves it at home?"

"She won't. That thing is probably glued to her hand."

"She might."

"Would you leave your phone at home?"

Olin shrugged, but it was halfhearted. Then he asked, "Where is she now?"

Connor already knew the answer to that question. The dot hadn't moved since he had first started tracking it. But, to illustrate for Olin how the app worked, he pinched the screen to zoom out. When he did, street names appeared on the map. "She's at home," he said, once again turning the phone around so Olin could see.

Olin bit down on his lip like he had in the laundry room of Dylan's house. It seemed to be his go-to move when he wanted to think. "How does that thing work?"

"What do you mean?"

"I mean—if you somehow managed to get an app installed on her phone, don't you think she might notice that?"

"Maybe. But she probably has tons of apps on that thing. I doubt she'll notice one more right away."

Olin considered this as well, then added, "So we just wait for her to leave and then what? Follow her?"

"Not literally, of course. We don't have to. But we should stay close. That way, when she ends up in a public location, somewhere she won't feel threatened, we can talk to her."

"Like we did Roland?"

"That was different."

"How?"

Connor put his phone back in his pocket. "You don't have to come if you don't want to," he snapped. He waited ten or fifteen seconds for

Olin to say something, then turned to leave.

"No, no. I'll come."

"Are you sure?"

"At this point, what is there to lose?"

CHAPTER 35

IT HAD BEEN a long time since Oldrich Kozar had thought
about the Heather Callahan murder case, and a lot longer than
that since he had worked it. The case had stuck with him for a
while. At the time, he had only been a detective for eleven months, and
while it wasn't his first murder investigation, it was the first one he had
been told to lead.

It was a sink-or-swim moment.

Back in those days, Oldrich was lean and strong. He had an ease of
movement and a charm that made people think he was more confident
than he was. Inside, he was a ball of nerves. Not just about the case—
everything put him on edge, but the case only made it worse. He had
been determined to solve it. He'd believed by doing so he might feel
like the man everyone already seemed to think he was.

In retrospect, it hadn't taken long to make an arrest.

At first, perhaps just as a matter of course, he had suspected her
husband, Frank Callahan. But staff working the Intercontinental
Hotel's front desk had reported seeing him leave the building some ten
minutes earlier, and right about the same time he had learned that, a
love note had pointed him to a new suspect. A busboy for the hotel had
said that same suspect had been in Heather's room when he'd brought
fresh towels up. Guests in a neighboring room had heard screams not
minutes later. And, as if all that weren't enough, her husband admitted

during questioning that Heather had been having an affair. It was the reason he had left the hotel alone. He was angry and needed some time to himself.

They had fought, he said. She had promised to end it. Presumably, that was exactly what she was doing—or trying to—when she'd been killed.

Oldrich remembered these facts well. But these were what he thought of as top-level facts. They were not the kinds of things that would help Olivia now. If there was anything to be found in this long-closed case, it would be in the details.

Oldrich sat at his desk in a cavernous room on the second floor at HQ. The building itself was an ornate, grand structure and emblematic of the magnificent architecture the city was known for.

The first time he'd shown up here, Oldrich had considered himself lucky to work somewhere so beautiful. He hadn't minded that the desks on the second floor sat facing each other in claustrophobic, makeshift rows, or that, with the high ceiling and nothing to absorb the noise, the many sounds of the department—ringing phones, conversations, the clank of handcuffs, footsteps going every which way, the squeak of a chair's legs against the tile—would every day seem to swell into a relentless cacophony that left him with a headache more often than not.

But those days were long behind him. Although his confidence had grown, so had his waistline. His hair had receded. He'd taken to wearing glasses to read and drive. At least the noise on the second floor no longer bothered him.

An hour had passed since he had spoken with Olivia. The file he had referred to when he talked to her was still on his desk. She had called right before lunch, and since he did not expect to find anything useful in it, he had decided to eat first.

He opened the folder. As he browsed through the contents, he found himself thinking that this was about as much of an open-and-shut case as he had ever seen. There was only one thing about it that bothered him (he remembered now it had bothered him at the time, as well): Nothing had ever been dusted for fingerprints. Not even the knife Heather had been stabbed with. But that's just the way it was with a case like this. No need to run it, the chief of police had said. Forensics had been backlogged for months in those days, and they'd had to prioritize the cases where there wasn't a clear perpetrator.

He wondered if they still had any of the evidence they had collected from that room.

Oldrich took the elevator down to the basement. Here, the building transformed. It no longer presented itself as a part of the grand architecture that made Prague so beautiful. With cinderblock walls and low-hanging fluorescent lights, it was as utilitarian as the blocks of cement housing that had been erected in the name of communism on the outskirts of the city.

He followed the hallways past a boiler room and a janitor's closet. The evidence locker was behind the last door on the left. He used his badge to buzz himself in. A uniformed officer so young he might have just stopped wearing diapers manned a desk on the other side. Behind him were rows of metal shelves lined with boxes.

"Got a case I want to check into," he said.

The young officer, who was preoccupied by something on his phone, hardly looked up. He tapped one finger on the clipboard that was sitting on the desk.

Oldrich knew the protocol. He signed the log, registered the case number he was looking into, and the officer was supposed to go get the related boxes for him. It was about maintaining control of the evidence, knowing exactly what came in and what went out. But after Oldrich signed the clipboard, the officer mumbled, "Go on, get what you need."

Oldrich grumbled to himself about the man's attitude, but didn't bother to say anything. There were a lot of officers on the force like him. Part of it was because many of them—especially the younger officers—felt like the city didn't pay enough. Some, for the same reason, took the occasional bribe.

That's not why you get into a job like this.

He already knew the boxes were labeled by case number and that the cases were in order. He browsed to one labeled RA143352-054, carried it over to a small table in the back of the room, and opened it. There wasn't much inside. The blood-stained blouse Heather had been wearing. The knife that had been used to kill her. A bedside alarm clock that, the theory was, had been knocked to the floor during the struggle.

Although it hadn't occurred to him at the time, when he looked back now, he realized forensics had done a piss-poor job of collecting evidence. Maybe, as backed up as they were, they'd known they weren't ever going to test any of it.

He took out the knife, sealed in a plastic evidence bag, and sat down in the foldout metal chair facing the table. Would it be worth testing now?

What the hell? Why not? At least he could rest easy knowing he had been thorough. Oldrich had been a detective for all these years not because he hadn't been offered promotions, but because he had turned them down. He liked what he did. And if he was going to do his job right, being thorough was part of it, even when it didn't make any difference.

Oldrich pulled out his cellphone, called the forensics department. A perky young woman named Basia answered, and hearing her voice made him smile. The forensics department was across town, but he had seen her around his building a dozen or more times. If he was ten years younger, he'd thought more than once, he would ask her out.

Focus.

"What's your turnaround time for a DNA analysis right now?"

"Two months, I think."

"I've got an old case that's resurfaced. Any chance I could get this prioritized?"

"What kind of case?"

"Murder. First degree."

"How old?"

"Fifteen years," Oldrich said as he put the phone on speaker and placed it on the table.

"That's old. What makes it so important that you need it now?"

"There's been an abduction."

"Oh?"

Oldrich relayed the information Olivia had told him. As he spoke, he picked up the knife and, holding it at each end, turned it over. It was automatic, perhaps drilled into him from so many years of looking for clues. There were, of course, none he would find here with the naked eye. Still, he looked.

"Same people, huh?" Basia said.

"That's right. Why?"

"It's not my place to say. You're the detective."

"Tell me."

"The murder, then the abductions? Most people never experience even one of those things, let alone both."

Until now, Oldrich had thought only about the time that had elapsed between the crimes. But this was like getting struck by lightning twice, and how often did that happen? His cop senses started to tingle. There might just be something here, after all. "Can you do it?"

"For an active crime, you bet. Bring me the knife. It will take twenty-four hours. System matches?"

The system she was referring to had been established by the European Union ten years ago with the intention of sharing criminal DNA between countries. All current prisoners had been swabbed and catalogued. If the sample Olivia pulled off the knife was Matthew Jones's (which, of course, it had to be), there wouldn't be any issue coming up with a match.

"Run it against the system," he said.

"Understood."

Oldrich thanked Basia and hung up.

CHAPTER 36

THE DAY WAS a bust. Connor and Olin watched the dot go from Dylan's home to New York University and back. Hours passed in between. It was the longest block of time the two had spent together without having something to do.

"What's she doing there?" Olin had asked at some point.

Connor had frowned, thought about the notebooks he had seen on her desk. "Summer classes, I guess. Should we go down there and try to talk to her?"

"It's a big campus. She'd be hard to find. Besides, what would we do if we *did* find her? Drag her out of class? That wouldn't fly. And waiting in the hall outside would just draw unwanted attention. No way. We've been lucky so far, but luck runs out. If we're going to talk to her, we're going to do it somewhere smart."

Connor reluctantly agreed.

While they waited for an opening, they kept themselves busy watching TV. They talked a little about what life had been like for each of them before the abductions. But since talking around the abductions was the same as talking about them, that petered out fast. Until Connor could speak to Dylan, he didn't want to think about any of it, and Olin seemed to feel the same way.

By the time six o'clock rolled around, Connor realized he had spent the whole day doing nothing. He was ready to give up when the dot started to move again. His phone had been sitting on the arm of the sofa, tracking app open, and Olin was the one who saw it first.

"Look," he said, pointing to Connor's phone.

"Where do you think she's going?"

"I don't know. Not back to NYU. Not at this hour."

"A friend's?"

Olin shrugged.

Connor hopped up, grabbed his phone. "Come on. This might be our chance."

"Wait. We don't even know where she's going."

"We also don't know how long she'll be there."

Olin didn't move. "I think we should stay here until—"

"Let's get close. Just in case, okay?"

"*Fine.*" Olin followed Connor out the door, and they each headed for their own car. "I'll drive," Olin said, once he realized what was happening. "Your driving makes me carsick."

Connor suspected the real reason Olin wanted to drive was so that he could pull the brakes—literally and figuratively—on the operation if he wanted to. But since he was happy to have Olin with him, he didn't make a fuss about it.

Connor directed Olin to the Albright Mall in Brooklyn, a four-story glass building with an attached parking garage and a sprawling interior that dedicated most of the floor space to retailers. "Fashion-forward" retailers, if the sign above the parking garage entrance was to be believed.

Olin found a spot on the third floor, making a point of parking as far away from any other vehicles as he could. "I don't want somebody to ding the car," he said.

Connor didn't respond.

"What do we do now?" Olin said.

Connor didn't think that question had to be asked. As soon as he knew Dylan had gone to the Albright Mall, he had assumed the answer was obvious. "Let's go talk to her."

Apparently, this was all Olin needed to hear. He nodded and got out of the car.

They took the stairs down to street level and circled around the building to the main entrance, sandwiched between a Brooks Brothers and a DSW.

Olin shifted from side to side, trying to see around an endless wave of shoppers. "Where is she?"

From time to time since Dylan had arrived at the mall, Connor had noticed the little blue dot move this way or that. But he suspected that was the application struggling to pinpoint Dylan's location. It was unreasonable to expect it to tell them the exact place she was standing. Even if it could, it couldn't tell them what floor she was on. But instead of explaining all that, Connor summed it up by saying, "She's in here somewhere. Let's find her."

He looked around, trying to decide how to approach their search. Olin did the same.

"You remember what she looks like?"

"I think so."

"Let's split up. I'll start at the top. You start at the bottom. Call me if you see her."

CHAPTER 37

CONNOR TOOK THE elevator to the top floor of the Albright Mall. Even though he had checked the tracking app on his phone only a few minutes ago, he checked it again now. It was becoming something of a nervous tic. Dylan was still here.

This time, he also noticed he had a missed call from Austin. But now wasn't the time to call him back. Whatever Austin wanted to talk to him about, it could wait until he returned to the apartment.

The elevator opened onto a food court that sold every type of cuisine imaginable, and seemed to be twice as crowded as the first floor. Most of the tables were full. The most popular restaurants—Chinese Dragon, Chick-fil-A, McDonald's—all had lines at least ten people deep.

There was an AMC off to the side, and there was a line there, as well.

Connor made his way around the food court. He hoped Dylan was by herself, but that seemed unlikely.

As long as she's not with her dad . . .

There was no need to finish the thought. He knew if she was with her dad their only choice would be to call the whole thing off and hope they could get away without being spotted.

The search was not as difficult as Connor had expected it might be when he saw the crowded food court. Redheads were few and far between. He still had to consciously look at each person, but if the person wasn't a woman and didn't have red hair, he didn't have to look any closer.

After circling the food court and examining the lines (he saw only one redhead—a boy sitting on a barstool at the Johnny Rockets counter, chowing down on a plate of fries), he studied the people who were already seated.

No redheads.

This might go faster than he'd thought. He took the escalator down to the second floor.

He went store by store, thoroughly scouting the shops he thought would be most likely to interest her and peeking his head into the others. This method got him through most of the stores in mere seconds.

At The Gap, he caught a glimpse of a redhead stepping into the dressing rooms and, for the three minutes he waited for her to exit, he suspected he had found Dylan. Olin hadn't called yet, and a glance at the tracking app confirmed she was still in the mall. There weren't a lot of places left to look. But then the redhead came out of the dressing room modeling a burgundy top for a man who stood waiting, and Connor knew it was time to move on. Unless Dylan had aged twenty years overnight, this woman wasn't her.

He had nearly finished searching the second floor when he ran into Olin. "You didn't find her, huh?"

Olin shook his head.

"Well, we still have those stores to check," Connor said, pointing to half a dozen retailers in front of him.

"I just checked those. You sure that app works?"

"I'm sure. She's here somewhere."

"Where else could she be? I guess we can go through the mall again—"

"The theater."

"What?"

"There's an AMC on the top floor. She's been here for over an hour, right? I bet she's watching a movie."

"So, what? We're going to go scouting the theaters now? Don't you think that might draw some attention? Plus, what if she's not there alone? What if the whole family went?" It seemed Olin had also considered the risk of running into Dylan's father unexpectedly.

"Actually, I was thinking we would sit at one of the tables in the food court and wait for her to come out. That way, if the whole family went, we'll see them before they see us."

Olin seemed to like that. They took the elevator back to the food court and found a table with a clear view of the movie theater.

It won't be long now, Connor told himself.

CHAPTER 38

LOGAN WRIGHT DID not think like everyone else. He knew that.

Most people muddled their way through small lives, hoping for small rewards for small accomplishments. They were so distracted chasing their idea of the American dream, they missed the whole point. And they certainly didn't realize how fragile all of it was.

Not Logan.

He knew. He understood this world and his purpose in it. He hadn't gotten to that understanding easily, though, which was why most people never got there at all, he figured. Most people weren't as patient as he was. They weren't willing to do the research to understand the world or the hard work he knew he must do once he understood it.

It was that work that had brought him here, to the Albright Mall, this evening.

He took the elevator up to the food court and ordered a Number Two at McDonald's. He wasn't hungry, but he thought sitting in the food court alone without anything to eat might make him stand out.

Kind of like those two clowns over there, staring at the AMC like something exciting was about to happen.

What were they doing?

Whatever it was, if they were indeed looking for something exciting, they were going to get it soon enough.

Logan selected a table as close to the center of the room as he could get, then took off his backpack and placed it by his feet. He picked his way through his food for a good ten minutes before looking at his watch. It was eight-oh-three. *Tick-tock*, he thought. Why wasn't anything happening?

He told himself to be patient. Things don't always go as planned. He was about to be a part of something big, and big things were worth waiting for.

Logan had been on his journey to this particular big thing for years now. He still remembered the day that journey had begun. He had been mindlessly scrolling through Facebook when he saw a link that led to a website called BeyondUnderstanding.com. He'd clicked it mostly out of curiosity. And read.

At first, he'd thought the ideas he was reading didn't make any sense. But the more he read, and the more he thought about it, the more they did. He'd signed up, begun participating in the forum. He still had questions, but they were questions people in the forum had been able to answer.

By the time a popup had appeared on the site, warning him that the information presented here was not to be trusted, he was already a believer. He knew the site had been hacked. (What he didn't know was that he was now sitting only thirty feet away from the person who had hacked it.)

He couldn't imagine what the hacker thought he would accomplish, but he didn't spend much time dwelling on it, either. He'd notified the website owner through a contact form, and the popup was gone fifteen minutes later.

Hope it was worth it, he had thought at the time, imagining the hours someone must have spent, all to post a popup that became a running joke on the forum for months afterward. Well, whatever. They had a hacker of their own now.

Logan looked at his watch again. Eight-oh-seven. He shifted anxiously in his seat.

Come on, guys. Let's get this party started.

Last night, the hacker had received the phone call he'd been hoping wouldn't come. Whatever Aden was planning, it couldn't be good. While there were some people who deserved to die—deserved to *suffer*—he knew enough about Aden's philosophy to know he was likely targeting people who did not.

But, the hacker reminded himself, it was the deal he had made.

At seven-thirty p.m., he started a fresh pot of coffee and turned on his computer. The whole thing should be quick. He would just hop through the back door he had left, enter a couple of commands, and sign off.

However, as soon as he attempted to access the system he had hacked into the other day, he realized his back door was no longer there. It seemed the company's security team had found and closed it.

Shit.

If he didn't come through, Aden would think he had dropped the ball on purpose. Tonight's plan had been a long time in the making. Aden wouldn't tolerate failure. He would send someone after the hacker to—he didn't want to think about it. He had to get back into that system. Fast.

Like last time, he drank his first cup of coffee in one long swallow, and sat down at the computer with a second. It had taken him five hours to get in the first time. This time, he had only twenty-two minutes. Twenty-one.

Shit!

The coffee had lit his throat on fire and the stress had done the same to his brain. His fingers flew across the keyboard, retracing the same steps he had taken last time.

He hoped to be able to follow the routine that had gotten him in before, and at first that plan looked promising. But then he hit a wall—the company's security team hadn't just removed his back door, they had sealed shut his way in. He cursed a third time, now out loud.

He wished he had somebody to call, to warn them about the delay, but he didn't. Part of Aden's grand design had been to compartmentalize the people involved. He wanted to be sure that if anybody got cold feet, went to the police, got arrested, they would be unable to take down the entire group.

The hacker told himself to stay calm. There was almost always another open door. It was just a matter of finding it.

Logan picked his way through his food until he had finished, then slowly sipped his Coke. Eight-thirteen. He was growing anxious. He should have been done by now. How long could he sit here like this, doing nothing, without drawing attention?

He looked at the two guys sitting at the table in front of the theater. They were still there, also doing nothing—not even eating, not even *pretending* to eat—and no one seemed to notice. Then he glanced at the people around him. Nobody seemed to be looking at him, either.

It was just his nerves. These people were occupied with their own lives—their food, their friends, their shopping. If Logan was here for any other reason, he wouldn't think twice about lingering at a table in the food court.

He needed to be patient.

Aden had said it was important they wait for the cue, follow the plan. He said it would have more impact that way. Logan knew he was right.

CHAPTER 39

A COLLECTION OF people surged out of the AMC. A movie must have let out. Connor watched the crowd closely. "That's her," he said, nodding toward a woman in an oversized black tee and a pair of jeans, hair pulled back with bobby pins. She seemed to be with a guy about her age.

"Is she on a date?" Olin said.

"Doesn't matter." Connor got up and started to move. Olin fell in behind him.

Dylan and her friend were headed toward an escalator, Connor noticed. He pushed through the crowd, trying to catch up to them. When he thought he might be within earshot, he shouted, "Hey! TruthSeekers!"

Several people looked at him, clearly confused. But Dylan also turned around to look, and she didn't look confused. She looked worried.

"I need to talk—"

Dylan took hold of the guy's hand and started moving faster.

Connor caught up to her right before she got on the escalator. He grabbed her arm. "Listen—"

Dylan whipped around. "Let go of me."

That likewise got the attention of the shoppers around them, but no one moved to intervene. Everyone who looked at them seemed to immediately look away when Connor made eye contact with them. They were curious, but didn't want to get involved.

That might change, though, if Dylan decided to scream.

Connor let go. "I need to talk to you."

"What's going on?" the guy said. He had a thin sheen of stubble on his chin and was wearing a Yankees baseball cap turned backward. For some reason, he looked to Connor like he was trying too hard to be cool. It was an image he had no doubt spent years cultivating.

"It's nothing you need to be worried about," Connor said. He noticed Olin was standing about two feet behind him, saying nothing. "Your friend here hosts a website—"

"Okay!" Dylan turned to the guy she was with. "Just . . . wait for me." She sounded flustered.

Dylan led Connor and Olin over to a hallway perhaps twenty feet from the escalator. A sign directing people toward the bathrooms hung above it.

The guy likewise stepped out of the flow of traffic, backing up to the nearest table and taking a seat, his eyes still on them.

"What are you doing hosting a website like that?" Connor said.

"What do you care? It's just for fun. And how did you . . ." She trailed off. The wheels were turning. "You're the guy who hacked into my site," she said slowly, pointing at him as her eyes narrowed to slits.

"How did you—"

"I don't know what you're doing here, but you better stay the fuck away from me." She backed up a step, but didn't run away. If anything, she suddenly looked determined to stand her ground. And, as if to make sure Connor understood that, she kept her finger pointed at him like it was a weapon. She turned to Olin. "Who are you?"

"I'm, uh—"

Before he could respond she was on to her next question, this one once again directed to Connor. "How did you find me, anyway?"

That wasn't a question Connor was going to answer. But he figured he'd better say something before Olin did, and he was tired of being on the defensive. "How did you know about Matt?"

"That's what you're here about?" Dylan made a face. "Have you heard of something called the dark web? I can find out anything I want there. I was just trying to make sure you stayed away from me."

The dark web. Of course. Connor should have realized that from the beginning. If he hadn't been so wrapped up with everything that was going on, he would have.

"I figured you didn't want anybody finding out what you had been up to. I thought if I let you know I knew who your dad was, you would stay in your lane."

Connor suddenly felt overwhelmed. He remembered proposing to Olin he might be Matt's son. But he had said it in passing, hadn't actually taken it all that seriously. He shook his head. "That's got to be a mistake."

Dylan looked at the guy she was with. He was slouched over in his chair, occupied with his phone. "Leave me alone, you hear me? Or I'll tell your dad what you've been up to."

"He's not my dad."

She turned to leave. "Have you ever seen your birth certificate?"

Connor wasn't sure how to respond. Of course he had. Matt's name wasn't on it, which was part of the reason he hadn't seriously considered the possibility before.

The hacker was finally back in. He typed a series of commands. Hesitated. This was it. His middle finger hovered over the Enter key. There was no going back once he hit it.

He looked down at the half-finished cup of coffee beside him. His hands balled into fists. Then, in a quick series of events and without hesitation, he slammed his fists down on the table, finished the last of the coffee, and hit the Enter key.

Done.

Before Connor could decide how to respond, or if he even should, the mall was plunged into darkness. And for two long seconds, that darkness was accompanied by an equally unnerving silence. Shoppers had frozen where they were. The whiz and whir of so many machines had stopped. The escalators and elevators had ground to a halt.

Connor pulled out his phone and hit the flashlight app. He noticed other people, including Olin and Dylan, were doing the same.

The roar of excited conversation that had filled the mall just seconds before returned now as one of annoyance. "It's 1977 all over again," someone said, referring to a blackout that had darkened most of the city. Connor hoped he was wrong.

Dylan huffed. "That's just great. The perfect end to a perfect evening." She shined her light toward the guy she had come with. He was already on his feet, heading toward her, fighting against a sea of people who were all trying to get to the escalator.

Then Connor saw a man coming their way and moving faster than the rest. He was looking every which way but where he was going, so it was no surprise when he ran straight into Dylan's friend, knocking him to the ground. He didn't stop to help him up or even apologize. He just kept pushing people out of his way. But he didn't go to the escalator, like everyone else. He went through a door that led to a stairwell.

A few shoppers saw where he had gone and followed, seizing on the opportunity to get out of the mall more quickly.

Dylan rolled her eyes. "Jerk."

Her friend got to his feet while shoppers continued on around him.

Somewhere outside—a boom. No louder than the kick of a bass drum within these walls, but Connor noticed. The guy did, too. He instinctively turned his head toward the sound.

"What was that?" Olin said.

"Hello?" Dylan held out her hands and gestured at nothing in particular. "Power generator, probably. I swear, sometimes I think everything in this city is falling apart."

CHAPTER 40

MINUTES EARLIER, LOGAN had been sitting at the table in the food court, watching the two guys as they got up and followed a redheaded girl toward the escalator. He slurped the last of the Coke out of the paper cup, put it back on the tray, and slid the tray to the other side of the table. He wondered what they wanted with her. Were they siblings? Lovers? Friends?

Oh, to hell with it. What did he care? He just needed that damn hacker to do his job.

He watched as the guys caught up with the redhead, and then saw the three of them move together out of the flow of traffic. The friend she was with took a seat at a nearby table.

Logan imagined a variety of conversations that fell in line with his theories.

Finally, the mall went dark. He immediately forgot about the strangers' lives he had turned into his own personal soap opera. He unzipped the backpack by his feet, reached in, and felt around the device inside until he found a switch. He had practiced this move several times in his apartment, so even working in the dark, it took him only a couple of seconds.

Logan zipped the backpack up, placed it under the table, and pushed his chair in before walking away. He didn't want anybody tripping over it and seeing the backpack. It wouldn't take a genius to figure out what that bag was doing there.

He was more nervous than he'd expected to be as he headed to the stairwell. He worried about being spotted, remembered, identified later in a lineup. And even though he knew that was so unlikely as to border on absurd, he couldn't help but look around while he walked. Was anybody staring at him funny? Did anybody have an inkling of what he was up to?

He slammed straight into the guy he had seen earlier, but he wasn't about to stop. He went to the stairwell, pushed through the door.

Footsteps echoed down the stairwell behind him. Other people were coming. Although he had intended to sneak out this way alone, that was probably a good thing. He would be just one of many people exiting the mall this way. Harder to identify as anything more than a shopper.

Right when he reached the landing for the second floor, he heard a soft boom and knew exactly what it meant. Things were going according to plan.

When he got to the bottom of the stairwell, there were two doors. One led into the mall and one led to an open-air parking lot that extended off the garage. He expected this. He had scouted the mall a week ago, been down this stairwell. His Toyota Camry was parked in a handicap spot just beyond the door.

He went through the parking lot door, and then, once he was clear of the building, he turned around to watch. He saw some of the people who had entered the stairwell behind him follow him into the parking lot while others went through the door that led into the mall. He could only imagine that second group was trying to get their bearings now, looking for the way they had come in.

He glanced at his watch. It had been a minute and forty-two seconds, give or take.

The blast blew out the windows that ran along the food court and seemed to shake the whole building.

This couldn't have gone any better.

CHAPTER 41

CONNOR WATCHED THE blast come toward him in slow motion. A churning mass of flames stretching out, consuming everything. Olin was already safely within the corridor that led to the bathrooms—or as safe as anybody on this floor could be, anyway. Dylan was not. She had started moving toward the friend she had come with. And the friend—oh, God. He had just gotten back to his feet, but there would be no time for him to get out of the way.

It wasn't too late for Dylan, though. Connor could still help her. He grabbed her arm and pulled her toward him just as a wall of flames and searing heat roared past them.

He heard the windows shatter, people screaming. A crash, like some part of the floor had given way.

Dylan was screaming, too. Demanding Connor let go, saying she needed to get to her friend—Tom was his name. But Connor could barely hear her. There was a ringing in his ears that drowned out almost everything else. He refused to let go. "Help me hold her!" he yelled at Olin, as he caught a glimpse of the devastation left by the blast. A glimpse of Tom. It was a sight he would never forget.

"Don't look out there," he told Dylan, trying to turn her away, as he and Olin both fought to keep her from seeing what they had seen.

"I have to get to Tom!"

"Tom didn't make it."

She screamed, tried harder to break free.

"Dylan! Please! You can't do anything for him! It's not safe out there!" Connor said, and continued to hold her until she stopped struggling, stopped screaming. Once she did, he let go and asked if she and Olin could hear him. Olin made a face like he was trying to figure out what Connor was saying. Dylan, with her back to him, did not respond at all. He would know soon enough she was doing her best to hold back tears.

"We have to get out of here!" Connor shouted.

This time, Dylan nodded.

"What do we do?" Olin said. Something about it reminded Connor of when he and Olin were trapped in the laundry room of Dylan's house. Perhaps it was just that Olin was again looking to him for a plan.

Connor steeled himself for what he was about to do, then poked his head out of the hallway, using the flashlight on his phone to assess the situation. The food court was filled with smoke and getting worse. He couldn't see much besides the fires that seemed to burn all around them and the massive hole in the floor where most of the tables had been. That was a blessing. He didn't want to see any more of the bodies than he had already.

Then he remembered—"The stairwell." It was close. They could get to it without . . . He refused to think about what it would mean to go down the escalator. "Follow me, everyone. Keep your eyes straight ahead."

Another crack and a crash, like more of the floor giving way.

"We have to go."

The smoke was getting thicker, making it harder to see by the second, and all three of them were starting to cough. At this point, even if Dylan wanted to try to get to her friend, she wouldn't be able to see him. Connor led them to stairwell, navigating partly from memory and refusing to look down.

He pushed through the door and held it open until Olin had passed through. Not much smoke had gotten in. Connor was still coughing, his ears were still ringing, but at least he could see again.

The three shared a look, an unspoken confirmation from each to the others that they were okay. Then they hurried down the stairs and through the door that led them outside.

They ran until they were on the far side of the parking lot, where Connor slowed to a stop and leaned over to cough some more. It was getting better. So was the ringing in his ears. But neither was completely gone yet.

He turned around to see the mall. Olin and Dylan did the same. They weren't alone. There were people all over the parking lot, some standing dangerously close to the building. From here, the damage didn't look as bad as it was. Sure, the windows along the food court were shattered. You could see the restaurants closest to them in flames and smoke billowing out. Glass and debris were scattered across the parking lot nearby. Some tables, fully intact, had landed on cars, crushing hoods and shattering windshields. But you couldn't see the hole that had been blown through the floor, the small fires that burned all the way back to the escalator. You couldn't see the bodies.

And thank God for that.

Connor hardly noticed when Dylan turned away from the mall and toward the road beyond. "Guys."

"Yeah?"

"Look."

They did.

It wasn't fully dark yet, but it was on its way. The streetlights along the alley in front of them and the buildings beyond it should have been lit up. They weren't.

"The whole city's gone dark," Olin said.

Hopefully not the whole *city*, Connor thought. Then he remembered the comment someone had made about the 1977 blackout.

But this wasn't like that. This wasn't some random blackout caused by ancient and overworked equipment. This was planned. It had to be.

Now Olin was pointing off to the left. "What's that?"

Connor strained to see. There was a flicker. Maybe smoke. *Another fire*, he thought.

He remembered the boom he had heard outside the mall. That had to be where it had come from, which meant there had been two explosions, at least.

"There were riots in 1977," Dylan said. Apparently, she was also thinking about the comment Connor had heard in the mall.

Dylan pulled out her phone. She dialed nine-one-one, but the call wouldn't go through. Perhaps to report the bomb, Connor thought, even though it seemed unnecessary.

From where he was, Connor could hear a message from AT&T telling her all lines were busy and to try her call again later.

Then there was a flash of lights and sirens that caught their attention and all three turned again to a see a pair of firetrucks pulling into the parking lot. Firemen hopped off, even while the trucks were still moving. They worked fast, hooking up hoses to fire hydrants, suiting up, sending men in to look for survivors.

Connor hadn't realized he had put a hand on Dylan's shoulder to comfort her until he spoke. She didn't pull away. "We need to leave."

"I want to wait for them to bring him out."

"We don't know if this is over. We need to get somewhere safe."

Dylan didn't seem convinced.

"He would want us to do that," Olin said.

She looked down at her shoes. Red Nike sneakers. Later, Connor would wonder if she had picked the shoes to match her hair, if the outfit that looked thrown together had actually been thoughtfully coordinated for her date. Right now, he wondered only what she was thinking.

When she spoke again, she said, "You're right. We need to go. I can't do anything if I stay here."

"But where are we going to go?" Olin said. "I don't think we can make it back to the suburbs. Traffic's—"

"Going to be terrible." Connor had already considered that. "I've been staying with a guy. A friend. I don't think his apartment's too far from here."

He hoped Dylan wouldn't ask any questions. He didn't want to tell her what had happened to his parents. Or Olin's.

CHAPTER 42

TRAFFIC WAS WORSE than they thought it would be. The first block had taken them twenty minutes and, since then, they hadn't moved at all.

By the time Connor turned around in the passenger seat so he could see Dylan, the sun had set, and the street was lit exclusively by headlights. She looked like she was starting to do a little better. "You said you found out Matthew Jones was my dad from my birth certificate. But you must have gotten it mixed up with something else. I've seen my birth certificate."

She shrugged. "I know what I saw."

In the silence that followed, Olin turned on the radio and was met with static. He tried several stations. None of them were transmitting. Then he gave up and turned it off. "I saw a documentary about adoption once," he said a minute later.

"Sounds exciting," Dylan responded.

Olin looked at Connor. "Sometimes when babies are adopted the parents will amend the birth certificate to include their names instead of the original parents'. Something about creating continuity for the child. I didn't really get it, but . . . you were young when your mother remarried, right? So maybe that's what happened."

Connor had never heard of an amended birth certificate, but he also had no reason to doubt Olin. Could that be what had happened? It tied in nicely with the facts he already knew, and it certainly made more sense than the idea that his mother had had an affair.

Okay, but so what? This wasn't going to help him get his parents back. Of course, he'd known that when he came to the mall. This whole exercise had been little more than a distraction. But now it was worse than that. He had put Olin and Dylan in danger, not to mention himself. Or Tom, who would have made it safely to the second floor before the blast if Connor hadn't pulled Dylan aside to ask her a question he knew was irrelevant.

He was acting like an idiot.

Don't do that to yourself. You couldn't have known.

That was true, but it didn't make him feel any better.

"That site of yours. TruthSeekers," Connor said, desperate to think about anything else. "Why did you put it up?"

"Why did you hack it?"

"Dylan, come on. Answer my question."

Dylan crossed her arms over her chest, then defensively said, "It was just for fun. Bigfoot. Vampires. Who's going to believe that, anyway?"

"Sites like that—okay, maybe not yours, exactly, but sites like it— they change how people think. You have to be careful—"

"Hey, Connor," Olin said, cutting him off.

"What?" As soon as he asked, he realized he didn't need to. It was obvious what Olin wanted to draw his attention to.

On the sidewalk ahead of them, someone swung a baseball bat at the window of a Best Buy, smashing it. He climbed in, followed by a swarm of others, and emerged a minute later carrying a laptop. As Connor watched from inside the car, the mob emptied the store of TVs, monitors, iPads, cellphones, and a whole assortment of boxed electronics he couldn't identify from his vantage point.

Along the way, one of them must have set the business on fire, because it wasn't long before Connor saw flames inside the shop. He flashed back to the mall they had just fled, then willed the memory from his mind.

Olin hit a button, and all of the car's doors locked. "We should be all right if we stay here." He didn't sound confident.

"As if we have a choice," Dylan said. She was once again leaning forward so she could get a better view.

Connor tried to reason his way through the situation. To his surprise, he realized he had been good at finding his way out of tough spots lately. But he couldn't see a way out of this. Every street in every direction was bumper to bumper. Even if a cross street magically cleared, there would be no easy way to get to it. There were three lanes going east, and they were stuck in the middle one. There was nothing they could do but inch their way along.

Connor could tell Olin's whole body was tensing up. He was gripping the steering wheel so tightly his fingers had turned white.

Then a small group of men—three, it looked like from here—turned their attention to a car at the end of the block. They began pounding on it, rocking it. Connor cracked his window so he could hear what was happening. They were telling the driver to open the door, get out. The man with the baseball bat went over to see what was going on. After a minute, he nodded, handed his laptop to one of the other men, and held the bat up threateningly. Presumably, the driver still refused to get out of the car, since seconds later the man with the bat swung it at the driver's side window. The group of men got the door open, dragged the driver out, kicked him as he rolled over, and went to town on the vehicle.

Connor had no idea what had set them off, and it scared him. Was the attack random? Just part of the chaos from the blackout? A byproduct of the fear people were feeling? "We can't stay here."

"I can't leave the car. My dad will kill me if anything happens to it." Olin was still gripping the steering wheel as tightly as he could.

"Your dad's not coming back," Connor said. "We have to get the hell out of here now."

Finally, Olin loosened his grip on the wheel. "What do you mean?"

"I didn't mean anything. I'm sorry. But we've got to go."

"You meant something."

"Olin, please. If they come this way . . ."

"What happened to Olin's parents?" Dylan asked.

Connor saw the men move to another car. Through the cracked window, he heard them demand this driver get out, as well. This *was* random. "Olin! Come on!"

Other drivers—some with families and friends—began abandoning their vehicles. Perhaps that was what Olin needed to see, because he finally said, "Okay," and opened his door. Dylan and Connor quickly followed suit.

"Which way?" Dylan said.

"Right now, let's just get as far as we can from whatever's going on here," Connor said, and began moving away from the man with the baseball bat. It seemed everyone who had abandoned their vehicles had the same idea. A sizable crowd of frightened drivers and passengers was now hurrying away from the mob, some carrying crying children.

Olin and Dylan followed Connor down the street, trying not to lose each other in the gathering dark and the crush of people. They turned left at the first intersection, and the crowd thinned some.

"How far are we from your friend's?" Dylan asked Connor.

"Two miles. Maybe less."

"In this direction?"

"Yes."

Olin looked over his shoulder. Connor guessed he wanted to make sure the man with the baseball bat and his friends weren't behind them. They, of course, weren't the only people on the street vandalizing stores, but they did seem to be the only people randomly targeting strangers.

"Are you sure?" he said.

"I'm sure," Connor responded. But that wasn't true. He had used GPS to get him to Austin's apartment before and didn't spend enough time in the city to be sure. He was, however, mostly sure.

CHAPTER 43

THE JUDGE HAD handed down a ruling in Olivia's favor earlier that day. Erin would be living with her full time from now on. Olivia should have been happy. And she was. But she couldn't stop thinking about the Callahan case. She had stopped by Roland's office that morning, and the conversation had not gone as expected.

Roland worked in a modern monstrosity in a wealthy part of Manhattan. The firm was called Park & Manor Architecture and Construction. Which meant Frank worked in the same industry. If she needed to dig deeper, it wouldn't be hard to figure out how they knew each other.

At first, everything had seemed normal. The firm was on the fifteenth floor. A security guard checked her ID, called up to announce the visit, and told her Roland would be down to see her. She nodded, walked back to the tall windows that faced the street and watched people pass by until she heard a man's voice say, "Detective Forbes?"

She turned around. The man heading toward her was dressed for the office (really, what else had she expected?) and carrying a donut in each hand. When he got close, he smiled, and, holding one of the donuts out in front of him, said, "They bring them into the office every day. I can't help myself. You want one?"

That was probably the first sign that was something was off. When she came into a building like this, people rarely took the elevator down to see her. Even when they did, they would act put out when they arrived.

"I'm fine," she said.

Roland looked down at the donuts, disappointed. She could tell he was trying to decide whether it would be rude to eat one anyway. Then, he swiftly threw both in a nearby trashcan and said, "Good choice. I don't need it either. I've already had my fill. What can I do for you?"

"I need to ask you some questions about Frank Callahan."

His smile faltered. He glanced around, perhaps making sure no one he knew was within earshot. "Do I need a lawyer?"

Sign number two. Something was definitely off. Maybe he would need a lawyer at some point. But right now, she wanted to keep this as cordial as she could. You catch more flies with honey and all that crap. Olivia smiled back. "Of course not."

"Because whatever those two told you, it was bullshit, you hear me?"

"Oh, I don't know. I've got evidence that says it isn't all bullshit." That was true. Sort of. Connor and Olin hadn't told her much more than the fact that the two men knew each other. But being a little cagey probably wouldn't hurt her chances of finding out more.

Roland's flabby cheeks had turned a bright red and he was starting to sweat.

"I have a lot of debt, okay? And what I did isn't that bad, is it? I mean, why are you here talking to me instead of Frank? He's the one you should be talking to."

"I'm going to," Olivia lied, pushing her glasses back up her nose. She had gathered from Roland's last comment that he didn't know Frank was missing. But he was hiding something, and she wanted to know what. "First I want to hear what you have to say."

"I better get a lawyer."

"No, I promise. I'm not here about you. I just want to hear in your own words what happened."

Roland sighed, reached his hand into the trashcan and pulled out one of the donuts. He took a bite, chewing it slowly. "Frank was drunk," he said as he worked the donut around in his mouth before swallowing it. "We were at The Cork. You know it?"

Olivia didn't, but she nodded. She didn't want to slow the momentum of his story.

"Yeah, well, I saw him there a lot after work. It's a popular bar for some of the guys in our industry. Couldn't tell you why. Place is a shithole. But that's where everyone goes. So, anyway, one night, after everyone left, and it was just Frank and me still at the bar, he says he has something he has to get off his chest. I can't tell you why on earth he thought it was a good idea to tell me. Probably just the alcohol talking."

Roland took another bite from the donut. This time, at least he waited until he finished chewing before he spoke again. "I mean, what was I supposed to do with that information? I didn't have any proof it was true."

"You blackmailed him?"

"I wouldn't say that."

Olivia suspected the DA would.

Keep it cordial, she reminded herself. There was more here. "No, you're right. Like you said, you didn't have any proof. If you had brought it to the police, what would we have done with it?"

"Exactly."

"What did he tell you?"

Roland's smile, which had disappeared for most of their conversation, returned and grew wider. Then he leaned in, spoke at a whisper. Olivia could tell he was excited to share the story.

It was disturbing. So disturbing, actually, she was still thinking about it when she took her daughter to TGI Friday's that evening for dinner.

Olivia had thought a night out might make breaking the news to Erin a little easier. As much as her father disappointed her—cancelling weekend visits, forgetting her birthday, showing up late—she was always excited to see him.

After a lot of questions, Erin seemed to reluctantly accept the situation. She would likely pout for the next week or so, but there was no screaming, no tears. Erin rarely acted out.

It had gone as well as it could have, Olivia decided on their way out.

It wasn't until they were almost home, with dusk settling across the city, that the traffic lights went out and every intersection turned into a four-way stop.

The power was out in her home, as well.

Olivia didn't hear the blast and assumed this was a run-of-the-mill outage. She lit candles, hoped it would get better soon. There was no need to call Con Ed. They would already be aware of the problem.

And it wasn't all bad. Times like these, when she and her daughter were both free of distractions, were great for bonding. Tonight, that seemed like a particularly good idea. She made a fire in the fireplace and got some wire coat hangers from the closet.

"Let's pretend we're camping," she said to Erin. "How about we make s'mores?"

Erin liked that. Olivia was glad her daughter would end the day on a high note. Funny how things that otherwise might seem inconvenient, like a power outage, could sometimes be exactly what you needed, she thought.

CHAPTER 44

CONNOR LED OLIN and Dylan left at the next block. They needed to start moving in the direction they were originally going, and this turn meant they were now heading down a street parallel to the one where they had left Olin's car.

Here, more people seemed content to stay in their vehicles and wait. There was a mini-market and a hole-in-the-wall pizza joint, both with their windows smashed, but no major retailers to draw the sort of vandalism that was happening a block over.

"So your site—that's just for fun?" Connor asked Dylan, circling back around to the conversation they'd been having in the car.

She was walking with her hands in her pockets, looking down at the sidewalk. Or maybe the red shoes she had picked out for tonight. Maybe thinking about Tom. "Yeah, you know."

"I don't, actually."

"I'm going to be a writer someday. It's just fiction."

"Why did you call it TruthSeekers, then?"

She shrugged. "I liked how it sounded. Kind of like that show—what was it called? *X-Files*, right? I mean, nobody thinks that's a documentary or anything, so why would they take my site any more seriously?"

"Some people do."

"Yeah, right."

Connor told her about the article that had linked back to her website.

She finally looked up. "No shit?"

"No shit."

Dylan looked back down, thought about that for a while. "I guess that's a compliment." Then, to Olin, she said, "What happened to your parents?"

"Somebody . . . They were kidnapped."

Connor might have said something else if he had managed to speak first. Dylan didn't need to hear about the abduction. Then again, after what she had seen tonight, she could probably handle anything.

"Really?"

He nodded.

"Wow. That sucks." She turned to Connor. "But what does that have to do with me or Matt? Why did you come looking for me? Unless . . . unless someone came and took your parents, too."

Connor didn't answer.

"Holy shit! Do you know what they want? Has there been a ransom demand or something?"

"I wish," Olin said.

"You mean someone came and kidnapped both your parents." She looked from Olin to Connor. "And they didn't call demanding a ransom?"

"No."

"Huh." She frowned. "Well, this doesn't sound random. You two know each other, so your parents must also. At least that's something for the police to go on."

Connor didn't feel like prolonging this conversation, so he didn't bother to tell her that while, yes, their parents knew each other, he and Olin had just met.

Olin, however, wasn't ready to let it go just yet. Maybe he even saw this as an opportunity to circle back to his own question. "What did you mean when you said my parents weren't coming back?" he asked Connor.

"We don't know that they are." Then, for emphasis, he added, "We don't know yours are. We don't know mine are. We don't know anything."

"That's not what you said, though. You said they *weren't*, like you knew something."

Movement ahead of them drew Connor's attention away from Olin. "Crap." The man with the baseball bat and his friends were standing at the end of the street, staring straight at them. They must have circled around the block in the opposite direction. Perhaps drawn by something they saw or an idea of what they might find here. Whatever it was, Connor was sure they hadn't come searching for the three of them.

But now the vandals were here, looking at them in a way Connor didn't like.

"What you got for us?" Baseball Bat called. "What you got for us to let you pass?"

Connor glanced around, hoping against hope he would see someone else on the street, someone else Baseball Bat could have been talking to. But everyone else was too far away, moving in the wrong direction, or still in their cars.

If Connor thought Baseball Bat would simply accept their wallets and let them continue on their way, he would have handed his over immediately. But he knew Baseball Bat would take everything of value, including Connor's cellphone, his father's cellphone, and Olin's cellphone. Even though the kidnapper hadn't called yet, he *might*.

Once the power was back up, who knew? And even if he didn't, what if Roland had a change of heart, wanted to talk? Or what if Olivia found something out and needed to reach him?

He wasn't giving up the phones.

The mini-market—cleverly called Minnie's Mini—was directly to Connor's left. The windows were smashed and the door stood slightly ajar. He had an idea. "Follow me," he told Olin and Dylan, then sprinted toward the shop. They did as instructed.

The place was ransacked. Shelving had been toppled, racks emptied. To Connor's surprise, even most of the frozen food had been taken. "Find a place to hide!"

He threw open the back door, then ducked behind an overturned shelving unit near the wall. An attached sign read "First Aid and Cold Medicine." Olin crouched down beside him.

"Where's Dylan?" Connor whispered.

"I don't know."

Connor peeked over the shelving and saw Dylan hiding behind a rack of magazines closer to the front. The magazines were among the few things that hadn't been stolen. Those and the canes in a nearby plastic bin.

"What's the plan?" Olin whispered.

"If we're lucky, they'll see the back door open and think we went out that way."

"If we're lucky?"

"You have a better idea?"

Olin shifted his weight onto his knees. "What did you mean when you said my parents weren't coming back?"

"Does this look like the time?"

"Just tell me."

"Fine. There was a fire, okay? Two bodies were found. Olivia told me it was my parents, but I don't think so. Which means it was probably yours. Now shut up." Connor regretted saying all that as soon as it had come out. He had already considered the possibility that the ring *didn't* mean anything, that it *was* his parents, or that it was another couple entirely. They were the reasons he hadn't told Olin about the fire before. (Okay, the main reason he hadn't told Olin about the fire before was that he wanted his help. But the possibility that Olin's parents weren't the ones killed in the fire—that was part of it.) Either way, he couldn't take it back, and this wasn't the time to elaborate. All he could do now was exactly what he had told Olin to do—shut up.

At least, from the way they were positioned, he couldn't see Olin's face.

Connor listened for footsteps and eventually heard them.

"Come out, come out, wherever you are."

The words were delivered in a singsong voice that Connor recognized as belonging to Baseball Bat.

The sound of footsteps moved closer. "We just want our toll."

Connor, who had been crouching down until now on just the balls of his feet, put one hand on the floor to take some of the weight off his knees. He wasn't sure how long he could stay like this, but he was afraid if he moved, they would hear him.

"What's this?"

Connor sighed with relief. Baseball Bat must have finally realized the back door was open. It wouldn't be long now.

Then he heard Dylan scream.

CHAPTER 45

CONNOR IMMEDIATELY POPPED up from behind the shelving unit. Olin did not.

Baseball Bat had placed the laptop he had stolen on the counter beside the register alongside the bat and was holding Dylan by the hair. He spun her around, pulled her to his chest. She fought until he popped open a switchblade and held the knife to her throat.

"Well, well, well. There you are," Baseball Bat said to Connor. His friends were standing behind him, unarmed but equally menacing.

By exposing himself, Connor had resisted his instinct to stay out of sight. It had taken every bit of will he had, but he wasn't going to let something terrible happen to Dylan. Not after what had happened to his parents.

"Let her go." The commanding tone he had attempted to muster failed him. The words came out more like a question.

Baseball Bat smiled with genuine amusement. Said nothing. He didn't have to. As things stood, he was in control. If Connor wanted to change that, he would need a weapon of his own, and backup. He looked around, thinking fast. A few packages of gauze were scattered on the floor by his feet. Those wouldn't work. Then he remembered the canes. They weren't ideal, but they were the best he was going to get.

One step over to the wall and back. He grabbed the first cane he could get his hands on. It was aluminum with a hooked handle and a rubber tip. He held it out like a sword, the rubber tip aimed straight at Baseball Bat.

Connor kicked Olin. "Get up."

Reluctantly, Olin did.

Then Connor directed his attention to Baseball Bat. "We'll give you our wallets, but we're keeping our phones."

Baseball Bat bobbed his head from side to side, like he was thinking it over. Connor could tell he was mocking them. "I'll take everything."

Connor held one hand out to Olin, palm up. "Give me the car keys."

"What?"

"I'm serious. Give me the damn car keys."

Olin glanced at Baseball Bat, and then handed Connor the keys.

"These are the keys to a BMW. You'll find it abandoned a block over. It's yours."

Baseball Bat said nothing.

"I'm going to give this to you, and you let us leave. Let's not make this into a thing, okay?"

Still nothing.

Connor wasn't sure what he should do. It was like negotiating with a statue. "I'm going to throw these to you, and you'll let her go, all right?"

Baseball Bat's smile was back. In the absence of any other response, Connor decided to take that as a yes.

The little voice in the back of his head told him this was a mistake. But he tried to convince himself that was just his fear talking. Since he had no better plan, this had to work.

He gently tossed the keys into the air. Baseball Bat did not move to catch them. Once they landed on the floor, one of the man's friends leaned in and picked them up.

"Thanks. I'll take your wallets and cellphones also."

Connor silently cursed himself for not listening to that voice in the back of his head. He had just handed these criminals Olin's keys, practically making himself complicit in their crime, and for nothing. All he had done was make a bad situation worse. From the corner of his eye, he could tell Olin was furious.

He wished he had the courage to step forward, swinging the aluminum cane. With the bat on the counter, he had the advantage of distance. But Baseball Bat's friends would no doubt step in. If luck wasn't on his side, they would beat him senseless. (Or worse.) And he did not even want to think about what might happen to Olin and Dylan. As much as he might have been able to will himself to stand in hopes of helping Dylan, he could not will himself into a fight he would certainly lose.

Perhaps a subtle shift in his expression or some small gesture gave away what he was thinking, because Baseball Bat said, "I've had enough of this shit." He forced his hand into Dylan's pockets, found her cellphone, a small wallet, and a house key. He threw the house key in one direction and pushed Dylan in the other, then pocketed the phone and wallet.

He took a step toward Connor. "I dare you. Come at me."

And Connor knew right then he had no choice but to do just that. He swung the aluminum cane at Baseball Bat's torso, intending to knock the wind out of him and hoping like hell Olin would back him up.

Baseball Bat stepped back, dropping his knife, and then, moving with Connor's swing, grabbed the cane and ripped it from Connor's hands.

Everything else happened in only seconds.

As Baseball Bat closed in on Connor, two of his friends—pale, missing teeth, interchangeable in their hoodies—headed for Olin. The third, sporting a bright red Mohawk, produced a knife of his own and trained it on Dylan, who was moving toward the door. "Stay right where you are, Missy."

Baseball Bat swung the cane at Connor's head, and Connor ducked. He swung it again and caught Connor in the shoulder. The pain shot down Connor's arm and into his back. He stumbled, fell. Dylan screamed.

Then Baseball Bat kicked Connor in the torso twice and was just about to swing the cane at him again when Connor heard a voice from the street: "Keep moving, folks. It's just a power outage."

To Connor, that sounded like a cop. To Baseball Bat, it seemed to, as well. He threw the cane away, turned toward the two men in hoodies. All Connor could see of them now were their backs. Baseball Bat shouted to get their attention, and, faster than they had come, they exited back onto the street.

Connor was in too much pain to make sense of what had happened at first. Still on the floor, he moved his shoulder gingerly around to make sure it wasn't broken.

Then, Dylan was there, asking if he was all right.

"I think so."

"What the hell?" Olin said, now standing beside Dylan. "That was my car."

Connor slowly got back to his feet, using the arm that wasn't in pain to push himself off the floor. "File an insurance claim. You'll get the money back."

"That's not the point."

"What is the point?"

"Now they've got my car!" He held up three fingers and started ticking them off. "They've got my car, my wallet, my phone. I mean—what were you thinking?"

Connor immediately felt his pockets for his and his father's phones. He couldn't imagine how Baseball Bat would have managed to take either of them, but he still needed to know they were there.

They were. Apparently, he was the only one left with a phone or a wallet.

He took a breath. "I didn't want to give them our phones."

"Why not?"

"Why do you think?" Connor snapped.

Olin opened his mouth to respond, but didn't. He seemed to have figured it out. His face softened, and he turned away, walked toward the front of the market.

When Dylan tried to go to him, Connor grabbed her arm, shook his head no. He could imagine how Olin felt, and so he gave him his moment.

When Olin spoke again, he said, "They left the bat."

Connor had seen Baseball Bat grab the switchblade on his way out. But he hadn't thought about looking to see if the bat was still here until just now. Baseball Bat had also left the laptop, Connor noticed. He probably didn't want to explain to the cop why he was walking around with a brand-new computer.

"We should take it with us," Connor said, referring to the bat. "Just in case."

Olin nodded and picked it up. Then all three of them hurried out of the mini-market.

CHAPTER 46

CONNOR, OLIN, AND Dylan made it back to Austin's building without further incident. Connor tried the door, but it was locked. Which wasn't unusual. Austin had said he would make Connor a key, but he hadn't gotten around to it yet. So, of course, Connor knocked.

Austin opened the door immediately. Behind him, the apartment was lit with candles. "Where have you been? I was trying to call you before . . ." He trailed off, gestured to the darkness around them. "Why didn't you answer?"

Connor remembered the calls. They had come in while he and Olin were scouting the Albright Mall. "I didn't hear them," he lied. Well, half-lied. He hadn't heard them, but he had seen the missed calls. He could have called back.

"Who are these people?" Austin said, looking past Connor and stepping out of the way so all three could enter.

"Friends," Connor said, which, before he had said it, had seemed like merely an easy answer. But after he had spoken the word aloud, he realized it was true. More for Olin than Dylan, since he had just met her, but true nonetheless.

Dylan, however, was not at that same point yet. "Yup. All you have to do these days to make a friend is hack into their website." She plopped down onto the sofa and put her feet, still in those red sneakers, up on the coffee table.

Austin winced—Connor knew he didn't like people putting their feet on his coffee table even when they weren't wearing shoes—but he didn't say anything. Perhaps there was enough going on right now with the blackout and the explosions that it seemed trivial. "You hacked into her website?" he asked Connor.

Dylan jumped in to answer. "He hacked in. I kicked him out. He followed me to the mall." To Connor: "How did you know I was at the mall, anyway?"

Connor stammered. He wasn't ready to tell her what he had done.

Olin did not seem to have that same problem. "He hacked into your phone through your computer and installed a tracking application," he said as he leaned the baseball bat against the wall.

Dylan put her feet back on the floor and rocked forward. "You *what?*"

"I didn't know how else to find you."

She glared at him, then collapsed back into the sofa. "*Touché.*"

If any of this concerned Austin, he didn't let on. "Sit down," he said to Connor and Olin, and they did. "I'm just glad all of you are safe. I think there's something bad going on out there."

"We know," Connor said.

"We were at the Albright Mall when it happened," Olin added.

"What are you talking about?"

"There was a bomb that went off in the food court. We're lucky be alive."

Austin sighed. "I don't think I'll be able to sleep tonight. Anyone want some coffee?"

Olin said he would take a cup, and Austin disappeared into the kitchen.

Connor heard him open a cabinet and then turn on the tap. He knew the sounds meant Austin was making a fresh pot.

"Why do you think it was my parents in the fire?" Olin asked.

Dylan, who seemed to be staring at nothing, perhaps thinking about Tom, tuned in. "What fire?"

Connor summed up for her what he had told Olin just so they could move on, then apologized to Olin for what he had said. "It's just the ring. It still bothers me that it was on the wrong finger. And I just assumed if it wasn't my parents, it had to be yours. But I don't know that. I don't know that it was yours or mine. For all we know, it could have been another two people entirely."

"I guess so."

"Let's try to stay positive for now."

Dylan rolled her eyes. "Have you *been* outside?"

Connor wasn't sure what to say to that. Dylan was right. Things out there were bad. It would be easy to give in to the anxiety that had been hounding him since his parents were taken and had compounded when the bomb went off. But that wouldn't do him any good. Instead of explaining that to Dylan, though—which was a one-way ticket to feeding his anxiety—he went into the kitchen to check on Austin.

A pot of water was sitting on the gas stove, not yet boiling. Austin was leaning against the counter, watching it. He had set out three mugs and a tin of Folgers instant coffee. "It's the best I can do under the circumstances," he said.

The kitchen was narrow and cramped. There was no reason to hang out here, literally watching a pot boil. Connor figured he must have overheard their conversation and was giving them some space.

"What did you want to talk to me about?"

"Nothing. It doesn't matter now."

"Are you sure?"

"Yeah. Don't worry about it."

Connor shrugged as the water bubbled up to a simmer.

Austin turned off the stove, put a scoop of instant coffee into each mug, and then poured in the water. He handed two of them to Connor. "For you and your friend. I'll bring some milk and sugar in case he wants any."

There weren't enough seats in Austin's living room for all four of them, so Austin carried in a chair from the dining room. They drank their coffee while Connor and his friends filled Austin in on what had happened at the mall and afterward.

Dylan did most of the talking. Olin just nodded along, and Connor, regularly checking his phone for a signal, only spoke up when he thought he had something to add.

Although nobody said as much, Connor suspected they were all waiting for the power to come back on so they could find out how bad the situation actually was.

CHAPTER 47

OLDRICH WAS BARELY out of bed when Basia called. He must have sounded tired or annoyed when he answered (he was both), because the first thing she said was, "I thought you would want to know about this right away."

"What is it?"

"There's no match in the system for the knife you gave me."

Oldrich walked to his bedroom closet in just his underwear and pulled out a suit. It was brown and wrinkled. Brown because he liked the color, wrinkled because he didn't iron. "What are you saying? That you couldn't get any DNA off it?"

"I got DNA. Plenty of it. The sample I pulled from the blade didn't have a match, but I expected that. The problem is, neither did the DNA on the handle."

Oldrich tried to make sense of what Basia was telling him. He knew Matthew Jones had killed Heather Callahan. There was no doubt about that. So why wasn't his DNA on the knife? "Are you sure there wasn't a second sample you missed?"

"If there was DNA on that knife that had been in our system, I wouldn't be telling you we didn't have a match." Basia sounded insulted.

Maybe, because he was American, Matthew Jones had been overlooked when they had catalogued the DNA of current prisoners. "When you get to the office—"

"I'm at the office. How do you think I know what the results of the test were?"

"Could you look up a name for me? I want to make sure they're in the system."

"Matthew Jones?"

Oldrich had an uneasy feeling about where this was going. "Yes."

"I already did. He's there."

That was exactly what Oldrich had worried Basia was going to say when she'd rattled Matthew's name off so easily. Still, since the DNA wasn't a match, he had to consider the possibility that another sample had been miscategorized or that the record tied to Matthew's name had been corrupted. While neither of those things happened often, they had both been known to happen before. Especially with some of the original records, which, since Matthew was in jail at the time the system was set up, would have included his.

Oldrich decided he had better go down to the prison, get a fresh sample, and run it again.

Praha Pankrác looked a lot like the American prisons Oldrich had seen on TV. He parked in the lot along the north wall and flashed his badge at a guard on his way in.

The process of gaining access to a prisoner was pretty boilerplate. Oldrich filled out a short form at the front desk and then was taken to an interrogation room, where he would wait for Matthew to arrive.

The room was a perfect square. Eight by eight. Cinderblocks walls, peeling linoleum on the floor. A small foldout table and two foldout chairs. No windows.

Oldrich took a seat in the chair that faced the door and occupied himself with his phone while he waited. The news about the blackout in New York was just starting to hit his feed. There wasn't much information yet. Likely a problem with a transformer, one article speculated.

But the door opened before he could finish reading it. A guard stepped in. "Detective, we have a problem."

CHAPTER 48

I T SEEMED LIKE a strange thing to play cards in the middle of a blackout, with Connor's parents missing, Olin's parents missing, and Dylan's friend dead, but that was what they did. None of them could sleep, and it was better than staring at each other in the dark, waiting for the power to come back.

When it did return a couple of hours later, the whole apartment lit up at once. Austin placed his cards face down on the coffee table, then got up and went to the window. He peeked through the blinds. "It's not just us. Far as I can see, everything's back."

Connor didn't realize how stressed the blackout had been making him until it had passed. He picked up the remote, turned on the TV, and was greeted by a commercial for Pillsbury biscuits. As if nothing at all had happened.

Without saying a word, everyone turned their attention to the screen. They all wanted answers, and they all seemed to know that was exactly what Connor was trying to get them.

He pressed the up button, browsing from one channel to the next.

"Forty-seven," Austin said.

Connor moved his thumb from the arrow to the digits. When the channel changed, they saw a news anchor sitting behind a desk. ". . . reports are still coming in. So far, we are aware of five explosions at malls across New York City. The bombs were detonated within minutes of each other. Deaths and casualties combined are expected to be in the hundreds. New York City Health & Hospital has already reached capacity and is routing ambulances to other locations . . ."

All four stared in silence, watching the broadcast. The news anchor cut over to experts who speculated on the reasons behind the bombings and how they would change the country and shopping malls, in particular. Governor Flores would be addressing the nation soon. So would the president.

Connor didn't have to say this was bad, but he did anyway, and Olin agreed. Austin put a finger to his lips and shushed them. Even though the gesture was common enough to be meaningless, it still reminded Connor of the night his parents were taken and gave him a chill.

After an hour or so, Austin muted the screen. Governor Flores had just finished speaking. He had assured the public they would find out who had done this. He had urged everyone to stay calm. And, of course, thoughts and prayers for the victims and their families.

There was nothing else new. The information cycle was running on repeat.

They talked for a while. It was no doubt the same sort of conversation people all across the country were having at that moment. They tried to assure each other that Flores was right, that those responsible for the bombings would be found. They told themselves they were lucky to still be alive.

At some point, Austin's cat jumped on the sofa and curled up beside Dylan, which surprised Connor.

"Huh. That bastard never takes to anyone," Austin said.

Dylan smiled down at the cat, began stroking his back. She turned to Connor. "Can I . . ." She hesitated, like she was embarrassed, then blurted out, "Can I use your phone?"

"Yeah, sure," Connor said, fishing his phone out of his pocket. "Give it a shot. Why?"

"I . . ." Now she looked away. "I need to call my parents and let them know I'm all right."

Connor nodded and handed it to her. If he was in her position, he would want to call his parents, too.

The conversation was short. She told them she was safe and that, yes, she could stay where she was until everything calmed down.

When she passed the phone back, Connor saw he had a voicemail from a California number. It wasn't any of his friends, and he doubted it was anything important—probably a telemarketer—but he checked it anyway, just in case.

"Connor, hi. It's Isaiah. From Uncovered. I'm back in California. I saw what happened on the news. Shit, I hope you're all right. If you get this, there's something you should know. The show aired tonight, and we got a call. Got a lot of them, actually. Mostly a bunch of crackpots. You know, the kind that call in Elvis sightings and crap like that. There was one, though, that I think might be something. Seems there was a man in New York on business. He drove in from Boston, if I remember right. Anyway, he says he saw the same van that you saw. Probably. He was at a BP gas station filling up when a rusty blue panel van pulled up to the pump opposite him. He remembered it because something about the driver made him nervous. He couldn't say what. At any rate, the point is, we've got a description. Skinny guy. Late forties, maybe early fifties. Blond hair to his shoulders. It's not a lot to go on, but it's something. And I bet, when I call the police, they'll be able to get a license plate also. I think we might have found your guy. Here's hoping, anyway. Call me back when you get this, all right?"

Isaiah had never told Connor when the show would air, but that was hardly the most important thing about the message. It wasn't even the fact that they had a lead they could forward to the NYPD. It was the subject's description. Skinny. Blond hair to his shoulders. Okay, it wasn't much of a description, but there was only one person Connor knew who matched it.

Austin.

Connor thought back to the shushing gesture he had made while they were watching the news and how it had reminded him of the gesture the kidnapper had made when he'd returned for his phone.

"Everything all right?" Austin asked.

"Yeah, it's fine." Connor put the phone back in his pocket. "Nothing important."

Think. What are you going to do? He tried to keep his expression neutral, keenly aware that Austin was looking at him.

There was only one way out of the apartment, and that was the front door. He could probably make it if he ran. But that would mean leaving Olin and Dylan behind. Since they didn't know what Austin had done, they wouldn't move as fast. And once Austin figured out that Connor knew who he was, what would he do to them?

For now, Connor had only one choice. He collapsed back into the armchair like nothing had happened. He could feel his hands shaking, so he kept them in his lap, hoping Austin wouldn't notice.

Olin and Dylan certainly didn't seem to.

Connor tried to pay attention to the conversation, figuring the best thing he could do for now was to blend in. Play the role Austin expected him to. But how long could he keep that up?

There was no way he was waiting around until tomorrow. Even though right now nobody thought they could sleep, eventually somebody would say they were tired. Then Austin would pull out the sofa bed and Connor would be expected to retire to his room. And what if he did fall asleep? Would he wake up? And if he did wake up, where would he wake up?

He could feel himself spinning out.

Even if Austin had abducted his parents, he was as safe here tonight as he had been any of the other nights. He needed to stay calm.

Why would Austin abduct his parents, anyway? It didn't make sense.

"You all right?" Austin asked.

Shit. "Yeah. Just—it's everything that's going on, you know."

That was it. He had to figure out one way or another whether Austin was the kidnapper. But how? If he could just find the Taser or the driving gloves, that would be evidence enough. But he couldn't just get up and start searching Austin's apartment. For something like that, he needed Austin out of the way. Asleep, maybe.

Then the answer dawned on him: *asleep.*

"I'll be right back," he said as he casually got up. "I want to get my laptop. Maybe there's more online about what happened."

Everyone seemed to buy the excuse.

In the guest room, he took the bottle of Ambien out of his backpack and transferred a pill from it to his pocket. He told himself not to look over his shoulder, not to draw attention, but he couldn't help it. Fortunately, nobody would be able to see what he was doing unless they had followed him into the hall.

Then he grabbed the laptop and returned to the living room. Once back in his seat, he powered the computer up and made a show of looking for more news. He even made a point of reading several articles out loud when Olin asked if he had found anything.

The articles contained nothing they didn't already know, which he summed up by saying, "It's just more of the same," before closing the laptop and putting it on the floor beside him. "I'm going to get some more coffee. Anyone want some?"

Austin drank a lot of coffee, and Connor was counting on him saying yes. He did.

"I'll make it," Connor said, when Austin started to get up.

He went into the kitchen, filled two mugs with water, and put them in the microwave. While he waited, he used the blunt end of a spoon to crush the Ambien on the counter. This time, he had every reason to look over his shoulder. If he got caught, he would have no believable explanation for what he was doing, and the sooner he knew someone was watching him, the better.

He returned to the living room with the coffees, handed a mug to Austin, and tensed up as Austin took his first sip. Connor was counting on the naturally bitter taste of the coffee to mask the pill, and—thank God—it seemed to be working.

He wasn't sure how long it took before Austin started getting sleepy. It seemed like forever. Long enough for Connor to worry his plan wasn't going to work.

Eventually, though, Austin's head dipped forward. He jerked it back, looked down into his coffee cup like he was confused. "Instant's definitely not the same as the real thing. I think I need to get some sleep." He got up slowly, held out his hands like he was worried he might fall back into the chair, then tried to head toward his bedroom.

After a couple of steps, he turned to Connor. "What did you do?"

"What are you talking about? You're just tired, like you said."

Austin's hands had balled into fists. His teeth clenched. He took a step towards Connor, but his balance faltered. He grabbed hold of the back of the sofa to keep himself from falling over.

Dylan and Olin jumped up, as confused by what was happening as Austin had been seconds earlier.

"This wasn't another one of your stupid plans, was it?" Olin said to Connor.

"I don't know what's happening, I swear. I thought he was just tired." Connor likewise got out of his seat and moved to the other side of the room. "You need to relax, Austin. I don't know what you think I did, but I swear I didn't do anything."

Austin turned. Again, it was slow, his balance even less reliable than it had been a moment ago. "You're making a mistake," he slurred. Then he dropped to his knees.

CHAPTER 49

THE POWER HAD not yet returned when Olivia put Erin to bed. Normally, her daughter slept with a nightlight. Since that wasn't an option, Olivia placed a flashlight in Erin's closet and cracked the door so it let just about the right amount of light into her room.

That, however, did not stop Erin from tiptoeing into Olivia's room an hour later, saying she was scared. On any other night, Olivia would ask her what she was afraid of, help her reason through her fear, so she could go back to sleep in her own room. It was a part of growing up. That didn't seem like the right move here. Erin had been through a lot today. The truth was, they both had. The trial had been exhausting. And then there was that conversation with Roland.

Olivia wanted to snuggle with Erin as much as Erin wanted to snuggle with her. So she pulled back her covers, invited her daughter into the king-size bed, and they stayed wrapped up tight until the phone woke Olivia up sometime later.

Erin was a sound sleeper. She didn't move when the phone rang or when Olivia pulled her arm out from underneath her daughter's head, sat up, and swung her feet over the side of the bed. Still, Olivia carried the phone into the hall before answering.

"Ms. Forbes," said Oldrich. "I have some troubling news."

CHAPTER 50

CONNOR STAYED WHERE he was until Austin passed out, stretched out on his stomach on the living room floor. The only thing he said, over and over again, was, "You're making a mistake." It became a sort of gauge Connor could use to tell how close Austin was to falling sleep.

At some point, Dylan suggested they call an ambulance. Olin responded by saying they would be unlikely to get one anytime soon. Connor simply shook his head no.

"But he might be in serious trouble. We should at least try. Connor, give me your phone."

"He's not," Connor said.

That seemed to surprise her more than Olin. She asked, "How do you know?" At the same time, Olin said, "You told us you didn't do anything to his drink."

Connor gave him a look but said nothing. The look was enough.

For a moment, Connor worried Olin would charge out of the apartment, angry or afraid or maybe both. Instead, Olin walked to the window, cursing under his breath. After a few moments, he turned around to face Connor again, arms crossed over his chest. Connor could tell he wanted to say something. But if he wasn't going to speak, Connor wasn't going to make him. This would all make sense soon enough.

Connor nudged Austin with his foot once he was sure Austin was out. When he didn't get a response, he told Olin and Dylan about the call from Isaiah. "I have to know if it's him."

Olin was less annoyed than he had been before. He moved closer to Austin, looking at him in a way that made Connor think he was trying to figure out whether the man was physically capable of the crime. "Well, since you've already gone to the trouble of drugging him, I guess we'd better find out."

"What are we looking for?" Dylan asked as she headed to a nearby bookshelf. She started pulling off books one at time and riffling through their pages before dumping them on the floor.

"I don't know. If he's our guy, he obviously doesn't have our parents here. Look for a pair of leather driving gloves. A Taser. Just let me know if you come across anything unusual." It was almost the exact same thing he'd told Olin when they had started searching Dylan's house. But it had served them well then, so hopefully it would serve them well here, too.

Olin went to the kitchen to start his search there.

"We have to assume he could wake up at any time," Connor called after him. "Be as fast as you can." Then he went to Austin's bedroom.

It was the one room in the apartment he had never been in. He had never even opened the door—which, Connor now realized, Austin always kept closed. Did he keep it locked, also? Connor tried to turn the knob. Apparently, he did.

Austin might as well have hung a flashing red sign over the door that read "Secrets Galore."

But how was he going to get inside? Connor could hack his way into a computer, but a locked door was another matter entirely.

Austin had to have a key. Connor tried to remember seeing him use it. He couldn't. No surprise. Austin would have been careful not to draw attention to the locked door. So, time for a game of hide and seek. If Connor wanted to keep a room in his house locked, where would he keep the key?

The most obvious place was Austin's keyring. Since Austin always kept his keyring in his pocket—never in a drawer or on a table, not even for a minute—that seemed like a safe assumption.

It was also the last place Connor wanted to look.

He returned to the living room. Austin was still sprawled out on his stomach near the sofa, only now he was snoring. To get to his pockets, Connor would have to turn him over. Getting that close to the man made him nervous, but what choice did he have?

He dropped to one knee, and Dylan, who was now searching the TV stand's cabinets, said, "What are you doing?"

"I need to get his keys."

"Why?"

"His bedroom door is locked."

As far as Connor could see, Dylan had found only a few DVDs inside the cabinets. That didn't surprise him. Austin didn't like clutter.

"No shit? That probably means there's something inside."

Connor resisted the urge to respond with the same kind of wisecrack remark he might have gotten from her.

"Let me see," she said, already making her way to Austin's bedroom door.

Connor stood up and followed. "It's a locked door. What are you going—"

"It's just a simple pop lock, I think," she said, looking at the handle.

Connor wasn't sure exactly what she meant, but it sounded like she was referring to the same kind of privacy lock he had seen on the guest bedroom door. "So? Unless you want to break it down, we're still going to need the key."

"Do you have a credit card?"

"You mean to tell me you know how to pick that lock?"

"I've learned a few things here and there."

Connor thought she might be overstating her skills, but there was no harm in letting her try. He pulled his Mastercard out of his wallet and handed it over.

Dylan went straight to work, wedging it between the door and the jamb, wiggling the handle.

"Are you sure you know what you're doing?"

"Be patient."

Olin joined them, perhaps drawn by the rattle. "What's going on?"

"It's Austin's bedroom," Connor said.

Then he, too, repeated the same sentiment that had crossed Connor's and Dylan's minds when they had learned about the locked door. "That looks promising."

There was a whisper of a sound as the credit card slid further between the door and the jamb, and then the door glided open. "See?" Dylan said. "I told you. Patience." She handed the credit card back to Connor.

All three stared into the bedroom as if it were still inaccessible, sealed off by some invisible wall. At first glance, there was nothing unusual about the space. A large bed had been centered along the back wall, the dressing tucked and folded in all the right places. A pair of nightstands made of reclaimed wood with brass handles sat on either side of it. A matching dresser on one side of the room. A closet, its door cracked open.

Like the rest of the apartment, everything was free of clutter. Really, of personal belongings or knickknacks of any sort.

At least it would be easy to search, Connor thought. He led the charge through the invisible wall, made a beeline for the closet. Dylan and Olin were still standing in the hall. "Come on, guys. Let's get this done."

In the walk-in, bare plastic racks clung to the walls. There wasn't a single item of clothing in sight outside of the hamper sitting by the door. "That's a bust," he announced, as he exited.

Dylan pulled out the drawers on the nightstands and announced they were both empty, as well. The only item in the room that wasn't, it turned out, was the dresser. There, Austin had neatly folded a collection of tee shirts and jeans. Olin opened another drawer and found even his underwear was folded.

Something about this didn't feel right. This was more than just the obsessive neatness Austin was known for. But at first Connor couldn't put his finger on what it was. Then he remembered: Austin had said he used to be a software developer. Connor knew a lot of software developers wore jeans to work, but even those who did had at least one nice suit in the closet for interviews.

"I don't get it," Olin said, when he had finished going through the dresser. "There's nothing here. Why would you go to the trouble of locking your bedroom door if you had nothing to hide?"

Dylan looked thoughtfully at the dresser. "Can you guys move it back? I want to see if there's anything behind it."

Connor and Olin each went to one side of the dresser. It was heavy—Connor could tell that much just by looking at it. "On the count of three." Working together, they moved the dresser away from the wall a few inches.

Dylan peeked into the crack between the furniture and the wall.

"Nothing." Then she got down on all fours, looked underneath both it and the bed. This time, she didn't say anything, but it was obvious there was nothing there, either.

"Maybe you're wrong," Olin said to Connor.

Dylan seemed like she wasn't ready to give up yet, though. She pulled the clothes out of the dresser, examined the interior of each drawer closely, then pulled the drawers themselves out and turned them over.

"What are you doing?" Olin said.

Dylan didn't respond. Once she finished with the dresser, she did the same thing with the drawers in the nightstands. "Bingo!" She put the second of the two nightstand drawers on the ground and leaned in close.

Connor couldn't tell what she had found until she turned around holding a key with a strip of masking tape stuck to it.

"I believe this is what you gentlemen are looking for."

Connor took the key from her. He pulled off the strip of masking tape and let it fall to the floor.

Olin crowded in close to get a better look. "What do you think it goes to?"

"I don't know."

"Looks like a padlock to me," Dylan said.

Then Connor remembered something. "Actually, maybe I *do* know."

CHAPTER 51

AUSTIN'S REHABBING A house not far from where I live. There's a shed at the end of the driveway. Bigger than you're thinking, probably. It's got a pair of double doors on it that are secured by a padlock. That might be what this goes to."

"You think that's where he's been keeping our parents?" Olin said.

Connor hoped not, because he had never heard a peep from that shed. Not even when he had walked right up to it looking for a hammer. If his parents were in there—his or Olin's—they were probably dead. But Connor didn't want to tell Olin that, so he said, "I don't know."

"How are we going to get there?" Dylan said.

That was also a question Connor could answer. Austin drove a pickup so he could haul stuff to and from the work site. Connor had seen it parked on the street when they'd arrived earlier. "We'll take his truck," Connor said, nodding his head in the general direction of the living room.

"What if he wakes up?" Olin said.

"And finds that we took his truck?" Connor held up the key. "I think he's going to be more upset that we left with this."

"Fair enough."

As far as Connor could see, there was only one drawback to his plan. But there was no way Dylan was hotwiring a pickup with a credit card, so this time it really would mean going into Austin's pocket for his keys.

"You want me to do it?" Dylan said, once the three of them had returned to the living room.

Connor shook his head. "No." Dylan shouldn't even be here. "Just be ready in case anything goes wrong."

He and Olin rolled Austin onto his back.

Austin stopped snoring, mumbled something incomprehensible. Connor jumped to his feet, ready to start kicking if Austin woke up. But then he smacked his lips and started to snore again.

Connor quietly sighed with relief.

"You can do this," Olin said nervously. He was now standing a good three feet back from the body and didn't look like he planned on getting any closer.

Connor went about getting the keys in slow, methodical steps, the whole time listening to Austin's breathing pattern and keeping his eyes open for any movement. He got down on his knees. Paused. Leaned over. Paused. Slid his hand into Austin's pocket. Paused. There was more than just a set of keys in there—he could tell that much by touch—so he wrapped his hand around everything and pulled all of it out.

Connor immediately got back to his feet and stepped away from the body. Checked for movement one last time. To say he felt relieved would have been an overstatement—there was still a lot to be stressed about—but he felt something akin to that. He had made it.

He opened his hand to find crumpled receipts, a Swiss Army knife, and Austin's keys. He let the receipts fall to the floor, then pocketed the knife, because why not? There were four keys on the keyring. Three house keys, one that looked like it went to his bedroom door, and a car key. One of the house keys had to be for the apartment. The other two were probably for the house he was remodeling.

Connor and his friends headed for the door, Olin stopping only long enough to grab the baseball bat on his way out.

Once they reached the street, Connor pointed at a white RAM pickup. "That's it."

All three piled in without hesitation. Dylan took the middle seat.

Connor navigated his way to the interstate. Traffic was slow going in places, still blocked up completely in others, but he made every turn thoughtfully, staying off the busiest roads, and once he was on I-95, he was confident he could get to the house without further issue.

The house was dark, which was no surprise. Austin preferred not to leave any lights on when he wasn't there. But with the nearest streetlamp out, the lot was even darker than it should have been.

Maybe that was for the best. It was looking more and more likely Austin was the kidnapper, but they still didn't know that for sure. If the evidence didn't pan out the way Connor expected it would, he didn't want to be the person who had first drugged his boss and was then spotted by a neighbor breaking into the house the man was rehabbing.

They made their way past the rented dumpster to the shed at the end of the driveway. Connor had always thought of it as a shed because he wasn't sure what else to call it. It was bigger than any shed he had ever seen, but with the double doors, it certainly didn't look like a garage. If anything, it might be best described as a barn, if a barn had any place in the suburbs.

Connor pulled out the key Dylan had found in Austin's bedroom. "Stand back so I can get some light," he told his friends as he tried to work the key into the padlock.

The key fit, turned. The lock clicked open.

It was the moment of truth.

He tossed the padlock on the ground, grabbed the handles. There was still no sound from inside. God, he hoped his parents weren't in there. "You ready?" he said to Olin, who was holding the baseball bat and seemed just as worried as Connor was about what they might find.

Olin nodded. "Do it."

Connor pulled the doors open. As dark as it was, he couldn't see much. But he could see the van. Blue paint. Rusty. Old. It was the same van Connor had seen pull up to his house some weeks back. If there had been any doubt left, it was gone now.

"Austin is the kidnapper."

Neither Dylan nor Olin responded. Perhaps they were both in shock, or perhaps, since it was a simple statement of fact, there was nothing to say.

Connor pulled out his phone, turned on the flashlight to examine the rest of the space. The three friends stayed close, moving into the shed as one. The cement floor was dusty, the walls bare. As far as they could see, there was nothing here but the van.

Connor was glad he hadn't found his parents' bodies. But it also meant they were still missing, and Austin was the only one who knew where they were.

CHAPTER 52

AUSTIN DID NOT dream, and when he awoke, he had no idea how much time had passed. Everything was fuzzy at first. Why was he on the floor? What had happened? Slowly, his memory returned. Connor had denied drugging his coffee, but Austin had no doubt that was exactly what he had done.

He called Connor's name to see if he was still in the apartment. Connor didn't answer.

He groaned as he sat up. A wave of dizziness washed over him. He could tell the drug was not out of his system. Far from it. Because of that, he was careful getting to his feet. He worried his balance would again betray him. But he was not giving in to the drug again. He had to know what Connor and his friends had been up to while he was unconscious.

A look around the apartment answered that question right away. The place was a mess. Books were scattered across the floor in front of the bookcase. Everything was overturned or out of place.

Once he was certain he could walk, he went straight to the bedroom. The door was open. *Shit.* They had gotten inside. Still, the key to the padlock was well hidden, he told himself. They likely hadn't found it.

But just a glance at the bedside tables dispelled that hope. The drawers were pulled out completely and lay overturned on the floor. Even from where he was, he could see the key was missing.

It didn't take much guesswork to figure out where Connor would have gone. Austin had to go after him. He hoped he could get to the house before it was too late. If Connor found the van, he would no doubt draw the wrong conclusion. Austin wasn't a bad person. He was a person who had had a bad thing done to him.

He hurried across the apartment, grabbed his phone off the coffee table. He looked at the clock on the screen and determined he had only been unconscious for forty-five minutes. Good thing he hadn't finished the whole cup of coffee. If he had, he would probably be out for the night. Then again, maybe it was all the coffee he had drunk that evening that had kept the drug from being more effective. Not that it mattered.

He headed for the front door, reaching into his pocket for his keys as he went, and found nothing. *Shit.*

He had a spare car key in a junk drawer in the kitchen, but that wouldn't matter if Connor had also taken his truck. He changed course, went to the window instead. Sometimes, he had to park a block or two away. Today, he had gotten lucky and found a spot right outside his building. He would be able to see his truck from the window if it was there.

It wasn't.

So be it. He still had one more option—the old Mustang with the stolen plate he used when running errands that he didn't want to be associated with.

Connor tried the driver's side door and found it unlocked. He climbed into the van.

"What are you doing?" Olin asked.

"I want to have a look around. Maybe I can find something."

"Count me in," Dylan announced, and scurried around the vehicle to the passenger door. It was locked. She gestured for Connor to open it.

"Just stay there," he said.

"Seriously, Connor. Let me in."

Ugh. "Fine." He pushed the door open. "But don't touch anything."

Olin stared at the two of them incredulously. "Get out of there—both of you," he said. "We need to let the police handle this."

Connor wasn't listening. He was busy searching for evidence. Or, more specifically, information about where Austin had taken his parents. He checked the pocket in the driver's door, flipped down the visor, opened the console between the seats. Austin's preference for minimalism was on display everywhere he looked. There wasn't even a scrap of paper to be found.

Then he heard Dylan say, "Look."

The glovebox was open in front of her and a car key dangled from a ring she held between her fingers.

"I told you not to touch anything," Connor said.

Then the significance of the discovery hit him. This was not the key Connor had taken out of Austin's pocket earlier. Connor still had that one—now in his own pocket. Which meant this had to be the key for the van.

At first, he was surprised Dylan had found it where she had. But then it made sense. Austin wouldn't want to keep the key on him. If anyone asked, explaining it might prove difficult. *You have two vehicles? Where's the second one?* And he probably figured it was safest in the glovebox, since nobody knew the van was here and a person would need either the key to the padlock or bolt cutters to get past the double doors hiding it.

But the key wasn't the only thing in the glovebox. There was another black-on-black mass, barely distinguishable from the shadows surrounding it. Connor aimed the light on the back of his phone directly into the glovebox so he could get a better look. It turned out there wasn't one item, but two.

He pulled them out, knowing he probably shouldn't be touching them, but unable to resist the urge. The gloves and the Taser. If the van wasn't enough to convince the police Austin had abducted his parents, this sure would be.

But even so, it didn't do anything to help him answer the central question: Where were his parents? If he went to Olivia with this information now and if the police arrested Austin, would he tell them? Connor doubted it. Austin would likely claim he was innocent, despite the evidence. Since he was the man who had abducted Connor's parents, he was also the man who had burned two bodies in a parking garage. He was going to jail for the rest of his life if he admitted what he had done, so why not take his chances with a jury?

But that wasn't the biggest problem with telling Olivia about what he had found. If he called her to report the evidence, she would ask them to stay where they were until she could get to the house. She would want statements from all of them, would want to know exactly what had happened that had led to their discovery of the van. Connor doubted he would get into much trouble for drugging Austin, but it would cost them time. And once the police arrived, they would take the keys, impound the van, send a CSI team to investigate this house and Austin's apartment. Connor would lose access to everything. Eventually the machinery of the NYPD would spit out his parents' location, but would it do that while they were still alive? Connor worried it might not.

And right now, they *were* still alive. They had to be.

Connor was so wrapped up in his own thoughts that, even though he had a clear view of the road, he didn't notice when a Mustang pulled up in front of the house and a man got out.

The man—Austin—charged straight toward the van. "Connor!"

Connor looked up just in time to see Olin spin around, raising the baseball bat to his shoulder like he was anticipating a pitch.

Austin put up his hands, but kept coming. Slowly now. At least until he reached the dumpster, where he stopped to pull out a broken two-by-four. The piece of wood was about three feet long and had nails sticking out of it on one end where it had previously been joined to an intersecting board.

Connor suspected it had been part of the wall they had demolished a couple of days earlier. He slid the gloves back into the glovebox and climbed out of the van. Dylan got out, as well.

"Where are our parents?" Connor asked.

"It's not what you think."

He held up the Taser so Austin could see it, then pressed the button, hoping the weapon was charged. Electricity flashed between the Taser's prongs. "I'm asking the questions here. Tell us where our parents are."

Austin backed up a step. His eyes darted from Connor to Olin.

In a move that surprised Connor, Olin screamed as if he were a warrior and charged at Austin, bat up. All this time, Connor had assumed Olin's repeated requests to advise the police of what they had found and his reluctance to, as Connor had put it, "stretch" the boundaries of the law were manifestations of cowardice. It seemed now that was not the case. It was a matter of ethics, a respect for the institutions and norms of society that drove his decision making. Because right now, when standing only feet from the man he knew had taken his parents, Olin had no trouble unleashing the testosterone-fueled energy that no doubt drove him when he was playing soccer and football.

He swung at Austin. Austin ducked and charged forward. He slammed his shoulder into Olin's stomach, knocking Olin off his feet, and ran.

Connor cursed and broke into a sprint. Olin leapt up and went after him without having to be asked.

Austin was moving faster than Connor would have ever thought possible. He darted across the front yard and disappeared behind the far side of the house.

Connor never heard the window break. But when he and Olin rounded the corner along the backside of the house, he saw the shattered glass and the two-by-four lying on the ground.

"He must have gone inside," Olin said.

That didn't feel right to Connor, but he couldn't say why. And he didn't have time to think about it. Everything right now was about split-second decisions. So when Olin crawled through the window, careful not to cut himself on the jagged glass, Connor crawled after him.

Once they were both inside, they stood as still as they could, listening. Trying to figure out where Austin was. But the house was quiet. If Austin was moving at all, he was being careful not to be heard.

Connor wondered what was so important that Austin would have broken into the house to get it. Was there additional evidence stashed somewhere in here? Something even more incriminating than what he had already found? It seemed possible.

The window had dumped them into the living room. Connor tapped Olin's shoulder to get his attention, then made a "follow me" gesture and quietly crept deeper into the house. If there was anything to be found here, he suspected, it would be upstairs. He and Austin hadn't gotten to remodeling the second floor yet. Actually, except for the time Austin had walked him through his plans for every room, Connor hadn't even seen it.

But he had barely put his foot on the first step when there was a scream from outside.

Dylan.

Connor's instinct had been right. Austin wasn't in the house. The broken window was a red herring, and Connor was pissed he had fallen for it.

Immediately, he and Olin broke into a run, this time heading straight for the front door. Connor pulled it open and they stepped outside, then turned as they heard an engine start. Connor looked toward the shed. Dylan was nowhere to be seen.

The van's headlights came on, and the van lurched forward a foot. Connor wasn't sure what that was about, but he was crystal clear on the big picture. Austin was behind the wheel of the van. He planned on getting rid of the evidence. And as an insurance policy, perhaps, he had taken Dylan with him.

CHAPTER 53

T HE VAN SPED away, veering off the driveway into the front yard to get around the dumpster and kicking up dirt as it went.

"The truck," Connor said, and Olin seemed to know what he meant. They raced for the GMC they had come here in. Connor knew there was no way they could keep up with Austin—by the time they got to the truck and got it started, the van would be out of sight, probably impossible to find—but they had to try.

Then a voice behind them: "Guys!"

Connor whirled around to look. It was Dylan. She was standing just beyond the shed doors, waving her arms over her head.

Oh, thank God.

Connor and Olin stopped running. Since Dylan was safe and the odds were they wouldn't catch Austin anyway, the best thing they could do was regroup. Maybe working together, they could figure out where he was going. After all, they had already gotten further working as a team than Connor ever would have on his own.

"I heard you scream," Connor said as he and Olin hurried toward her. "What happened?"

"Austin came around the corner over there." Dylan pointed toward the side of the house as she likewise trotted over to meet them. "He looked like he was going to come right up to me. It scared the crap out of me. But he got in the van instead, and I guess you know what happened next."

"Do you think he didn't see you?" Olin said.

"Oh, he saw me."

It sounded to Connor like what had happened to him when Austin had returned for his phone at Connor's house.

Dylan looked at the Mustang. "Did you know he had another car?"

Connor shook his head.

Olin put his hands on his hips, took a series of deep breaths. "What do we do now?"

"I'm pretty sure he's going to go dump the van somewhere it'll be hard to find. Maybe even sink it. He's going to get rid of the evidence."

"Can you put a tracker on his phone like you did Dylan's?" Olin said.

"No. Certainly not without a computer, and even then, it might not be possible."

"We need to get him to tell us where our parents are," Olin said.

A thoughtful expression crossed Dylan's face, and she cocked her head just an inch. "You know, I hate to be the one to tell you this, but if he's getting rid of evidence and your parents are still alive, they might not be for long."

It seemed like a fair assumption. Connor would kill his parents, too, if he was in Austin's place, then find somewhere he could get rid of the bodies. "Maybe we don't need to get him to tell us where our parents are."

"What do you mean?"

"Austin has four keys on his keyring, not counting the one for the truck. Two we know go to the apartment, and the other two I assumed must go to this house. But he told me once he has a cabin somewhere. I bet only one of those keys goes to this house, and the other one is for the cabin. That's probably where he's keeping them."

"Do you know where it is?" Olin said.

"I'm not sure if he ever said." Connor turned to Dylan. "But you can find out, can't you?" She had found his original birth certificate, after all. And since all property sales in New York were a matter of public record, he was certain she could find this, too.

Dylan smiled. "Can I see your phone?"

Connor handed it over. Then he and Olin waited while Dylan tapped the screen, scrolled, and tapped some more. Connor paced back and forth impatiently. With nothing to do but think, he asked himself the same questions he had already asked himself a thousand times. Now, though, they came fully formed with a clarity he hadn't had before.

He no longer wondered: What did the *kidnapper* want? Why had the *kidnapper* taken his parents?

Now he wondered: What did *Austin* want? Why had *Austin* taken his parents?

They also came with a new question: Why had Austin befriended him before the abduction?

He knew he would not be able to think his way to the answers, but he couldn't help trying.

"Full name?" Dylan said, her fingers poised over the screen.

"Austin Jones."

She hesitated. "Jones? Like Matthew Jones?"

Connor blinked in surprise. He hadn't put that together until now. "Jones is a pretty common last name," he said. But he knew there had to be more to it than mere coincidence. In truth, because the name was so common, this was a connection he hadn't made until Dylan made it for him. Now that she had, he could see clearly it was part of the puzzle—and went a small way toward answering the question of why

Austin had taken his parents. But since it went *only* a small way toward answering that question (and seemed to raise more than it helped answer), he wanted to stay focused on the task at hand. Whatever Austin's relationship to Matthew was, it wasn't going to help them find the cabin.

Dylan tapped and scrolled some more. "Well, that's interesting."

"What?"

"I've got the address. But I don't think you're going to like how I found it."

Connor was about to ask her what she meant when his phone rang. For no particular reason, he had a feeling it might be Austin and grabbed it out of Dylan's hand to check. "It's Olivia," he said, which made more sense, but not by much. It was the middle of the night.

She must have something important to tell him.

"Listen to me," she said when he answered. "Your father isn't who you think it is. Your real father went with your mother and four other people to Prague on that trip you told me about. This is going to be hard to hear, but you need to know." She took a breath. "He never came back. He was having an affair with Frank Callahan's wife. She tried to call it off while they were overseas, and he killed her. He has spent the last fifteen years in a Czech jail. But . . ."

Connor had a bad feeling about this. "But what?"

"He was supposed to be there for much longer. But something happened. It's not clear what. Oldrich Kozar, the detective I spoke with over there, is looking into it. Either way, Matthew got out. No one knows exactly what happened to him after that, but I think he came back here. I think he's the man who kidnapped your parents. I don't know what he wants with them or what this has to do with Olin's parents, other than that they were all on the trip together. He's been locked up a long time. Maybe he's got it in his head that they are all responsible for what happened to him and wants revenge. Either way, you need to be careful out there. He might come back for you, so stay away from people you don't know. I doubt he would use his real name, but in case he does, it's Matthew Austin Jones, got it?"

Connor flashed back to the marriage certificate he had found. Matthew A. Jones. It seemed so obvious now, but he could still hardly believe what she was telling him. "He's here."

"What do you mean?" Olivia sounded alarmed. "Do you mean you're with him right now?"

"No, I mean he's here, in the country. I've met him. I . . ." He decided his working relationship with Austin was beside the point. It would only prolong the conversation, and what mattered right now were two things: Austin was his father, and Austin had his parents—or the parents who had raised him, anyway. "We think we know where he's taken my parents. We're going there now."

"What? Where? Who's we?"

"I don't have time to explain."

"Connor, don't do that. Let us handle it. I don't want you—"

He hung up. There was nothing Olivia could say that would stop him from going to the cabin.

"What was that about?" Olin said.

Connor wasn't sure how Olin would react if he said Austin was his father, so he decided to keep it to himself. Besides, no matter what their genetic relationship might be, Austin wasn't the man who'd raised him. "Nothing we didn't already know. Let's go."

He passed the phone back to Dylan as he led her and Olin to Austin's truck. "Put the address in the GPS."

CHAPTER 54

OLDRICH HAD LEFT the prison angry and confused. When the guard had told him the prisoner had been released, he had demanded to see Matthew's cell, to verify for himself that the guard wasn't making a mistake. Then Oldrich had demanded to see the paperwork authorizing said release.

It was all in order. Requested by the chief of police, Anton Mira, and approved by the warden.

And that may have been the only unusual part about it. Although Anton had the right to request prisoners be released early (and what warden would refuse a request from the chief?), he had never known Anton to use it. Even when a prisoner came forward with information that might help an ongoing investigation, the best he could have hoped for would have been a reduced sentence.

So why this time?

Oldrich had a sickening feeling he knew the answer, and decided to do something he had never done to find out for sure. Before Anton had gotten married, he and Oldrich had been friends, regularly hitting the bars on Friday nights and taking in the occasional game of billiards. Because of that, he knew the man banked with Ceska Sporitelna. He had seen Anton's debit card often enough. Anton had liked to pay for the drinks. Oldrich had thought it was a subtle way of showing off how much money he made. But he also hadn't cared. If Anton got off on buying their drinks, that was fine with him.

Oldrich stopped by HQ long enough to call Olivia, then walked to the nearest Ceska Sporitelna branch. It was only two blocks over. More trouble to take the car. Besides, the weather was pleasant this morning, and he figured a few extra steps wouldn't be bad for his waistline.

He stopped at the ATM outside, then went in and waited to speak with a personal banker. He showed her his badge, placed a stack of bills on her desk without saying a word about it, and asked if she could pull the records for one Anton Mira.

Oldrich had never taken a bribe himself, but he had been on the receiving end of enough offers when he had worked traffic to know how it was done. *Speeding ticket? Oh, Geez. I'm really sorry, Officer. It won't happen again. What? You want to see my license? Sure. By the way, pay no attention to the money I'll attempt to hand you at the same time. As far as I'm concerned, it doesn't even exist. Wink, wink.*

As he hoped, the banker didn't acknowledge the money. She didn't even look at it. She did, however, say she would see what she could do for him. And he, in turn, asked if he could use the restroom while she got the documentation together.

When he returned, the money was gone. In its place: bank records for Anton Mira going back eighteen months.

Oldrich thanked her for being so helpful, picked up the stack of papers, and left.

He wanted to review them somewhere private. Last thing he needed was for someone in the department to figure out what he was up to.

Oldrich found a dive bar far enough from his home and HQ that it was unlikely he would run into anyone he knew. The place smelled of cigarette smoke, and everyone looked like they were well past "one too many."

He ordered a beer from the bartender and took a table as far from everyone else as he could get. He perused the documents line by line to make sure he didn't miss anything, starting with the most recent month and working his way backward. Most of what he found was exactly what he expected to: deposited paychecks (no wonder Anton always got the drinks), utility payments, trips to the grocery store. But it didn't take long before Oldrich found what he was looking for. Right at the top of the fifth page, there was a deposit that had come in via wire in the amount of 2,335,499.00 koruna and dated two days before Matthew had been released. The sender was Aden Tindol.

Oldrich was devastated. He had hoped there would be another explanation.

He folded the papers, slid them into his coat pocket, and finished his beer.

The right thing to do would be turn Anton in. This wasn't even close to accepting a bribe for a traffic ticket (or to offering one in exchange for bank records), but he wasn't sure he could bring himself to do it. At least not without talking to Anton first.

There had to be an explanation. He had to be missing something.

CHAPTER 55

AUSTIN'S CABIN WAS in a remote part of the woods. His nearest neighbor was a mile away, and more often than not he had the small lake on the edge of his property to himself.

The road that got him there transitioned from two lanes to one to gravel to dirt. And by the time he was within sight of the house, it was so tight there was no turning around. At night, with that last stretch of road visible only thanks to his headlights, it looked like something out of a horror movie.

He pulled up to the cabin, left his headlights on while he made his way up the wooden steps to the porch. Connor still had his keys. But there was always another way in. And here he could do it without breaking a window.

At the far end of the porch there was a statue, about eighteen inches in height. A stone frog standing on two legs, wearing a tuxedo jacket. It was just the sort of kitsch Kim loved, although she had never seen it. Not until recently.

Austin had bought the cabin a month before their trip to the Czech Republic. And, yes, he had done it without telling his wife. But it was cheap, and he had been able to pay for it outright with an inheritance he had gotten when his mother passed away years earlier.

At the time, he hadn't planned on keeping the cabin a secret forever. He had intended to bring Kim and their young son Connor up here for a surprise trip to celebrate their anniversary in September.

Ever since Austin had known her, Kim had talked about having a place like this. Somewhere they could go to get away from the noise of the city. (In those days, the three of them had lived in a walk-up much like the one Austin lived in now.) He was sure she would love it and, from the stone frog to the afghan throw on the sofa, had decorated it with her in mind.

He picked up the frog with two hands and moved it to the side. Underneath was a spare key to the front door. Not exactly high-tech security, but this far out, it hardly mattered.

Austin turned on all the lights. He stopped in his bedroom to remove a pair of keys and a gun from a small safe, then headed for the cellar. The door creaked. So did the stairs. He could hear muted voices whimpering. He flipped the light switch.

There were two wire cages in the middle of the room, not quite big enough to sit upright in. Kim and Frank were each locked in one of them. They were wearing gray sweats Austin had made them put on when he had taken their clothes. The sweats were too big on Kim, too small on Frank. Their hands were bound.

Each cage had a water bowl on one end (although his guests couldn't drink from them with their mouths gagged) and a pot on the other for use as a toilet. The room stank.

They looked weak and tired—no surprise, since they hadn't eaten in days—and they were squinting from the sudden light of the bare sixty-watt bulb in the ceiling. Also no surprise, since they had been kept in darkness just as long.

Kim's pleas for release came out incomprehensible and muted.

Frank, who was sitting cross-legged and hunched over, his head pressed against the top of the cage, said nothing. He seemed to understand Austin did not intend to let him go.

"Today's your lucky day," Austin said.

Finally, Frank made eye contact. A look that said he would kill Austin if he could.

There was a small wooden table along the wall next to Austin. It had been here when he had bought the place and was the only piece of furniture in the cellar. Rotting and discolored, it looked just as old as it was.

He used the keys he had taken from the safe to unlock the cages, then tossed both the keys and locks onto the table. He stepped back and pulled the gun from the waistband of his pants.

"Come out slowly," he instructed.

They did. But, bound as they were, there really wasn't any other way for them to come out.

Kim continued to try to speak through the gag. It annoyed Austin. He couldn't understand her, and he wasn't taking it off. "Shut up."

She didn't.

Austin slammed one hand down on the table while, with the other, he kept the gun trained on the couple. "I said shut up!"

This time, she got the message.

"Up the stairs."

Kim and Frank complied.

From behind, Austin directed them out of the house and to the van. When Kim saw it, she turned around to stare at him. Her eyes were wide with alarm. She shook her head, again tried to speak. She didn't want to get back in the van.

Perhaps in a show of support, Frank turned around, too. Chin up, he puffed out his chest.

Austin didn't have time for this bullshit. He spun the gun around and whacked Frank across the top of the head with the grip. Frank fell to the ground as if some invisible puppeteer had just cut the strings that were holding him upright.

Kim did her best to scream.

Austin pulled open the back door. "Get in the damn van!"

Her eyes darted between Austin and Frank. She shook her head no.

Austin had had enough. He slid the gun back under his belt and forced her into the vehicle. Then, with considerable effort, he managed to get Frank inside, as well.

He slammed the door shut, then went around to the driver's side door, climbed in, and started the engine. He drove to the edge of the lake. But it wasn't until he got there that he realized he had a flaw in his plan. Unless he stayed in the vehicle, foot on the gas, he had no way to send it careening into the water.

Although he wanted their deaths to be terrifying events that seemed to go on forever, Frank was already unconscious. He would drown without ever knowing what had happened. Austin should probably just shoot them both and be done with it. Burn the bodies. Drop the van in some sketchy neighborhood.

No matter what Connor told the police, the vehicle wasn't in his name. So if it was gone, Austin's link to it was gone, as well.

Yes, he decided. That's exactly what he should do. But he wasn't going to shoot Kim and Frank in the van for the same reason he hadn't shot the other couple in the van. You can't completely get rid of blood. And if the police ever found the vehicle, he didn't want them uncovering that sort of evidence.

If you're going to kill someone, you can never be too careful.

Austin put the van in park, went around to the back, and pulled Frank out of the rear door. "You, too. Get out," he instructed Kim.

This time, she did what he asked her to. Maybe because getting out seemed like a safer idea than getting in. How wrong she was.

It didn't take her more than a few seconds to realize that, either. Austin hadn't aimed the gun at either one of them yet, but she already looked terrified and, it seemed to Austin, a little confused.

At first, Austin thought it was the in-and-out instructions he had given her. Why bother putting her in the van at all if he was just going to tell her to get out a few moments later? Then he noticed she wasn't looking directly at him. Actually, to be more specific, she was looking *past* him.

That was strange. The van was behind her. The cabin was off to her left. As far as he knew, there was nothing in her line of sight but him. He turned around to see what had gotten her attention and immediately wished he had turned around sooner.

CHAPTER 56

DYLAN KEPT HER eyes glued to Connor's cellphone. Go left, go right. Connor began to doubt the directions when the road turned from two lanes to one, and was almost certain they were going the wrong way when it turned to dirt a few minutes later. But by the time he decided to say something, they were too far down the narrow road to turn around.

"This is what the phone says, okay?" Dylan responded. "If we get to our destination and there's nothing, we're probably going to be too late to save them, wherever they are, so we might as well keep going."

That wasn't what Connor wanted to hear, but he knew she was right. He pressed down on the gas. The truck bounced over the uneven ground in jaw-jarring thumps. Then, between the trees, he saw another set of headlights, also in motion, but not headed toward them. They were headed toward—Connor looked closer, noticed the way the headlights seemed to twinkle on the distant ground—a lake.

He stopped, killed the lights on the truck.

"What are you doing?" Olin said.

Connor pointed at the other vehicle. "You see that?" Its shape was impossible to make out in the darkness, but everyone got the point: If they had come to the right place, that was almost certainly Austin's van.

"What do you want to do?" Dylan said.

"We can't keep going in this thing. We can't take the chance Austin will hear us." He turned off the engine. "We need to get up there on foot, deal with him first. Then we'll figure out where our parents are."

Olin and Dylan agreed that made sense, and they all got out of the truck.

Olin reached over into the bed and grabbed the bat. "Let's go."

Connor nodded, and they hurried up the road. He wished he had the Taser as well, but somehow in all the excitement back at the house he had lost it.

The trees thinned out as they neared the cabin. With the moon reflecting off the water and the lights in the cabin casting a warm glow onto the porch, the sight would have been picturesque in another context.

Connor noticed the van had stopped at the edge of the water and was just sitting there.

"Should we go check it out?" Dylan said.

Connor took a deep breath, answered only by stepping off the road. The new course he was on would take him directly to the vehicle. He didn't think Austin had an accomplice, so it was almost certainly Austin driving the van. The three of them had taken him down before. They could do it again.

The driver's door opened. A figure got out.

Connor stopped where he was, held a hand out for Olin and Dylan to do the same. It was inevitable that the van would eventually move or someone would step out, but Connor suddenly felt more exposed than he had before and he needed a moment to reassess their situation.

First question: Was it Austin?

He watched the way the man moved around the van and decided it probably was.

Second question: What was he up to?

They had come this far with their only plan being to "deal with him." But Connor still didn't know exactly how they were going to do that. If they could figure out what Austin was doing, they could anticipate his movements, form a plan to close in without being seen.

"Do you think he's dumping the van in the lake?" Olin said.

Connor shrugged. It did indeed look that way. What else *would* he be doing there? "If he is, he's going to have to go back to the front of the van eventually to put it in gear and weigh down the gas pedal."

"And that's when we'll get him," Dylan said, punching her right fist into her left palm.

"Calm down." Connor watched Austin open the van's rear doors. "But, yes, that's when we'll get him."

Austin dragged something big and bulky out of the van and let it fall to the ground. Then he gestured as if he might be talking to someone.

"He's not alone," Olin said.

A figured emerged. Connor strained to see through the darkness. As the person awkwardly climbed out of the van, Connor could see enough of the person's silhouette to know it was a woman. He also noticed she moved both hands as one. It was as if . . . "Her hands are tied. That's got to be my mom." He turned to Olin. "Or yours."

Then Connor realized the big and bulky thing Austin had dragged out of the van was a body. Dead or unconscious, there was no way to know.

"What is he doing out there?" Dylan said.

Connor suspected Dylan's question was rhetorical. There was only one answer, and he was sure all three of them knew what it was. "We need a plan right now."

Olin, however, wasn't waiting around to make a plan. He broke into a run before Connor even finished his sentence. Connor and Dylan immediately went after him. As he closed in on Austin, he raised the bat, swung.

Austin turned around right before Olin made contact. He doubled over, fell to the ground. Connor and Dylan caught up with Olin as he was lifting the bat over his head, about to swing again.

"Don't do it," Austin said. He was lying on the ground, half propped up by the body Connor still couldn't identify and struggling to speak. He had one hand wrapped around his torso. And in the other, a gun aimed in Olin's general direction.

Olin froze.

The woman, Connor noticed, was his mom. He felt himself go dizzy like he had on the stairwell as so many emotions fought for dominance. He wanted to run to her, to hug her, to let her know that everything would be okay. But he couldn't do any of that. Not with Austin holding that gun. For now, he just had to take solace in the fact that, while she looked bad, at least she was alive.

And that, he realized, probably meant the man Austin was propped up against was Frank.

"Put it down," Austin said.

Olin did, moving slowly so as not to spook him. The man's hand might be shaking, but Olin clearly understood Austin was close enough to hit one of them if he pulled the trigger.

"Get over there with the rest of them," Austin said to Kim. Then he grunted and groaned and pushed himself back up to his feet. Still holding one hand around his stomach, he stepped back. When you have a gun and your enemy has a bat, distance is your friend.

He looked down at Frank, who was still lying in a heap on the ground but seemed to be regaining consciousness, and swung the gun toward him only long enough to fire a single round.

Kim screamed.

"The rest of you get into the house!" Austin shouted, jabbing the gun at them as he spoke.

CHAPTER 57

USTIN TOLD CONNOR to hand over his and his father's cellphones. Then he directed everyone down to the cellar. He said he needed to think. It wasn't supposed to happen this way. None of it was.

When Connor saw the cages, he knew that was where Austin must have been keeping his parents. But with only two cages, he also knew it meant he was right when he had assumed Olin's parents had been the ones found burning in the parking deck.

But why had Austin killed them and kept Kim and Frank alive?

Austin put Kim back in a cage, then tied Connor, Dylan, and Olin up, binding their hands behind their backs and then securing them to one side of the empty cage.

They all had gags on now—rolled-up socks Austin had stuffed into their mouths, held in place with bandanas and rope. Connor felt like he was going to choke to death if he didn't keep fighting the sock away from his throat with his tongue.

There had to be a way out of this. If Connor had been keeping a scorecard, he would have to admit that he had gotten himself and Olin (and now Dylan) in more trouble than he'd gotten them out of, but it was never too late to try to turn things around.

He had only one tool at his disposal—the Swiss Army knife he had taken off Austin back at the apartment—but it would be enough if he could get to it.

The problem was the knife was in his front pocket, and he couldn't exactly reach a hand in and pull it out. He might, however, be able to shake it out, he thought.

He put his feet flat on the floor, lifted with his knees so that he could get the pocket at a forty-five-degree angle, then began to shake his hips. Dylan raised an eyebrow in his direction. He could only imagine what she was thinking.

Connor felt the knife slide closer to the top of the pocket. Eventually, though, it hit a fold in the fabric and refused to go any further. After several attempts, Connor gave up. There was nothing they could do. They were trapped.

He wished he had thought to text Olivia the address before they came up here.

Connor wasn't sure how much time had passed before Austin came back down into the cellar. When he did, though, he didn't say a word. He just walked over to Connor, untied him from the cage, and pulled his gun.

Connor wasn't sure where this was going. He worried Austin might take him outside and shoot him like he had Frank. Maybe his plan was to kill them all, one at a time.

The rational part of him insisted that was unlikely. No matter how he felt about Austin now, Austin had gone to a great deal of trouble to find Connor and get close to him. There was something he wanted. Maybe Connor was about to find out what that was. This couldn't be all about family. If Austin had only been interested in getting to know his estranged son, he could have introduced himself honestly when they'd first met.

But the rational part of him also insisted he treat the situation like he *was* going to be killed. Because if this was the last chance he had to help his friends, he had better take it.

When Austin gestured for Connor to go upstairs, Connor instead took a step toward him, placing them only inches apart. He could hardly believe what he was doing. Stepping right up to him like this seemed suicidal. But he also didn't know any other way to pull off his plan.

"Get upstairs," Austin demanded.

Connor stood there, eye to eye, for several seconds, before turning and following Austin's instructions.

When they got upstairs, Austin removed Connor's gag. He gestured toward the sofa, told Connor to sit down. Then he locked the cellar door and took a seat himself. The chair he had chosen put him as close to Connor as he could get without actually sitting on the sofa with him. "I wish you hadn't come here."

Connor didn't respond.

"But since you did, there are some things you need to understand. All this isn't what it looks like." Austin put the gun on the chair beside him. Too far away for Connor to grab if he tried. Which he thought about doing.

Austin lifted a mug off the coffee table, which was made of pale, unvarnished wood, and took a sip of what looked like coffee. Connor had been so distracted by the weapon he hadn't noticed the mug until now. It was one of two. Both on coasters, of course.

He assumed the second mug was for him. There was no way he was drinking that coffee, though. God knows what might be in it. After all, it wasn't as if Austin had let him choose which mug he wanted to drink out of.

"It looks like you kidnapped my parents and killed my dad."

Austin sighed. "You need to understand what's really happening here. Frank was not your dad."

"I know."

Austin suddenly looked surprised. "You do?"

"I saw my birth certificate. But he's the man who raised me. Not you. And at least he never killed anybody."

"You know I'm your father?"

Connor didn't feel like elaborating on how he had learned that information, so he shrugged and said, "I put two and two together."

Austin took another sip from his coffee. "Frank had it coming."

"I'm not just talking about him."

"You mean Olin's parents? They had it coming, too."

"Why? What did they do?"

"It's what they didn't do."

"I don't understand."

Austin leaned forward. "Now we're getting somewhere. I think there's probably a lot you don't understand. Fifteen years ago—"

"I already know about Prague."

"You do?" He considered that. "You have been a busy bee, haven't you?"

The comment got under Connor's skin. Had Austin really expected he wouldn't go looking for answers after his parents were kidnapped? Did he think the police were so inept they wouldn't eventually make the connection between the murder in Prague and the abductions in New York?

"Let's skip the history lesson," Connor said. Minutes earlier, he would have warned himself about letting his emotion get the better of him. But he didn't regret saying it. Not one bit. Either Austin was going to kill him or he wasn't. Connor had already cowered before this man once. He wasn't going to do it again. "You were already having an affair with Frank's wife, so you weren't exactly stellar father material to begin with. Then she tried to call it off and you killed her. Am I up to speed enough for you now?"

He saw a flash of anger behind Austin's eyes. "That's where you have it wrong. There was no affair. I didn't kill her. Frank did. Kim and Frank set me up to take the fall. So this—this was payback. It was their turn to spend their lives in a cage. As far as I was concerned, they could stay there until they died of old age. I planned to be there for you. To take their place. To finally have *my* chance to be your father. I was never going to tell you how we were related, but I figured with time you would come to see me as family anyway."

Connor tried to wrap his head around this. He wasn't sure whether to believe Austin. Was it like Olivia had said? Had all those years behind bars twisted his memory? *No*, Connor thought, *they didn't*. He knew Austin well enough to know he wasn't crazy. Even as part of Connor rebelled against the idea that Frank and his mom had killed Frank's wife and conspired to frame Austin, he knew there was something true about what Austin was saying. And it was enough to make him lean back and listen—really listen—to what Austin had to say next.

"I made sure you were taken care of, didn't I?"

"What are you talking about?"

"Do you think that money you found on the dining room table just came out of nowhere?"

Austin was talking about the money that was now stashed away in the back of Connor's sock drawer. Thinking about the money also made him think about Roland. Whatever secrets he and Frank had, there was now no doubt in Connor's mind that he wasn't involved in this.

But there was that word: secrets. This whole thing was about secrets. And didn't it make it just a little more plausible that if Frank had secrets with Roland, he had darker secrets, as well?

Yes, it did.

Then Connor remembered something else. There was a question he had been asking himself since the night of the abduction. In the big picture, it didn't matter very much. But he still wanted to know, and this seemed like it might be his only opportunity to find out. "How did you get into the house so fast?"

Austin leaned forward, resting his elbows on his knees and intertwining his fingers. "I'm not very proud of that. It's the only time I've ever manipulated you, and I'm sorry for that. But it was necessary."

"What do you mean?"

"Remember when I told you I kept a spare key hidden under a statue here in case I got locked out? And I asked if you did something similar at your house?"

Connor hadn't thought about that conversation since it had happened. At the time, it had seemed just like one man giving advice to another. Now he saw it for what it really was. "And I told you we had a fake rock hidden in the bushes by the door."

"Kim told me that's where her mom hid hers when she was growing up, so I thought she would probably do the same thing, too. But I needed to be sure."

"How did you get out?"

"What do you mean?"

"Of prison. In the Czech Republic."

"I would rather not talk about that."

"You want to be my dad. You want me to trust you. Tell me how you got out."

Austin looked down, shook his head, then took a sip of his coffee. "You should try it." He nodded at the second mug. "It's good."

Connor didn't respond.

"Do you remember when you were four, you wanted to know what I did at work? And when I told you I was a programmer, you asked me what that was?"

"No."

"Anyway, we sat down at the computer together and I taught you just enough so you could write an if/then statement on your own. You were so excited. I'm glad to see you're still using those skills."

That part Connor remembered. But up until now, he would have sworn it was Frank he had been sitting with.

"In those days, I was as a senior software engineer for the city," Austin said. "My primary job was upgrading and maintaining the code used by the New York Independent System Operator."

Connor suspected he looked confused, because the next thing Austin said was: "I wouldn't expect you to know who they are. Not a lot of people do. It's complicated, but basically, they manage the flow of electricity up and down most of the East Coast."

If Austin had stopped right there, Connor would have had enough information to sketch together the basics of what had occurred—it was a horrifying thought—but he kept going. "While I was in jail, I met a man named Aden Tindol. He was the only other American I ever saw there. He said he was Army. Busted for solicitation. He was out after only a few days. I figured he would forget about me a week after he was gone. But then, about a year ago, he paid me a visit. Said if he got me out would I be willing to do something for him.

"I wish I could tell you I asked what it was. I wish I could tell you I even cared. But I just wanted so badly to be back here with you that I would have done anything."

"What did he want you to do?"

Austin wasn't ready to answer that question yet. "You know, when it all went down, I asked Mark and Hillary for help. They could have afforded to get me a good lawyer, but they bought into Frank and Kim's story and just turned their backs on me. I had known them for ten years and they didn't even consider the possibility that I might be innocent. If they had helped me back then, none of this would have happened."

Connor knew Mark and Hillary were Olin's parents. Another piece of the puzzle fell into place. But he wasn't going to let go of the question he had asked before, so he repeated it. "What did this Aden Tindol want you to do?"

"He wanted to see if I could take out the city's power for a while."

It was exactly what Connor thought he was going to say. He also now realized it was why Austin had wanted him to come home early. He hadn't had anything to talk to Connor about—he'd just been trying to get him out of harm's way. Not that it did anything to make up for all the horrible things he had done.

"Aden said he would get me out and set me up with enough cash to start over."

"That's how you bought the house you're flipping now?"

Austin nodded. "He told me it would be smart to stay off the grid. That meant no company paperwork, no nine-to-five job."

"And that's how you were paying me, too, wasn't it?"

Austin nodded again.

Connor didn't have to ask if the money Austin had left for him at the house had also come from Aden. "Did you know what he was going to do when you shut down the city?"

"No, I didn't. I didn't think the power outage was the end game, but I didn't think it would be as bad as it was." Austin paused, then added, "I tried to stop him. Before everything went down, I found a guy. Carlos something. Took about a month, visiting sketchy bars at night and discreetly asking around. He was supposed to go into Aden's liquor store and take him out. I told him to make it look like a robbery gone wrong. I hoped to put an end to this whole thing before it started. But he screwed it up.

"Aden had told me what would happen if I didn't go through with my end of the bargain. He would kill you and me both, he said. So at that point I didn't have any choice."

Connor took a deep breath, tried to process all of the information. Then he asked perhaps the only question that really mattered right now. "What are you going to do with all of us?"

CHAPTER 58

DYLAN WAS TERRIFIED Austin would shoot Connor when he turned around and got right up in Austin's face. She couldn't figure out what he was thinking. Not even she would do something like that. Then she saw him contort his right hand, trying to move it only at the wrist and get it into his pocket. And she immediately understood. When Connor had lifted his legs earlier and shaken his hips, he had been trying to get something out. Now he was trying again.

"Get upstairs," Austin demanded.

Connor stayed nose-to-nose with Austin while he worked the hand around in his pocket, pulled out a pocketknife, and flicked it over to Dylan. It hit her chest with a soft thump—too soft to hear, she suspected—and slid down to her waist.

Her first instinct was to move, shake it off, hide it under her thigh. But that would be a lot of activity. It would draw Austin's attention, for sure. Connor had put himself at great risk to get her that knife. The best thing she could do was stay still and hope Austin didn't look down.

She didn't realize Olin was looking at her, had probably seen the whole series of events unfold, until Austin and Connor were upstairs. He glanced at the knife and then his eyes returned to meet hers. He nodded. The message: *Go for it.*

Behind Dylan, Kim was making excited noises through her gag.

Apparently, she had seen Connor toss her the knife, too.

No shit I'll go for it, Dylan would have responded, if she could speak.

She shook the knife off, then trapped it between her thigh and the floor and slid it back an inch. She lifted her leg, repositioned, and slid it another inch. The process was painfully slow, but eventually she could feel the knife with the tip of one finger. One more push, and she was able to grab it between her pointer and middle finger.

Cutting through the rope was challenging. Twice she slipped and nicked her hand. Olin watched anxiously, unable to see what she was doing from his angle. Kim, who likely had a better view, made sounds of encouragement.

Dylan pressed her wrists against the rope while she cut to keep it taut. Finally, she cut through enough of the rope that the remaining fibers snapped and her wrists sprang apart. She untied the bandana Austin had used for a gag and spat out the sock. Then she untied Olin and, while he was removing his own gag, grabbed the keys Austin had left on the table by the stairs and unlocked the cage Kim was in.

Whispering, each asked the other if they were okay, and determined, considering the circumstances, they were all holding up about as well as could be expected. Kim, of course, was in the worst shape. But because of that, she also seemed like she was the most angry, the most ready to do whatever it took to escape.

"Let me see if I can figure out what's going on up there," Dylan said. "You guys stay here. I don't want to make too much noise on those stairs."

Olin and Kim looked at each other. Olin nodded. "Okay."

Dylan crept up the stairs slowly, stopping every time one of them creaked. When she reached the top, she put an ear against the door and listened. She could hear voices. It sounded like Austin was doing most of the talking, but she couldn't make out the words. He and Connor were too far away from the cellar door.

As much as she wished she could hear what they were saying, she was glad he and Connor weren't standing right outside the door. At least it gave her a chance to get Olin and Kim upstairs without being seen.

She turned the knob to see if the door was unlocked. It wasn't. But that wasn't going to stop her. She knew how to pick more than one type of lock. It was a skill she had learned when she was a teenager, going through what her mother called her "spy phase." At first, her mother had thought it was cute. "You're going to be our very own double-oh-seven," she would tease. That came to a halt when Dylan had gotten caught trying to steal a can of cranberry sauce from the Whole Foods near her house. Dylan had insisted she was just practicing what she had learned. She said spies had to do all sorts of things, and she wanted some real-world experience. Her mom had believed her because it was, well, a can of cranberry sauce. But that didn't make it any better.

Dylan pulled two of her bobby pins out of her hair. She slid one into the keyhole and fiddled with the lock's pins until they were all in place, then used the second bobby pin to turn the lock. Easy as pie.

She pinned her hair back into place, turned the knob. She let the door swing open only a few inches before she stopped it. Just enough to get a peek at the main floor.

She could see Connor sitting on a sofa, facing her. He didn't seem to notice she had opened the door. Austin was sitting in a chair facing him. He would have to turn almost all the way around to see her.

She quietly pulled the door shut and went back downstairs. "They're both up there."

"What are they doing?" Olin said.

"They're in the living room. Just talking, it looks like."

"What about?"

"I don't know. I couldn't hear much."

"What are we going to do?" Kim said.

Olin looked up the stairs. "I think we should stay here. We can wait until he comes back down and then take him by surprise."

Dylan shook her head. "No way. We don't know where this is going. Connor took a risk getting me that knife. We can't take a chance that Austin will kill him before he comes back down for us."

"What do you suggest?" Olin said.

"I'll go back up there first. You two stay right behind me. They're far enough away from the door that he won't hear us coming up the stairs. Then, as long as they're still sitting where they were before, we should be able to sneak up on Austin from behind."

"What about the gun?"

"We'll figure it out."

Kim didn't seem to like that answer.

"We have to do *something*."

"Damn straight we do. I still need to know what he's done with my parents." Olin held out his hand. "Lead the way."

Just before Dylan went up the stairs, she turned to Kim. "Actually, I want you to stay back. Let Olin and me handle this."

"What? Why? That's my son up there."

And that was exactly the problem. Kim had lost her husband, might lose her son. Add to that the fact that she had been locked up for a long time in that little cage, and Dylan didn't trust her to keep her cool. But she didn't want to tell Kim that, so she said, "If something goes wrong, we'll need another shot, and you might be all we've got."

Kim needed barely a second to think about it. She nodded.

Dylan nodded back. She led Olin up the stairs, being just as slow and careful as she had been the first time. "I'm going to take a quick peek first, just to make sure nothing's changed," she said once she reached the door.

Olin was right behind her and biting down on his lower lip almost hard enough to draw blood. He gestured for her to go ahead.

"Okay, here we go." She opened the door.

CHAPTER 59

WHAT ARE YOU *going to do with all of us?* Connor had asked, and Austin still hadn't answered it. He sipped his coffee, seemed like he was about to say something, and then sipped again. Finally, he spoke. "I guess that depends on you."

"What do you mean?"

"I can't let them go. You know that. But you and I—we can still start over if you would like to."

Connor was about to tell Austin that he wasn't going to let him kill his friends when he saw the cellar door creep all the way open. Dylan and Olin stepped out. They looked like they had a plan, like they were counting on him to be a distraction, so he played along. "I get it. After what my mom and Frank did to you . . ." He nodded thoughtfully. "I can't lose my whole family. If we have to get rid of Olin and Dylan, too, so there aren't any witness, then I guess that's what we have to do."

Austin was looking at him funny. Like he could tell something about Connor's answer wasn't right. Had Connor agreed with him too quickly? He wasn't sure. But it also didn't matter. While he was talking, Dylan and Olin had quietly crossed the room and were now standing directly behind Austin.

They grabbed him. Austin screamed, started to fight, reached for the gun, but Connor grabbed it first. Then Austin twisted and flipped out of the chair and got free of Olin and Dylan. "What the hell?" he screamed, stumbling backward as he tried to find his balance.

"Where are my parents?" Olin demanded.

Balance restored, Austin lunged at Olin even as Connor shouted to get his attention. They fell to the floor, each fighting to be the man on top. When Austin managed to pin Olin down, Dylan jumped on top of him, wrapping her arms around him and trying to pin his arms to his side, but he shook her off.

Connor fired a shot into the ceiling. "Hey!"

Everyone turned to face him.

Although they all looked surprised, Austin was the only one who also looked bewildered. Probably because Connor now had the gun aimed at him. "Son, what are you doing?"

"Son?" Now Dylan looked a little bewildered, too.

"It's a long story." To Austin: "Get the hell off him."

"But . . . what about what you just told me?"

"Why do you think I told you that? Get off him."

Austin reluctantly stood up, took several steps back so as not to crowd Olin when he, too, got to his feet.

"Where are my parents?" Olin said again.

"Tell him," Connor said.

Austin glanced nervously between Connor and Olin. "They died. In a fire."

"In a fire you set," Connor clarified.

Olin's face twisted with rage. "You son of a—"

Connor could tell he was about to launch himself onto Austin again, so he fired another shot into the ceiling to regain control of the situation. "That's not the way we're going to handle this."

"Why not?" Olin sounded like he was doing everything he could to control his anger.

"I don't want you going to jail."

Olin looked at Dylan as if asking for a second opinion, and she gestured as if to say she agreed.

"We need some rope," Connor said.

Dylan crossed to the cellar door. "Come on up!" she shouted. "And bring some rope with you."

Kim emerged, holding a length of rope in one hand. It was so long that it dragged on the floor behind her.

Connor figured it must have been one of the ropes Austin had used to tie them up. Fitting, he thought, that they were now going to use that same rope on him.

While Connor kept the gun aimed at his father, Olin bound Austin's hands. Then, as Connor looked around for something to tie him to so he couldn't escape—the handle of the stove, perhaps—he had a better idea.

They weren't just going to use Austin's rope.

He shoved Austin forward to get him moving. "This way," Connor said, directing him toward the cellar door. "Let's go."

CHAPTER 60

CONNOR FOUND HIS cellphone on the kitchen counter. He used it to call Olivia, gave her the address for the cabin, told her they would be there waiting. She asked where Austin was, and Connor responded only by saying that she didn't have to worry about him. He wasn't going anywhere.

The reason he wasn't going anywhere, Olivia found out when she arrived, was that Connor and his friends had locked Austin in a cage in the cellar. "They are the cages he kept my parents in," Connor explained. "That's where they've been this whole time."

Olivia had arrived with half a dozen black-and-whites in tow for backup and a second detective Connor didn't recognize but Olin did.

"That's the man who was working my case," Olin said when he saw him.

The detective looked like he had stepped right off one of those CSI shows—tailored suit, trim, his hair just so. He walked up to Olin. "So they found his parents," he said, gesturing to Connor. "What about yours?"

Olin couldn't get the words out, so Connor stepped in to explain what had happened.

The detective's only response was, "Shit. I'm sorry." At least he sounded sincere when he said it.

Getting back to a normal life was difficult. Connor followed the news for a while, hoping the police would catch the bombers. At first, things seemed promising. Using blast-radius technology and video surveillance from Albright Mall, they were able to identify a man named Logan Wright as their prime suspect and even made an arrest. So at least there was that. The other four bombers, though, would likely never be found. The talking heads on the major news networks speculated one or all of them might be dead, but there was no way to know for sure.

Olivia checked in with him and his mom regularly while she wrapped up her investigation. Mostly crossing the Ts and dotting the Is. Matt, or Austin as he now called himself, was in jail. Frank was dead. So the only thing that seemed to really be in doubt was who had killed Frank's wife, Heather, in Prague. Connor wasn't sure how much that mattered anymore. The story Roland had told Olivia tracked almost entirely with the one Austin had told him. The only difference was that, according to Roland, Frank had operated alone.

He never got the details of the murder, though. Those Olivia kept to herself. Connor didn't need to know them and didn't want to. All he cared to hear was that his mother was innocent.

Frank's motive: That was simple enough. Kim made good money as a doctor and had inherited even more. Frank had wanted the lifestyle she could provide, and had set out to leverage the grief Kim believed they shared to get it.

When Connor asked Olivia why she hadn't told him Matt had been set up the night she called to warn him he had escaped from prison, she said she hadn't been able to confirm whether it was true and didn't want to alarm him unnecessarily if it wasn't. Besides, no matter who had killed Heather Callahan, Matt had abducted Frank and Kim, and at the time she was convinced Connor might be in danger as well.

The details of the murder Olivia put into her case notes, of course. And, if Roland was to be believed, it had been surprisingly simple.

Roland said Frank had ordered room service the night before and stashed the steak knife they'd delivered with the meal in his suitcase. He had also ordered fresh towels that morning and every morning previous to get an idea of how long it would take room service to come. The answer was, on average, ten minutes. So the morning of the murder, with the steak knife hidden in his suitcase, he waited until Heather was in the shower, then called Matt and asked him to come over to the room. Frank needed to run down to the little shop in the lobby, he said, and asked if Matt could wait for the towels that were on their way. He made a point of being vague about what he needed, trusting Matt's imagination to fill in the blank, and even then he knew the request probably sounded odd. But Matt was a friend, so even though he seemed a little confused by the whole thing, he agreed to wait.

Then Frank took the elevator down to the first floor, grabbed a toothbrush from the lobby shop (it was the first thing he saw), and, as he exited the hotel, made a point of waving to the receptionist.

He came back in through a side door he had scouted out on their first day and took the stairs back up to the twelfth floor. The towels had arrived while he was gone. He thanked Matt, sent him back to his room.

When the murder was complete and he had showered off the blood, he left the same way he had come and meandered around the city long enough to make sure the maids found the body.

As he had hoped, the facts seemed to fit perfectly with his story of an affair. Bada-bing, bada-boom. Matt was in jail. Frank was married to Kim. And little Connor was already starting to forget he'd had a father before Frank had entered the picture.

There were only two questions Olivia felt like she couldn't answer by the time she closed the file, but neither mattered all that much.

The first was why Matt had been released from prison early. Oldrich had never given her a good answer, because unbeknownst to her, he had questioned the chief about the bribe and was told, quite pointedly, to keep his trap shut. The chief was tired of not getting his, he said. And what did it matter anyway? They were Americans. In other words—not his problem.

The second was what had motivated Aden to organize the attack. Matt didn't know, he said. Aden had kept everything compartmentalized. But, at least in this case, she had a theory. A search of Aden's computer pointed strongly to a website called BeyondUnderstanding.com. The name sounded like hippie bullshit. But when she browsed the content, she noticed a lot of cult-like language that endorsed mayhem as the route to freeing society from its "materialistic bonds."

Kim struggled with her emotions. She was angry with Matt and Frank and, maybe most of all, herself. She cursed herself for believing Matt would cheat on her, then cursed Matt for locking her in a cage. She cursed herself for spending the last fifteen years with Frank, then Frank for putting all this in motion.

At least her brother Henry had come back up from Florida to help her through it.

Connor was surprised when, this time, the big man gave him a hug. But he was dealing with a lot of the same issues his mother was and probably looked like he needed it.

When Henry finally released Connor, he looked over at Olin, who was standing on the far side of the living room, and said, "Who's this?"

Connor told him and added that Olin would be staying with them for a while.

"As long as he needs to," Kim clarified.

But the invitation to stay had not come immediately. Connor had been in touch with Olin and Dylan regularly after they got back from Austin's cabin, but had put most of his energy into dealing with his own emotions and making sure his mom was okay.

All things considered, Dylan seemed to be managing (which didn't surprise Connor), and Connor was glad to hear the police had been able to track down Olin's car.

But eventually Connor had learned Olin wasn't handling things as well as he pretended to be. He didn't have any family outside of his parents and, like Connor, no close friends. It was him and his pain, alone in the house twenty-four-seven. That wasn't okay, so Connor had asked Kim about having Olin come and stay, and Kim had readily agreed.

The only thing Connor wasn't sure how to handle was the money Austin had left him. (Even though Connor had come to terms with the fact that Matt and Austin were the same person, he still referred to him as Matt when he was talking about the time before Prague and as Austin when referring to recent events.) Austin had only had that money because people had died, and Connor didn't want anything to do with it. But he couldn't bring himself to throw it away, either.

No matter how it had come to him, it still had value.

Maybe for some more than others, though. Because there was one other victim in this whole thing. Two, actually. Adriana and her daughter.

Connor had a suspicion the "Carlos" Austin had told him about was Adriana's husband. And when Dylan, who seemed to be pretty good at tracking down information on the web, confirmed he was the man who had robbed Aden's liquor store, he was certain of it.

The only problem was Adriana had said she didn't want to see Connor again, and he doubted she would answer the door no matter how long he stood there knocking. Leaving the cash in an envelope on her porch wasn't a good idea, either. Odds were it would be gone before she ever had a chance to find it.

However, there was one more option. Adriana might not open the door for Connor, but she might open it for someone else.

He was right.

When Kim knocked, Adriana answered right away.

From the car, Connor couldn't hear what the two women said, but the body language told him everything he needed to know. After waving her hands in front of her chest and shaking her head, Adriana finally accepted the money. She looked down at it like she couldn't believe it was real.

"You did a good thing," Olin said, who had come along for the drive.

Connor didn't respond until he saw Adriana hug Kim and close the door. "I'm just glad all this is over."

Then Kim got back in the car, and Connor saw something he hadn't seen in a long time. Kim was smiling. It was like a glimpse into a world that used to be and, he now knew, could be again.

It was just a matter of time.

Things are just getting started for Connor and his friends.

Get the sequel *A Good Plan* here:

http://reagankeeter.com/agoodplan

Turn the page to start Connor's next adventure right now.

A GOOD PLAN

CHAPTER 1

DYLAN SAT AT a table in the corner of Cafe de Flore, a small, French-style eatery right in the heart of Midtown Atlanta. The food was served on small plates and cost too much. It was all very chic. And *very* crowded.

Dylan's cell phone was sitting face-up on the table. She tapped the screen, noted the time. Aleshia was late. That wasn't like her. Dylan told herself not to worry. Aleshia would have called if anything was wrong.

They'd been friends for two years now, and Dylan imagined Aleshia was the kind of girl she would be friends with all her life. She had a lot of spunk, a little sass. Dylan liked that, perhaps because they had those things in common.

She took a sip from her coffee and looked toward the door.

Dylan had met Aleshia while working at this very cafe. It was the first job she had gotten after moving down here, and she had needed the money.

Aleshia, however, was just killing time while she figured out what she wanted to do with her life. She was the daughter of Andrew Thompson, a world-renowned impressionist who'd been covered by all the major publications many times over and still—even after his death—had a standing exhibit at the National Gallery of Art in Washington, DC.

In other words, he was loaded.

It had not always been that way. When Maddie—his first daughter—was born, Andrew was an art teacher at Middleton High School. In those days, he and his wife could barely afford one child. Had he not become a national sensation, they would likely never have had a second.

But he did (albeit fifteen years later), and as one of two heirs, now Aleshia was loaded, too.

It was because of Maddie that Dylan was meeting her here today. Maddie had disappeared a month ago. Aleshia put in a missing person report with the police but that had gone nowhere, so Dylan told her she would see what she could find out.

This wouldn't be the first missing person Dylan had helped locate, she'd said. What she didn't mention was that when she had done it before, she hadn't done it alone. She had help from her friends Connor and Olin. Having turned up nothing on Maddie so far, however, she wished she could call on them again.

But Dylan had moved to Atlanta after graduating college because she was tired of the cold, and New York was just too far away.

Dylan tried to call Aleshia to see where she was. The phone rang three times, then rolled over to voicemail. She didn't bother to leave a message. Instead, she gave it another thirty minutes, paid her check, and headed for the door.

If Aleshia wasn't here by now, she wasn't coming.

Dylan was on edge all the way to Aleshia's house.

Two months before Maddie had gone missing, someone tried to mug her in a parking lot outside the Ink Well.

The Ink Well was an art studio in the suburbs. It had a small gallery in the front and a large, open room where Sofia, who owned the studio, taught classes on weekends. Maddie was one of her students.

Dylan knew about the attack because Aleshia had told her, and she knew the details because Sofia had filled them in.

As the story went, Maddie was halfway to her car when a masked man came out of nowhere and attacked her. He was all over her, grabbing her arms, her purse. She'd screamed and fought back and eventually managed to work her pepper spray out of her bag. She'd fired the pepper spray at her attacker, and then he started screaming as well. He backed away, and an old Ford rolled up beside them. The attacker fumbled his way into the front passenger seat, and the driver took off.

At the time, the attack seemed like nothing more than a robbery gone wrong. After Maddie went missing, though, it took on new dimensions. Was the attacker really after *her*, not her purse? If so, why? Had he come back? Tried again?

According to the police, they reviewed the footage from the parking lot, but it was a dead end. The attacker could have been anyone. They couldn't clearly see the driver, and the car had exited the lot in a way that never revealed the license plate.

And now Dylan had another question: *Had Aleshia been taken, too?*

Dylan told herself she was worrying for nothing.

She pulled up to a modest house in a quiet Dunwoody neighborhood. People who'd known Aleshia's father would have been surprised to find her living here. They would have expected something with more flair, more drama. Dylan, however, thought the gray-and-white bungalow suited Aleshia perfectly. It offered plenty of space, didn't draw a lot of attention. After spending her childhood in the public eye, the last thing Aleshia wanted was more attention.

Dylan noticed Aleshia's BMW in the driveway. She made her way up the stone steps to the front door and knocked. When no one answered, she tried calling Aleshia again. Like before, the call went to voicemail. She stepped off the porch, moved along the side of the house, and squeezed between the shrubbery so she could get close to the window. She had to hold her hands over her eyes like a visor, blocking out the sun, to see anything. Even then, the blinds obscured most of her view.

Oh, God, she thought, once she could make out what she was looking at. This was bad. She should have called Connor, after all.

She pulled her cell phone out of her pocket and dialed a number.

CHAPTER 2

THE TWO-BEDROOM apartment in Manhattan was tight. It was also almost exactly as far from Connor's office as it was from Olin's, which had a lot to do with why they had selected it as opposed to the more spacious options they'd seen that were farther from the city.

Each bedroom was barely big enough for a bed and a nightstand, so Connor and Olin had agreed Connor could set up a small desk in the living room. It was at that desk that Connor was sitting now.

When Connor was in college, he had imagined himself getting a job at Google or Facebook. Any prestigious firm, really, would have been fine. When it came to computers, he certainly had the skill for it. But life hadn't shaken out that way. Instead, he was refactoring code for a small shop called TexRaid in the data analytics space.

Connor had tried on more than one occasion to explain to Olin the specifics of what the firm did. Olin, whose degree was in finance and who (perhaps inevitably) had taken a job as an accountant at another small company, didn't get it. Neither did most people outside of the tech space, Connor had come to realize. So, these days, he simply stuck with calling it "data analytics," which was usually enough to avoid any follow-up questions.

All that was fine with Connor, since he, too, found the work boring.

In college, Connor had entertained himself by hacking into

strangers' websites and disrupting their service. Not just anybody's site, mind you. Just those he determined were promoting violence, encouraging cult-like behavior, or disseminating lies he considered harmful for society. He felt a rush when he was doing that, driven by the idea that he was one of the good guys fighting back the evils of the world.

How could the day-to-day grind of any job compare with that?

It was the question Connor asked himself whenever he felt like quitting, followed by: *Where else would I go?* It wasn't as if another firm, even a Google or a Facebook, would be any different.

So, on some nights—those like tonight, when that longing for more meaningful work overtook him—he would fire up his laptop and hunt down the same kinds of websites he had in college.

Olin never asked what he was doing at the computer. Connor suspected he didn't want to know. He also never asked Connor if he would like to watch a basketball game—which was what Olin, who was sitting on the sofa with the TV on, was doing tonight. Connor had no interest in sports.

They shared the occasional conversation, acknowledging each other without talking about either's specific interest. That's probably how the whole night would have gone had Connor's cell phone not rung.

The caller ID read "Dylan Naese."

Dylan had entered Connor's life through the same tragic events that brought Olin into it, and even though Connor did not live with her, he felt his bond with her was just as close.

He looked at the time. It was after ten p.m. Too late for her to be calling. But she was also a night owl. He picked up the phone and crossed the apartment to his bedroom to get away from the TV.

"What's up?"

"Can you—" She stopped short, sounded like she was choking up. "Connor, I've got a problem. Can you come to Atlanta?"

He felt the hairs on his arms stand up as his mind raced through all the horrible things that might have happened to her. "What's going on, Dylan? Are you okay?"

"I'm fine. You know, as fine as I can be. Considering . . ."

"Considering what?"

"I have a friend whose sister went missing about a month ago."

That was bad enough, but Connor could tell Dylan wasn't done. He held his breath, waited.

"Now she's gone, too."

This all reminded Connor too much of what he had been through before. He could feel himself getting lightheaded. He sat down on the edge of his bed. "Are you sure? How long ago did you find out your friend was missing?"

"This morning."

"Well, maybe she's—"

"She hasn't been answering her phone all day. She's not texting me back. She's not at home. Something's wrong."

Okay, that didn't sound good. "You've gone to the police, right?"

"They went by her house to do a wellness check. Since she wasn't there, that was a big waste of time. And when I told them I wanted to file a missing person report, they told me I had to wait twenty-four hours. Can you come—help me figure out what happened to her? I can't sit around and just wait for the police. They still haven't found her sister, and, well, I'm worried."

Connor nodded to himself. *Yes, of course, I'll come*, he thought, as his gaze shifted to the window and the night sky beyond it. Somewhere in the back of his mind, he could feel himself already plotting the trip.

"I'll get a flight out in the morning. File a missing person report as soon as you can. At least it will put her on their radar."

"Okay, I will. Thank you."

"I'll call you as soon as I land." Connor hung up. He hurried back into the living room. "Olin."

"One second," Olin said, leaning forward, watching a player in a white jersey bounce the basketball as he prepared for a free throw.

Connor moved in front of the TV.

"What are you doing?"

"That was Dylan. She needs our help."

The look of annoyance on Olin's face immediately transformed into concern. "What do you mean?"

Connor relayed the story Dylan had told him. "I'm flying out in the morning. Are you coming?"

"What about work?"

"Seriously? Tell them you're sick. Who cares? It's Dylan. Just come up with something."

Olin licked his lips. A twitch turned into a nod. "Yeah. I mean— yeah, you're right. I'll come up with something."

Connor then went to his computer to search for plane tickets. The earliest flight he could find that had room for him and Olin departed at four o'clock tomorrow afternoon. It would have to do. He had no idea how long they would be gone, so he made reservations for only one way.

CHAPTER 3

CONNOR SQUEEZED ENOUGH clothes for a week into a carry-on and tried to get some sleep. It didn't come easily. He tossed and turned. He would force his eyes closed, and they would pop back open.

He kept thinking back to his parents' abduction: the man driving up onto the lawn, attacking Connor's parents in their home, and loading them into the back of his van.

For a long time, he had thought about that horrible event every day. Although time had dulled the sharpest edges of the memory, the months that followed that event had changed him forever.

Now, here he was again—facing a mystery that he knew would take him places he didn't want to go and force him to see things he didn't want to see. If he could, he would turn his back on it. Let the police solve it. Every missing person couldn't be his problem.

But Dylan had asked . . .

He got out of bed and went to the kitchen to make some chamomile tea. That would usually help him sleep, calm his dreams. He wouldn't be any good tomorrow if he didn't get some sleep.

There was a half wall that separated the kitchen from the living room and three bar stools on this side of it. Olin was sitting on one of them in a pair of plaid pajama pants, nursing a beer.

"Can't sleep either, huh?" Connor asked.

Olin spun around, startled. He must not have heard Connor open his bedroom door. He immediately calmed down once he saw who it was. "No, I guess not."

Connor filled a kettle with water from the sink and put it on the stove. "You're thinking about . . ." He let the question hang in the air. It was easier for them both if they didn't speak directly about the events that had bound them together.

Olin shrugged.

"It's not going to be like that," Connor said.

"How do you know?"

Connor didn't. But dwelling on how things might go wrong wasn't going to help either of them. Wasn't that the whole reason he'd come into the kitchen to make tea? To clear his head? To push out the bad thoughts? To get some rest? Sometimes the best you can do is tell yourself, "This time it will be better." Tonight was one of those times.

Olin's gaze shifted to the Budweiser in front of him. He picked at the corner of the label with one fingernail. He took a deep breath, a sip of his beer. Connor wasn't sure Olin got his point until he said, "You're right. Things are going to be fine." Then he directed the conversation toward the new *Avengers* movie, and Connor changed gears right along with him.

He was happy to pretend for a while that tonight was like any other.

When he finally went to bed—groggy from the tea and his mind calmed from the conversation—he was able to get the sleep he knew he needed.

His last thought before he nodded off was, *This time it will be better.*

CHAPTER 4

CONNOR AND OLIN stepped off the escalator in the Atlanta airport near the baggage carousels and saw Dylan standing in the waiting area.

Connor hadn't been face-to-face with her since she'd come up to New York to visit them six months ago. She'd looked well. Atlanta agreed with her, he had said.

Today, he felt like he was standing in front of a different woman. Dylan had her hair pulled back into a ponytail, which probably drew more attention than she wanted to her bloodshot eyes. She looked tired. Weak. Her flannel shirt was wrinkled and stained. When they hugged, she collapsed into Connor.

"It's going to be okay," he said, with more confidence than he felt.

Her head was pressed to his chest. He felt her nod.

She hugged Olin next. When she let go, she wiped her eyes with the heel of her hand. "You probably want to go to a hotel first, right? Get settled?"

Connor and Olin looked at each other. "No," Connor said. "We can do that later. Take us to Aleshia's house."

"Why there?"

"Do you have a better place to start?" When Dylan didn't answer, he added, "I'd like to see what we're dealing with."

Dylan led Connor and Olin to an old white Volvo in the parking deck. The interior was a mess. Fast-food wrappers littered the floor. A makeup bag was poking out of the center console. Hairbands and bobby pins were everywhere.

Olin made a face as he pushed the fast-food wrappers aside and climbed into the back seat. Connor pretended not to notice.

Dylan drove them to a small house in the suburbs. She parked along the curb.

"This is it?" Olin asked, gesturing toward the house.

"Yes."

Connor saw a BMW in the driveway. "There's a car here."

"That's Aleshia's. It was here yesterday, also."

"All right," Connor said. "Here we go." He got out first and headed straight for the front porch. Dylan and Olin fell in behind him. He pounded on the door.

"What are you doing?" Dylan said. "I told you—she's not here."

"I know. But before we start looking in her windows, I just want to be sure no one else is either."

When no one answered the door, Connor squeezed through the shrubs along the side of the house, exactly like Dylan had done the day before. Since it was just after seven o'clock, the sun had already set, meaning he did not need to try to block it out like she had.

The darkness, however, presented its own complications, and getting closer to the window hadn't improved his visibility.

Connor pulled his cell phone out of his pocket. He clicked the flashlight app, hoping it would help. It didn't. Not much, anyway. No matter how he angled it, the blinds blocked out most of the light.

He sighed. "We've already lost a day." Then, to Dylan: "Were you able to put in a missing person report on Aleshia finally?"

"Yeah, but—"

"I know," Connor said, as he slid back between the shrubs. "At least it's done." He stepped onto the porch, looked at the front door. "The police probably aren't coming back here anytime soon."

"So, what do you want to do?" Olin asked.

Connor looked at him. "I think you know what we have to do."

Olin groaned.

"What?" Dylan asked.

Connor tried the doorknob. The door was locked. Then he shined his light on the ground around the porch to see if he could find one of those fake rocks people sometimes hid a key in. He had one outside his house growing up, so maybe he would find one here, too. When he didn't, he gestured for Dylan and Olin to follow him. "Come on." He walked around the gray-and-white bungalow to the backyard.

He tried to open the first set of windows. They wouldn't budge. Neither would those on the other side of the back door, or the back door itself. The house was locked up tight.

"We're *not* breaking in," Olin said, glancing at the surrounding houses.

"No, I guess we're not," Connor said, disappointed.

"What do you want to get inside for?" Dylan asked. "I already know she's not there."

"I wanted to see what we could find out. It doesn't sound like the police are going to go in there looking for clues anytime soon, and right now, I can't think of anything better we could do to find out what happened to her."

Dylan considered that. "Hold on." She scurried away.

Olin got a worried look on his face. Connor suspected they both knew what she was about to do.

Dylan returned less than a minute later with a pair of bobby pins she'd no doubt found on the floor of her car. "I can get us into the house," she said, as she twisted the bobby pins into place and then wiggled them into the lock on the back door.

Dylan had learned a lot of unusual skills when she was going through her "spy phase" as a teenager. Picking locks was one of them. It had come in handy for Connor before, and he was glad to see she had kept it up.

"We shouldn't be doing this," Olin said.

"Aleshia's my best friend. She'd want me to."

"What if the alarm's set?" There were ADT signs by both the front and back doors, so there was no question Aleshia had one.

"It's fine. Even if it is, I know the code."

Dylan continued to apply pressure to the cylinder until it rotated as far as it would go. Then she slid the bobby pins back into the pocket of her jeans and turned the knob. The door opened.

Connor followed Dylan inside. He heard Olin—who, no doubt, was still unhappy about what they were doing—step in behind him.

The living room featured modest furniture and a warm feel. A sofa was positioned along one wall and a TV stand was pressed up against the wall opposite. There was barely enough space between them for the rustic coffee table that occupied it. Most of the art looked uninspired— kind of like what you might expect to find in a hotel room.

Most of it.

Among the small, store-bought paintings that hung in a mosaic above the sofa, there was one that gave Connor chills. The frame hung from a rope. The woman in it was wearing a blue dress and sitting in a cafe. The left side of her face seemed to be melting off.

Connor could tell this was an original.

"That's one of Maddie's," Dylan said. "The one to the left of it is their father's."

Connor shifted his attention to the painting beside it and realized what he had mistakenly assumed was one of many generic prints was actually another original. The watercolor of two men walking along a cobblestone street was so meticulously detailed that the rain gathering in puddles by their feet looked almost real.

"You'd never guess how much that thing is worth," Dylan said.

Connor had no doubt that was true. He didn't know much about art.

He turned his attention back to the room. Clothes were strewn about. Loose hangers littered the floor. Books and magazines were stacked up in an unorderly heap on the coffee table. The place was a mess, but not the kind that would point to foul play.

Dylan seemed to know what he was thinking. "There's more," she said, and led Connor and Olin toward the dining room. From its position in the house, Connor could tell this was the room he was trying to see into from outside.

Dylan turned on the light.

The chair closest to the window was pulled back from the large ebony table that filled the space. The place was set with a plate, a fork, and a glass of milk. On the plate was a half-eaten omelet. There was an assortment of makeup on the table around it—lipstick, foundation, eyeliner—and a freestanding mirror to apply it. Two other chairs were askew, with more clothes hanging over them.

"That's what I saw yesterday," Dylan said. "That's how I knew something was wrong. Aleshia might not be good about her clothes, but she would never leave food out like that. And she certainly wouldn't go anywhere without her purse."

Connor noticed the Louis Vuitton bag hanging over the back of another chair. He picked it up, started rifling through its contents.

"What are you doing?" Olin asked.

Connor didn't answer him directly. "Dylan, do you know the code for Aleshia's cell phone?" Since she knew the code for the alarm, it seemed reasonable to assume she might know this one, also.

"Yeah. I saw her enter it once." She repeated the word "one" six times in a row. "I teased her about the simplicity of it for a while. She said that was the whole point. You only get a few tries to enter the passcode for an iPhone before it locks up for good, so who's going to waste a guess on something so obvious?"

In most cases, a password like that would be a terrible idea. But there was a certain logic to Aleshia's reasoning, Connor thought.

When he couldn't find the phone by touch, he dumped the contents of the purse onto the table. More makeup, hand wipes, iPhone earbuds, keys. No phone.

Even if you wanted to argue that she might have left in a hurry—that this *one* time she had left without her purse—the door had been locked. She couldn't have done that without taking her keys.

Unless . . .

He circled around to the foyer to check the front door. The latch on the knob had been turned, securing it in place, but the deadbolt was unlocked. However, he cautioned himself, anybody could have turned that latch before exiting the house. Including a kidnapper. And if someone really wanted to hide an abduction, they just might have.

"All right, let's see what we can find," Connor said.

Olin looked around like he was lost. "What are we looking for?"

"Anything. If you see something suspicious—or even weird, I guess—just let the rest of us know."

"Gotcha." Olin made his way back toward the living room. He might not have wanted to break in, but now that he was here, at least he was willing to help search the place. Connor wasn't surprised. They had broken into a house once before. Olin had been just as reluctant then to cross the threshold. And then, like now, he became a team player once they were inside.

Since there was nothing of interest in the purse and the dining room contained only the table, Connor went into the kitchen. It was the next closest room. He intended to search all of them, so he might as well start there.

Dylan followed him.

Before they could begin their search, though, Olin popped his head in. "Should we be wearing gloves for this?"

Connor shrugged. "She's Aleshia's friend," he said, referring to Dylan. "If the police ever bother looking for prints, they shouldn't be surprised to find hers. And we're Dylan's friends, so . . ." He trailed off, looked from Olin to Dylan and back, then disappeared down the hall. When he returned, he was carrying three towels. "Still, probably better to be safe." He handed one towel to Olin as he passed and tossed another to Dylan, who was on the opposite side of the kitchen. "Wipe down everything you touch."

Then, to avoid (as he called it) "compromising the scene," he returned to the dining room, swept the contents of Aleshia's purse back into her bag, and hung the bag back over the chair. After carefully wiping the bag down, he did one last visual inspection of the room to make sure everything looked like it had when they'd entered. "Done," he said when he came back to the kitchen.

While Olin searched the living room, Connor and Dylan scoured the cupboards and the pantry. Connor spoke only once before they were finished, and that was when he saw Dylan clearing plates off a shelf and moving on without putting them back.

"What are you doing?" he asked her. "We have to leave everything like it was when we found it."

Dylan gave him a look but followed his instructions.

The house consisted entirely of one bathroom, two bedrooms (one of which had been converted into a home gym), a living room, a dining room, and the narrow kitchen. There was no basement, and the only way to get to the attic was through a set of pull-down stairs, making it less than ideal for any sort of storage.

After Olin finished searching the living room, he went up there, anyway, just to be sure. As Connor suspected, he found nothing. Not even a box of Christmas decorations.

"If we're going to find anything here at all, it's got to be in the bedroom," he said when Olin came back down.

Dylan nodded. "I think you're right. How about you two check that out while I give the bathroom a once-over?"

With nothing more than an elliptical machine, a yoga mat, and some free weights, there was no reason to spend any time on the gym.

The three friends moved down the hall together. Connor and Olin broke off at the bedroom. Connor checked the nightstands and Olin the dresser, both diligently using the towels to wipe down everything they touched.

The bed was unmade, which made it easy to tell which side Aleshia slept on. In that nightstand, Connor found a Chapstick, earplugs, and a dog-eared copy of James Patterson's *Honeymoon*. The other one—no surprise—was empty.

He turned around. "Nothing. What about you?"

Olin was on the third drawer from the top. "Nothing here, either. Not yet, anyway."

Dylan had finished searching the bathroom and was now standing in the doorway. "Did you check the closet?"

Connor did. It was also a bust.

He was just about to give up when a flicker of light on the bed caught his attention. A hard piece of plastic glinted in the light from the overhead lamp. Although only the corner of the object was visible, he knew what it was right away. He pushed the blankets aside to reveal a laptop. "Hey, guys."

Connor sat down on the bed with the computer in his lap and pressed the power button. The computer came to life. Olin and Dylan moved in close so they could see what he was doing.

When the computer finished booting up, it presented them with a login screen.

Connor glanced at Dylan. "Do you know the password?"

"No, not to this."

Connor took a deep breath. He knew from experience people kept all sorts of secrets on their personal computers. They had to find a way to get in. However, that could take some time.

He shut down the laptop to preserve the battery and closed it. He tucked it under one arm as he got to his feet. "Let's take it back to the hotel. We'll work on it there."

"What about leaving things like they were?" Dylan said.

"I think we can make an exception for this."

CHAPTER 5

WHILE CONNOR HAD made reservations for their flight, Olin found a hotel: The Grand Hyatt in Buckhead. He'd cleared it with Connor, then booked a suite. He also made a point of paying for it in advance. This came as no surprise to Connor. Olin had inherited a lot of money, and whenever a big expense came their way, he insisted on taking care of it.

On their way there, Connor asked Dylan to stop by Target so he could pick up an external hard drive. He'd found an article online about a heist in Chicago a few years back where a hacker broke into someone's computer using just such a device. The details of the article were sketchy, but he knew more than enough about how computers worked to understand the contours of the scheme. While he was there, he also grabbed three pairs of gloves in case they decided they needed to break into anyone else's house.

The suite was even bigger than Connor expected. He and Olin each had their own bedrooms. They dropped off their luggage and joined Dylan at the small dining table in the living room.

Connor placed the laptop and the external hard drive on the table. While he was at Target, he'd also bought a universal power cable. He wanted to make sure the laptop wouldn't run out of juice before they were finished with it. He plugged the power cable into the computer and said, "This is going to take a couple of hours. You two should find something to do to entertain yourselves. Dylan, if you need to go . . ."

She waved him off. "Are you kidding? I'm staying here until we get into that thing."

Olin looked at Dylan. "Is there anyone else you and I could talk to while we wait? What about Aleshia's parents?"

"Her father died of cancer a few years ago. Her mother went in her sleep not long after that. Something with her heart. I think it was probably grief. Either way, all Aleshia has left is her sister Maddie, and, as you know, she's missing too. Even if she wasn't, she's fifteen years older than Aleshia, so I don't think they have much in common. And she's kind of a recluse on top of that. They don't see each other very often. Which only makes this whole thing stranger, doesn't it?"

Olin didn't respond, and Connor understood why. There was nothing to say. First a woman goes missing. Then her sister disappears. They have no other family, so there would be no one to pay a ransom if that had been the goal. And even though their father had been famous, Aleshia and Maddie lived quiet lives out of the public eye, minimizing the number of enemies they might have. With Maddie a recluse and her relationship with her sister limited, the number of *shared* enemies would have to be nearly zero.

In other words, the question answered itself. Yes, the situation was strange. Yes, the fact that Maddie was a recluse made it stranger. However, none of that mattered until they had a lead.

Olin looked at his phone. "There's a basketball game on," he said to Dylan. "Kentucky versus Auburn."

Dylan looked from Olin to Connor.

"Really," Connor said. "There's nothing you can do right now. I'll let you know once I'm in."

Olin and Dylan moved to the sofa and Olin turned on the TV.

Connor hardly noticed when they put the game on. He was in the zone.

First, Connor used his own laptop to download a recent version of the Windows operating system. He installed it onto the external hard drive and booted his computer from that drive to make sure it worked. When it did, he switched laptops and booted Aleshia's computer from the external drive using the same technique.

He browsed through recent files and folders, looking for anything that stood out. She didn't have a lot on the machine. Several dozen pictures. A spreadsheet for bills. And an assortment of miscellaneous files. Nothing that would explain her disappearance.

He opened her browser to check the history. She was a frequent user of Facebook and Twitter, so he started there first. She hadn't posted anything in the last two days—from here or her phone. There were no intimidating messages, no suspicious activity of any kind, actually.

That was a bust.

Next on the list: CupidsCorner.com.

It sounded like a dating site to Connor, which, it turned out, it was.

Connor started with her profile. She had uploaded a nice closeup of her face as her primary photo and filled out every question in exhaustive detail.

She liked beaches more than mountains, thought small towns had a lot of charm, ran three miles every day. She liked to travel and wanted a partner who would go with her.

There was no indication from the profile she had a job, which fit with what Connor had already learned from Dylan. Instead, she seemed to do a lot of volunteer work at Helping Hand, an agency that delivered meals to the poor and elderly.

"Did you know Aleshia was on a dating site?" Connor asked.

Dylan leaned forward on the sofa, turned to face him. "You're in?"

"Yes."

"You were supposed to let me know." She got up and came over to the table.

Olin turned off the game and followed her.

"Did you know?" Connor asked again.

"Yeah. I even helped her set up her profile."

That made sense, Connor thought. Dylan never half-assed anything. If she was going to fill out a profile on a dating site, she would answer every question in detail, exactly like Aleshia had.

Connor browsed through her recent messages. There were several from a guy named Tyler921. According to the messages, Tyler was a trainer at Power Fitness who also liked to travel.

"Did you know Aleshia had a date with a guy named Tyler the night before she disappeared?"

Dylan's eyes grew wide. "Let me see that." She turned the laptop toward her, read their exchange. "It doesn't say where they went."

"Aleshia gave him her phone number," Connor said, directing Dylan to that part of their conversation. "They probably worked that out on the call."

Dylan clicked on Tyler921's screen name. She was redirected to Tyler's profile. Like Aleshia's, the profile included a large photo with several smaller ones underneath it. In the primary picture, Tyler stood facing the camera. He was visible from the waist up and wearing a tight shirt that made it clear he wasn't lying when he called himself a trainer. He had a square face that worked for him and a sharp jaw line. His hands rested on his hips. One corner of his mouth was turned up in a half-smile that made him seem both serious and approachable.

The pictures underneath suggested he lived an active life—sailing, running, playing tennis. Connor had no doubt he did all of those things. Although he doubted they comprised as much of his life as the pictures might have you believe.

"Did you talk to Aleshia the day she went missing?" Connor asked.

Dylan shook her head. "No. We'd made plans to meet at the cafe the day before."

"So as far as you know, Tyler may have been the last person to see her."

Her face dropped. "She should have told me she was meeting him."

"At least we know where he works," Olin said.

"We'll go by Power Fitness first thing in the morning," Connor said.

"What if he's not there?"

"Then we'll track him down."

Connor finished perusing the messages on the dating site. As far as he could see, Aleshia hadn't met with anybody else.

CHAPTER 6

JAKE AVARNATTI ENJOYED his morning run. Especially in winter. The beach along Lake Lanier was quiet at this hour, and he often made the run without seeing another soul. Dressed in gray sweats and Nike tennis shoes, he would park in the public lot, then tread his way through the sand down and back. Twenty minutes in all. Enough to work up a sweat and loosen up the muscles that used to ache from too many hours at the computer.

Today, however, he didn't even get a quarter of a mile down the beach before he saw somebody stretched out along the edge of the water. With the sun just over the horizon and facing him, he couldn't make out any details at first.

Once he could, he realized the woman wasn't on the edge of the water—she was in it. And she was fully dressed. Nothing fancy. Just jeans and a tee shirt. But it was too cold to be dressed like that, and even if she liked the cold, that wasn't what you would wear if you were going into the water.

Perhaps she wandered down here drunk, Jake thought. There was a hotel not far away. Even a neighborhood within walking distance. That made the most sense, he decided. He figured he'd better check on her.

Jake jogged up to the woman. Once he was close enough to see her in detail, the scene changed from merely unusual to alarming. The woman had blood smeared across her forehead and her shirt.

Jake dropped to his knees, instinctively pulled her farther onto the sand, shook her shoulders. "Ma'am. Ma'am, are you okay?"

No response. He leaned in close to check for breathing, heard none, and then realized how cold she really was. That wasn't just from the water.

With his heart pounding faster than it ever did when he ran, Jake pulled back. He fumbled to get his phone out of his pocket, dialed 911. "I need to report . . . Well, I don't know. A body, I guess." He didn't want to say "murder." He didn't want to imagine a killer dumping a body along his running route. Even though he knew there was nothing else it could be.

There was a halting jerkiness to his voice as he answered the operator's questions. When she was done, she asked him to stay where he was, and he said he would. Once he got off the phone, he stepped far enough away from the body that he could no longer see the blood on the woman's forehead.

Although he tried to keep his attention on the road, his gaze kept shifting back to the woman. There was a part of him that felt like he had to watch her, to make sure she was still there when the police arrived. It was absurd. Even as alarmed as he was, he could think straight enough to be sure of that. But it didn't stop him from looking.

There was also a part of him that worried the killer was still out here, that simply by being close to the body he would become the next victim. Which was also probably absurd (although somewhat less so).

Road. Body. Road. Body.

What the hell was taking the police so long?

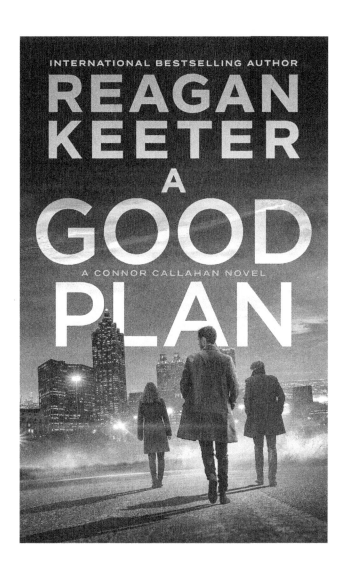

GO HERE TO ORDER:

http://reagankeeter.com/agoodplan

ABOUT THE AUTHOR

Reagan Keeter is the author of multiple Amazon bestsellers and a National Indie Excellence Awards finalist. He has worked as a writer and editor at Georgia newspapers. From Georgia State University, he earned his undergraduate degree in Journalism and from Southern Polytechnic State University his master's in Technical and Professional Communication. He lives with his wife and their two dogs in Atlanta, Georgia.

You can connect with him via reagankeeter.com.

GET AN EXCLUSIVE COPY OF *THE LAYOVER*

Connor Callahan is back in this exclusive novella. Everything he has been through has left him with an overdeveloped sense of justice. Perhaps that is why when he sees a man discreetly tag a stranger's suitcase with a black magic marker, he sets out to discover what is going on. It's a decision that will thrust Connor into a conflict far more dangerous than he could have imagined, and when it's over he will know one thing for sure: You're not always safer on the ground.

When you join my readers club, you will immediately get a free and exclusive copy of *The Layover*, not available elsewhere.

I usually e-mail once or twice a month with things I think you'll find interesting, such as behind-the-scenes stories, new releases, and fan discounts. Of course, you can unsubscribe at any time.

Join the readers club by signing up at
read.reagankeeter.com

ALSO BY REAGAN KEETER

The Redwood Con

High-rolling illegal gambler Liam Parker finds his girlfriend dead in her apartment, and it's not long before the police charge him with her murder. Desperate to avoid a lifetime behind bars, Liam's hunt to clear his name uncovers unexplainable secrets about the woman he thought he knew. And with the police revoking his bail and his freedom under threat, he goes on the run in pursuit of two strangers . . . and their deadly answers.

Misery Rock

Sharron Freeman's world gets shattered when she learns her husband, Ben, is a killer. Worse than that, he kills as part of a group. Desperate to keep herself and her daughter safe, Sharon sets out to discover who else is involved and find evidence against them before they meet to kill again. It's a journey that will require her to draw on courage she didn't know she had and come face to face with enemies she didn't know existed. And in the end, it all might prove to be in vain.

Printed in Great Britain
by Amazon

17753857R00190